# Mea puppet cabaret

## steve Beard

**R/W DOG SCREAMING PRESS**

Meat Puppet Cabaret © 2006
by Steve Beard

Published by Raw Dog Screaming Press
Hyattsville, MD

First Paperback Edition

Cover: Terry Rentzepis, www.alltenthumbs.com
Book design: Jennifer Barnes

Printed in the United States of America

ISBN: 978-1-933293-31-8

Library of Congress Control Number: 2006928349

www.rawdogscreaming.com

for Victoria Athenee Halford

## Quotations from occult sources

"Death, who can take either male or female form, fucks the young Corn God and the Corn God ejaculates 400 million years of corn from seed to harvest and back. This operation requires actual corn and an actual human body to represent the young Corn God. This is an endorsed check signed by the young Corn God. Once he has signed the check any number of zeros can be added."
—William S. Burroughs, *Ah Pook Is Here*, 1975

"Perhaps this is the purpose of all art, all writing, on the murders, fiction and non-fiction: Simply to participate."
—Alan Moore, *From Hell*, 1999

"The desire for death and joy of living mix in a terrible way in the eyes of lovers who have no future."
—Unica Zurn, *The Man of Jasmine*, 1977

"Should a certain percentage of women be set aside by force to serve as brood mares for the species? Obviously this will not do. The answer is laboratory production of babies."
—Valerie Solanas, *SCUM Manifesto*, 1967

# Context

(0)  Quotations from occult sources                    5

(1)  Interview with King Charles in exile              9

(2)  Testimony of an ancient Shadwell psychogeographer  21

(3)  Sado-masochistic lessons in magick               27

(4)  Confession of Professor Natasha Supanova          53

# Interrogation of Eddie Boy Krishna

(1)  Anglo-Caribbean sex slave trade                   17

(2)  Child abduction at Shadwell Dock Stairs           60

(3)  Royal assassination in Paris road tunnel          69

(4)  Five century pattern killing in East London       86

(5)  Conspiratorial plots of the secret Osiris Club   145

(6)  Infant sacrifice planned on Hampstead Heath      165

(7)  Pollution of the divine source in Shadwell       190

# Secret Ukanian Combine: Rave Nation 2

(1)  Game on                                           39

(2)  White Lotus ascent                               101

(3)  Contingency operation                            124

(4)  Secret level                                     170

(5)  Pink Lotus descent                               215

## Survivor's dream

(1) Transplantation     62

(2) Trepanation     79

(3) Assault     93

(4) Abortion     114

(5) Crash     207

## Voices of Afro-Atlantean ancestor gods

(1) New Deal     73

(2) Secret Deal     193

(3) No Deal     233

## Mark 23 & his Consensus Reality Studio

(1) Wet sari number     89

(2) Kiddie brothel expose     97

(3) Dream girl circuit     150

(4) Offworld power games     183

(5) Alpine dance sequence     201

(6) Space station insurrection     229

## Last prophet of Allah's text messages

(1) Tracking the water serpent Ashtoreth     160

(2) Exorcising the inner demon Jack     181

## Interview with King Charles in exile

The dozens of Rockwell engines on board the *Britannia* began the complex pattern of thrusting sequences required to insert us into polar orbit and we hung at a low altitude in the disputed Ukanian/Argentine corridor above Antarctica. The little window revealed dark space. The vid display showed an image of the fly-back booster *Atlantis* falling away from us with the spent fuel tank. She was a big, angular craft. Her whiteness showed up against the dark. She was looping back over the fiery rim of the earth.

The canned voice explained: "*Atlantis* is on a ballistic trajectory which will secure her atmospheric entry and return her to St John's old US Air Force base in the Caribbean Sea. So long, baby bird."

The twenty other passengers strapped on board *Britannia* fluttered in irritation as the announcement of our separation interrupted their viewing of the in-flight entertainment—Theda Bara resurrected from the Hollywood image graves for Chris Cunningham's Old Egyptian-themed musical *Don't Fuck With My Mummy*. The prestige of extra-terrestrial flight may have become routine for Russian people traffickers, Korean money traders and American internet robber barons, but this magazine's humble correspondent was used to commuting by train. I continued to be fascinated by the live video footage.

A message from *Atlantis* over the cans: "So long mama *Britannia*. You've been the perfect host."

The departing booster lobbed us a farewell image of the *Britannia*—with her snub nose, long narrow fuselage and abruptly curved tail-wings—as she adjusted her position. Theda Bara returned to the screen. I closed my eyes and rested my head against the seat. Once in free flight, the orbiter would breathe fire from her propulsion nozzles and begin the delicate line of approach which led to the rarefied orbit occupied by the Ark of Old England. This spaceship was the hub of the New Ukanian Combine. It was His Majesty's own little semi-permanent autonomous zone. I had been told there was always a queue to land at one of the ten perimeter docking ports.

"Remember…whatever you do, don't mention Diana." The whispered caution from the Rogers & Cowan PR boy employed by the Ark hissed in my ear. I turned and put him down with a look. How could anyone reckon I would make such an uncool move? It was unthinkable. The King's bitterness towards the surviving memory of his ex-wife and mother of his eldest son, William, is legendary. He has never forgiven Diana for failing to live up to her role as brood-mare by appointment and still has deeply ambivalent feelings about her bastard son, Harry. When Diana died in that tragic car crash in Paris at the end of the last century, Charles was obviously relieved that her embarrassing career as a celebrated prostitute was over. He may also have been pleased that her final suitor, the Anglo-Egyptian money launderer Emad "Dodi" Al Fayed, died in her lap.

Charles's sensitivity over his dead wife is perfectly understandable and something that will be respected by this loyal Jamaican Crown subject. *D&S* is a publication that has always been sympathetic to the plight of royalty. We are proud to have been commissioned to help spin some good news from the most recent spate of scandals to beseige the Saxe-Coburg-Gotha firm. We would neither mention Diana nor stoop to the level of embarrassing our host with questions about his recent forced withdrawal from England. Still less would we pause to mention the betrayal of his legacy by his turncoat eldest son, the self-styled 'Cheikh' William. The recognition of the Islamic Republic of New New England by the UN is nothing short of a sacrilege.

The old man may no longer be sovereign of the latest new England, but he's still boss of all those islands in the Caribbean sea. Who'd have guessed that those self-righteous towel-heads in the Mosque of Westminster would have been so stupid that they actually gave away the off-shore tax shelters and black bank addresses that go with Ukania? But they did. The dumbfucks got so carried away banning the sale of sex, drugs and money that they forgot what keeps their pensions topped up.

"Thankyou for flying Virgin Orbital. We wish you a pleasant onward journey."

The vid feed closed with a picture postcard image of the Ark of Old England. It floated in space against a backdrop dusted with stars. Its multi-recursive icosahedral architecture was ugly but stupendous. With its nodal spheres and connecting struts, it looked like a giant model atom. The structure had originally been designed decades ago as an air structure for nesting lizards. Now it was being used to house a different kind of dinosaur.

O Rex Mundi! How the mighty were fallen.

The *Britannia* was powered down and parked in one of the docking port airlock hangars of Perimeter Sphere Ten. As the PR boy and I quit the tiny flight cabin with the other passengers I could see the orbiter's fuselage splitting apart on low hinges either side to reveal the payload bay within. Dockside cranes joined the mechanical arm of the orbiter in busy activity as the *Britannia* prepared to deliver up its mundane cargo and import a rare payload of Duchy Original Organic

Cannabis for the return flight. There were thirty airlock hangars at this docking port and they were all serviced by a collection of warehouses, a light industrial railway and various commercial offices of His Majesty's Customs & Excise. There was the acrid smell of burning weed in the air.

"Don't forget the duty-free shop on the way back!"

The PR boy directed me to the port exit and we took a service travelator in through the Ark's storage and interchange zones until we hit the Home Sphere at the dead centre of its recursive structure. As we rode past the sewage plants and garbage units I couldn't help wondering if this was where HRH stashed his loot. When William had put together his snap coup down below he had grabbed the 300,000 acres of prime real estate which comprise the Crown Estates. Under the tutelage of his crazed Anglo-Egyptian tycoon mentor Mohammed Al Fayed, he had gone on to consecrate it to Allah and designate it an international refugee zone. Charles had managed to get out with his Holbeins, Rembrandts and Vermeers intact—along with a whole pile of tapestries, porcelain and antique furniture—but was obliged to leave behind the family's personal papers.

The opening of the locked vaults which housed the Saxe-Coburg-Gotha archives in Windsor Castle had coincided with William's declassification of all Ukanian secret state papers. Smart move. The vigorous young Cheikh looked like a dragon-slayer, while the ageing King was left carrying the can for the criminal failures of a whole political class suddenly revealed to be up to its neck in the atrocities of the twentieth century.

The sad thing is that throughout all this, young Wills has merely been a puppet in the hands of Mohammed Al Fayed. Some say the paranoid old devil is taking his revenge on those he holds responsible for the death of his son in that bloody car crash in Paris. Others reckon he's the head of a worldwide Muslim conspiracy. *D&S* is quite ready to believe that he's a jumped-up arms dealer who got lucky by manipulating a confused young man's desperate need for a father-figure.

Whatever. It was my job to spin the shit of history into the pure gold of media dissimulation. The King had instructed his Lord Chamberlain to invite the editor of *D&S* to attend only his eleventh Royal Interview with a member of the press. We were only too pleased to accept.

Actually, things weren't so bad for the Saxe-Coburg-Gothas. All the Nazi stuff was old news which was explained by the fact that the King's mum's great-grandmother was the aunt of the Russian Tsar murdered by the Bolsheviks. As for the drive-by shootings of unarmed civilians by Frank Kitson's psyops mob in the Irish low-intensity conflict of the 1970s…well, that could be handled with an out-of-court settlement. Quite a generous offer really when you think about it. After all, like the old boy has said, he can't really be held responsible for the cavortings of his mum's ancient ministers. Half of them were mad.

No, it was this whole Argentine business which was really threatening to blow things out of orbit. He wouldn't hear a word said against his dear departed papa. That was the problem. Too loyal, see?

A court eunuch from the Royal Protection Unit ushered us into a Bristow helicopter and we fluttered round the super-structure of the Home Sphere on a brief tour of its simulated open-air environment. The roll-out polo fields, pocket golf courses and floating game park unscrolled beneath us. The trees were dripping with ice and the hills were thick with snow. There were track-marks on the white crunchy floor of the game park.

"His Royal Highness still enjoys a shoot." Uh huh. By this time, I was feeling physically sick from all the bobbing around in semi-micro-gravity. Holograms of late-afternoon fair weather cumulus were projected past us on to the concave roof screens of this tiny orbital kingdom. We scudded over the genetic sequencing pharm which housed the Royal Extra-Terrestrial Biological Entities—rows of demountable sheds with clip-on mock-Tudor facades—and I watched the boom-supported observation decks sliding gracefully over their lab specimens on poised steel adjustment feet. The snow was melted and churned on the ground. This was a working environment.

The whole internal volume of the Home Sphere was really one big operational matrix serviced by travelling gantry cranes, mobile platforms and multi-level suspension grids. Tucked away deep in the back-stage infrastructure of the whole show were the grace-and-favour accommodation units which housed the King's entourage of stewards, clerks, steganographers, Oxford-schooled quantum mathemagicians and tame Soviet genetic engineers. The old buzzard's private apartments were enclosed at the centre of the Home Sphere within a modest floating White Palace camouflaged with blanket holograms of zero-field space.

The copter pulled up away from the sculpted ice forest below and passed through the weather projections and the invisibility holograms to plonk itself down next to a fold-out observation deck. I was thoroughly disorientated but staggered after my two companions through an infrared motion detector curtain into the grounds of the Palace. We crept through a maze of audio-visual surveillance stalks into a silent pleasure-garden and passed through an entrance gate into a gloomy ante-room which somehow connected to the Presence Chamber.

"Shhh!" The PR lad had his finger to his lips. There was the pungent smell of caviar and aftershave in the air.

I was immediately conscious that it was only the earth's distant gravitational pull which prevented us from falling into the sun. Somehow the thought eased my distressed metabolism.

A footman appeared and watched silently as I was patted down by the sexless bodyguard. Then we all trooped into the Presence Chamber and I stood beside a ritually placed table. It was very dark and extremely cold. My breath condensed in the air.

The PR boy and the footman began conferring together in sibilant whispers. There was much snickering and rolling of the eyes. Soon I was informed that HRH would be ready to join us for tea as soon as he had finished watching an old tape of one of his charity polo matches at Cowdray Park.

His arrival was announced by his genetically modified dwarf dogs who bundled into the room in a baying and yapping pack. Everyone started bowing and scraping and sneaking glances at each other. Suddenly he was sprawling in a high-backed chair while I was eased into an over-stuffed couch by the coded movements of the footman's white-gloved hands. The table was between Charles and me.

I can't recall much of what happened next. It's possible that I'd been subject to some form of post-hypnotic command by the bodyguard or even worked over psychoactively during the flight. Who knows? Not me. I've only got flashes.

There was a butler serving us Earl Grey tea and darling little jam sandwiches made from processed white bread. Except that the old buzzard was knocking back the Black Forest cherry brandy and smoking marijuana cigarettes straight from the packet. Wasn't he? We followed protocol and talked about the weather. No, he kept moaning about Diana and how she'd ruined his life.

I was standing there with no clothes on talking to myself. My hands were held out in front of me and my knees were bent. Someone was dropping food on the carpet for the dogs. There was shit everywhere.

"Now! Now! Now!" The PR boy was hissing at me. It was time for me to do my thing. I was able to remember the access protocol deal. No embarrassing questions.

"Some say that Diana was eight months pregnant when she died. What is your comment?"

No…that wasn't what I was supposed to say.

"We are glad you asked us that question. One is now ready to reveal that one had a private autopsy conducted on one's first wife immediately before her burial. The report shows definitively that she exhibited no signs of disease or any other significant change in her condition."

HRH was casually dressed in a scarlet Gieves & Hawkes dressing gown and green Wellington boots. His discreetly exposed collar and cuffs showed he was wearing royal blue striped pyjamas underneath. He kept crossing and uncrossing his legs throughout our interview and readjusting the hang of his gown. He seemed uncomfortable. One of his slavering little dogs jumped on his lap in the middle of one of his homilies and began to nuzzle his master's groin. HRH gently massaged the creature's dark testicles. Then he brushed the animal off without pausing for breath and finished his lecture about the benefits of organic farming to the drugs economy. The whole room pretended nothing had happened.

This is probably a screen memory.

What the fuck. I got my exclusive on the whole Argentine business. Remember that? The Argentinians claimed sovereignty over the orbital territory occupied by the Ark of Old England spaceship and had been only too pleased to be graced with a request from the United Republic of Eire to extradite Charles in his capacity as the Commander-in-Chief of the Ukanian armed forces. The charges related to crimes against humanity committed on Irish soil. Can you believe those treacherous South American scumbags? Official international recognition of their disputed borders with Ukania meant they might eventually get their hands on oil rights in Antarctica.

Well, I guess you can't blame them. It all goes back to oil in a way. See, the Argentinians were extra pissed off by the release of Ukanian cabinet papers from 1962 which the Saxe-Coburg-Gotha mob—quite properly—had originally ordered sealed until 2057. That little sneak Wills again! Suddenly all the old Commies were saying that the real reason Charles's deadbeat dad went to Buenos Aires in March 1962 was to aid and abet the military coup which got rid of President Arturo Frondizi and his crazy plans to nationalise the US oil companies.

What a joke! If only the stupid sack of shit had been that far in the loop. Anyway, the King finds he can no longer protect the memory of his long gone papa in the way he would have once preferred. How about that? HRH is now prepared to admit that when his dad fucked off on a tour of Argentina's polo fields in 1962, the randy old goat sired a love child with rich bitch socialite Magdalena Nelson de Blaquier in her groovy *estancia*.

Or as he put it to me in the only unscripted moment in the interview: "One had a half-sister one never knew. She died of a drugs overdose, don't you know. Cunting tragoedia!"

Indeed. I'm sure even the most cynical old Fleet Street coke-head could not fail to be touched by the King's halting Latinate resort to the final taboo word. Such a fine manifestation of human frailty!

Once the interview was over I was invited with other guests to attend a party to celebrate the completion of the Sirius Leyline and the opening of interplanetary trade between Old England and the Sirius star system. I had a wild time. The highlight of the festivities was a little show of twentieth century Ukanian folk art in the pavilion theatre. There was a tatty old shark in a tank and old tabloid newspaper headlines blown up on a board. It was hilarious. The climax of the evening was an appearance by the distinguished court concept designer Sir Martin Creed, who offered us a reprise of his famous works *The lights turning on and off* and *Everything is going to be just the way it used to be*.

I stood near the back but still had a great view. I could clearly see HRH in his deck-chair at the front of the stage, looking relaxed and alert in his Armani shades. It was unfortunate his mood was spoiled by what happened at the climax of the show. An Extra-Terrestrial Biological Entity was hauled in from the pharm to offer a display of her charms. But it all went badly wrong. Maybe it was a tasteless idea to begin with. After all, these chimerical entities are quite controversial. The Royal biologists guard them very closely. We don't really know how they're produced. Some say they're grown in test-tubes using Sirian DNA. Others say they've beamed down in teleportation chambers. They're a Crown secret.

I couldn't see too much of what was happening on stage. The curtain went up to reveal a white-walled stage-set bathed in coloured lights. Nothing happened for a while and people started giggling. Maybe they thought it was another of Sir Martin's outrageous concepts. But then something began to take shape amidst the whirling pink and blue spotlights. It looked like a sad little girl. Except it only came into focus from a certain angle. It was like a hologram of flesh and blood and bone. It was weird. It seemed insubstantial. But it had an animal magnetism.

I could feel myself falling into its large white face. It was a female. They all were. She had eyes like pin-holes. She was looking directly at HRH and he was rigid with fear. He was gripping the sides of his chair. Noone said anything. The creature was flowing across the stage. Her tiny bones rode under the surface of her skin at unexpected angles. She was wearing a white bikini together with some kind of green belt. Her hair was thick and black. But then it began to change colour.

The little girl was shape-shifting before us. This was the special talent of these creatures. It was the first time I had ever seen it occur. It was like another figure was projected on to the little girl in a double-exposure. But then she began to adapt herself to the new image and fade out her original form. She was looking down at HRH the whole time she was transforming herself. Like she was doing it all for him—changing her hair, her facial features, changing her posture, even her clothes. Only her eyes didn't change—those relentless green orbs drawing all the energy from the surrounding environment into a deep internal void.

HRH was choking. It was as if he couldn't breathe. People gasped in the audience. We all saw what was there on the stage—the image of his dead wife. It was only there for a moment. But it was recognisable enough. There she was with that sheeny blonde hair, that over-groomed Versace look, that insufferable expression of piety and need on her smiling docile face. Only now it was mixed up with something else. Hatred and fear and guilt and spite. It was horrible.

The King screamed in the end. He just couldn't take it. The curtain came down like a shot. But not before I had the chance to see the shape-shifting chimera revert to its natural state. It abandoned its Diana impersonation and passed through some kind of liquid mercury interval, where it hung in the air like a molten silver snake that had been charmed to raise itself up on its tail. Then it phase-shifted again and became this small and wizened little old crone with a scarred face and flashing green eyes. She stood there swaying from side to side as she laughed at the stricken King.

People were rushing to support the King as he lay there gasping. His aides needed to give him oxygen and rush him back to the Palace. I was bundled away from the scene and dumped in a Waiting Room with the PR boy and other confused guests. Once the King had recovered, his official media speaker dismissed the whole affair as an instance of heat-stroke. No mention was made of the evening's entertainment or the performance of the Royal Extra-Terrestrial Biological Entity. But I know what I saw.

It was only when I got back earthside that I made some discreet enquiries about the fate of the creature I was convinced had bewitched the King. I was led to believe it had been taken away and destroyed. Perhaps it's just as well. These strange entities have such brief lives anyway. We know so little about them.

No matter. The important thing is that HRH emerged from the whole episode fitter than ever. He remains Charles the Third, by the Grace of God of the New Ukanian Combine of Old England, the Channel Islands and of his Downworld Territories of Anguilla, Bermuda, the Cayman Islands, the Falkland Islands, Gibraltar, Montserrat, the Pitcairn Islands, the Royal Antarctic Territory, the Royal Indian Ocean Territory, the Royal Virgin Islands, St Helena and its Dependencies, South Georgia and the South Sandwich Islands and the Turks and Caicos Islands King. Who would dare to begrudge him that?

## Anglo-Caribbean sex slave trade

Eddie sweating under the lights in a Ljubljana safe-house in Slovenia. Reckons he's been hauled in to add lustre to recent dark events.

*A True and Faithful Relation of What Passed at Clarence House between Dr John Dee and the Devil*. Extract 1.1: It is found by prophecy that the haunted ride east from the wretched Tower Gateway was to give testimony unclean.

It was not long before the Juggler turned left off the endless Ratcliffe Highway, to go up and along the deserted Cable Street into the silent realm of Shad. Bounded in the west was Shad by the eerie Church of the White Devil and in the east by the subterranean Osiris Club.

Three ancient Wells comprised the hermitage of the shadow women of the Devil Osiris.

And the Juggler slowed his pace and came unto the dank outskirts of the venerable Well of the Third Weird Sister near Glamis Road.

Know ye that the Well of the Second Weird Sister in the north was large and ornate, with a door extravagantly barred; and that passage unto the Well of the First Weird Sister in the south was covered by dark trees; but that the Well of the Third Weird Sister opened onto the broken stones of the street.

The Juggler had pressed his sliding key into the sunken locks of the First Well and the Second Well. But the morbid Isis and the demoniacal Nephthys responded had they not. Only the neglected Satis bestowed on him a low ironic bow.

It was here in the Third Well, according to his demented instructions, that he would find the Devil's Hoof.

EK Exegesis 1.1: It's amazing that toilet interface is still working at St Mary's church in Shadwell, ain't it? The old man made a point of avoiding the area ever since that whole Christopher Marlowe business went sour. But he wasn't averse to sending me down there, was he? Oh no.

Well, I didn't mind. I had a little thing going with Satis, didn't I? She always was the most grateful of Osiris's women, if you know what I mean. Very hard to shake off. Blimey, it was that often she was down on her hands and knees to me, I could see her mooning face in the shine of me boots.

It was painful.

In the end getting hold of Osiris's Magic Wand was a bloody relief. The thing only used to squirt pure Sirian germ-plasm, didn't it? I tell you, when the old man wasn't looking I used to strap it on as a dildo.

Got some very strange results. That Satis wasn't as daft as she looked.

*A True and Faithful Relation...* Extract 1.2: It was an occupational hazard for any desperate child star groomed by the Silver Birches to be unnamed upon discovery of their corpse.

Always the Morning Star collected the paper money before she appeased the pawing clients. Little idea had she how to use her skills to meet their odious demands. She was simply an expensive status symbol.

One of the older girls ran the dismal orphanage single-handed. The Elephant Priestess was the only girl fully acquainted with its benighted privacies.

The dripping outer court opened unto a shocking red rotating light. And it was here where the nocturnal girls found new work.

The hollow inner court contained the personal sanctums with pitiful divan beds. And it was here where degenerate clients spent the night in closeted violation of the terms of the lease.

The Morning Star had suffered from needs both infantile and shameful since she was separated from her unhinged mother. And the Clown Jack had not been able to provide for her when his idea of accommodation had extended no further than squatting a single unwelcoming room.

Mouldy it was, and foetid, in the Glamis Road. Only her battered young companions offered the Morning Star the comfort of a home.

EK Exegesis 1.2: The Silver Birches? I never actually went into the dorms there meself, so I can't comment. I was just the waterman.

I'm not saying I didn't have occasional relations with the old girl who ran the place. But they were strictly of a business nature. Well, we've all gotta make a living, ain't we?

*A True and Faithful Relation...* Extract 1.3: Now the Elephant Priestess had ledgers vast of ruled paper containing double entry book-keeping. She wrote down everything.

She had a regular client who was one of the oldest firms in the Atlantic Ocean. They had a rotten palace. Atlantis was their name.

Atlantis issued a sightless craft to collect the disturbed girls from Shaddock

Stairs and take them unto the other side of the Atlantic Ocean. Help the girls had with the hellish journey. They were obliged to pay the Juggler before they left.

The director of this prodigious old firm was certainly peculiar and occasionally mad. The Doctor, as he was called, was fastidious about what Atlantis received. He was looking for special girls and promising them miracles inconceivable.

The abnormal business procedure was understood too well by all interested parties. The Juggler beseeched the Elephant Priestess to this time send a girl who comparable was at least to the bewitching image advertised. And she despatched whomsoever of her sullen girls was unoccupied and open to guileful persuasion. The psychopathologies of client and victim never did coincide. Each withstood the other til the unspeakable torment ended.

None of the girls ever returned. It was chilling.

And the Elephant Priestess never did let the Juggler persuade her to accept less than the full asking price; nor ever did she fail to be impressed that she could dictate her own grisly terms. She earned carrion commission on every abhorrent transaction. A fiendish deal it was.

The East End orphanage continued to exist in business because the rates it charged the ancient Department of Health and Religious Security were more modest than those charged by other children's homes. But still the Elephant Priestess was made to feel that the nasty accidents of the Caliphate were somehow her own fault. Often did she console herself with a sigh.

The Elephant Priestess never could decide whether she loved or hated her orphan girls. Deprived were they from the moment they were old enough to open their legs. Most of those who became sexually active at sixteen became hypocritical converts and raised children supported by the Caliphate. The Elephant Priestess persuaded herself there was more dignity in learning to become a mute commercial asset at eleven in an orphanage.

An unhealthy expertise with varied types of devilish practice offered a girl the pick of the jobs. Sometimes a leering client might even offer fulgurous treats to persuade her to make contributions even more sordid.

The belief of the Elephant Priestess in the lofty deceitfulness of her slithering clients did combine with an inability to cope without them. Her life was marked by a panting struggle to retain those few maniacal girls in her orphanage who could actually want to have sex with decrepit and eaten-away old men.

EK Exegesis 1.3: Why are we wasting time with this?

Most of the girls from the Silver Birches were just rubbish. Hardly any of them were up to scratch. Mind you, I never made the final selections. Like I say, I was just the waterman.

Are you getting all your lines from the old girl's account books? Yeah, well, she didn't know the half of it, I can tell you.

## Testimony of an ancient Shadwell psychogeographer

Now I come in again to these parts on the old river, the Thames, crawling in from the Atlantic and all points west, the Caribbean and even beyond, the old space station where the King holed up, yeah I come in again. So this is it, your new East London, this is what happen to the old neighbourhood, sure looks like a mess to me.

Cos what I see is all sad cunts hanging in my walk-in cribs, my old dens where the pipe was loaded up good by my man Sal from Chinatown, now dead and gone. No more opium here, sad to say, just this new thing not to my taste, no way, this powder cuts you a sex high over a death trip, fuck that, mana they call it, a drug for tossers, you got no memory you smoked it, (okay, I tried it once). What kind of fool gonna take the publican's word for this one, oh yeah, noone knows shit about it from the inside, except they see their good old pals go off their heads, the orgasm of their lives.

So that's one thing, for sure. They don't make the drugs like they used to, take it from me, I've been around here when the Shadwell docks were full of cargo ships, the warehouses spilling perfumes and incense in the air, just look around for some action and there it was, fine old times, you don't wanna hear this again, I know. You wanna hear about the old gods, the ones who got here before you, what they done and how they built their lives, see what's in it for you, whether there's something to learn.

Well, you gotta remember Jack the Mack. He's the most famous deity round these parts, god of infanticide, with his skull-face and his black top hat, his gentle-man's rags and his doctor's bag where he keeps all his knives. Watch out for Jack, he jumps on girls walk the streets at night, he cuts them up and sucks out their insides. Some reckon he snatches the babies of all the good time girls get knocked up and don't want the kid, takes away the little bundles, stores them in a sack nailed to his closet under the baths, round the back of St George in the East, where Ratcliffe Highway meets Cannon Street Road. Others say he lingers in the old Great General on the Whitechapel Road, there in the abortion clinic got no name, smells like a cancer on the maternity ward.

The girls don't like Jack, they scared of him appearing each and every month, when they have no blood to offer him, no dirty old egg to flush down the toilet to the place where he lives. So that's why the Eleven Merry Maidens teamed up to form a union all those years ago, sitting round pub tables with glasses raised and smoking dope together in neat flatshares, they all had enough of opening their legs for Jack the Mack once a month, a tax on earnings honestly earned. They all together got the courage to fob him off with knitting needles and rubbers and stained tampons, left as offerings in the gaps between the bricks in Angel Alley, where he known to play at night.

It worked for a time and the union was strong and the Eleven Merry Maidens got on with their lives, out buying designer hats and imported shoes, only the very finest, they got to look their best, it's all part of the job. There was Carrie Shakespeare-Brown, always with her head in a poetry book, knew how to put a man down with a single glance, mistress of the acid quip, she cracked all the girls up. Then there was Red Nell KFC, opium addict from way back, it kept her in the game, her eyes were full of sorrow, she hardly ever said a word. Lady Lydia was just a baby, still found it all exciting, scored some really deep pockets, but was holding out for something true.

Crackpipe Ali was another. She was the one came up with the idea for the union, wrote the articles and covenants, the toasts and the jokes, she was a real talker, knew how to use her mouth, was gonna go to college, soon as she got the time. Big Mama Em did the cooking, getting busy with the veg and the aromatic rice, she worked nights in a dungeon, real hard labour, was saving for her op. Lollipop Liz never ate a thing if she could help it, except canapes from private views, she had her name on the books of a couple of modelling agencies, turning tricks was just a way to keep herself in diet pills and fashion magazines.

Now Motown Anne, she was a raver, always out on the town with dealers and promoters and assorted sacks of shit, wanted to pull down a rock star, figured she was worth at least that. Pollyanna Goldenshower got into it by accident as the quickest way to pay the rent, could hardly believe it, grown men paying her to piss on them, well she gotta do it anyway, she developed a whole stand-up routine.

Then there was Kit-Kat Kate, a bit of a dreamer, floated around doing little things for the girls, they all loved her for it, she never talked about her work. Mary J Kelly was a star, never understood what she had, an ability to fascinate, it gained her loads of admirers, but she never cared a damn. Last there was Little Fanny Annie, who was always on the hustle, hardly ever got work, she used to listen hard to what the big girls said, but she never got anything she could apply to her life.

Well, that's the Eleven Merry Maidens, goddesses of prostitution, worshipped by homeless alcoholics starved of affection, moody celebrants with collection money standing at bars. Yeah, the Merry Maidens still got their sex temples going round these parts, near the church crypt at Spitalfields, they ain't so hard to find, they're tricked up with disco music and spot-lights, but the piss-poor glamour smells exactly the same.

Some say there's a Twelfth Merry Maiden betrayed the others to Jack, took all their money and stole their contraceptives down flat. But I reckon you don't wanna hear about that one, she long gone from here, Ada Babyface Wilson disappeared and left hardly no trace. No, you wanna hear all about the Karma Twins, they still around, long shadows at night in deserted car-parks and pub toilets, sheltered courtyards and block stairways, wherever there's a score needs settling the quick way, all in and out the old Whitechapel Road.

The Karma Twins always recognisable from their sharp suits and ties, their crooked grins and their solemn eyes. One was big and strong, with a wide face, and a large bosom taped down under her plain white shirt. That was Rhona, she stand on the corner polishing her razor with a handkerchief. The other was tiny and compact, with a mischievous expression and all frills down the front of her silk blue shirt. That was Regina, she always writing with a pencil in her little black book, keeping score on what she reckons she and her sister was owed.

The Karma Twins look after their own but they got this thing about tribute, you gotta pony up exact or get your arse striped. Rhona love flowers and guns and sentimental songs, while Regina like glitter and cigarettes and fancy words of praise. They lie underground in the old Osiris billiard hall, used to be there in Maidman Street at the end of the Burdett Road from St Anne's in Limehouse, sleeping on altars draped in cloth of green felt. Rhona got the word 'HATE' tattooed on her knuckles, while her sister's fists are inked with 'LOVE' instead. They go at it together when nobody is watching, jumping round the room with hands darting between them, hugging each other as they wheel round and round.

Thing about the Karma Twins is they so mixed up nobody knows where one of them begins and the other one ends. Put them together and what you got is a monopoly of violence in the local area, an old-fashioned system invented by the Kings, it works real well, you kick up your tribute to the Karma Twins and they come down hard on your disbelieving enemies, but you gotta point them out. So that's why the Karma Twins are the deities of street justice, what else you gonna call it when good boys go unpunished and bad girls are repaid?

Now as for other gods and goddesses round these parts, you gotta know at once about the Elephant Woman. She a big old girl covered in rolls of fat, the hide on her rump over one inch thick. Well, she covered in a black sari goes from head to foot, all you see above the veil is eyes pricked out in a wad of flesh, they send out a message says, coochy coochy coo. The Elephant Woman shuffle the underground corridors of the old Great General in her carpet slippers, pausing every other step to lean on her metal stick and catch her breath, she puffing and wheezing as she waddle along.

There's a furnace in the old Great General where they burn the parts of dead bodies, it right at the bottom of the tall brick chimney takes all the smoke and sends it away. This where the Elephant Woman sometimes sits in her old camp chair, fanning herself with adoption papers, waiting for Jack to drop on by, he opens up his sack and they do a roaring trade. The Elephant Woman sharpen Jack's knives on her grinding stick, she make a criss-cross sound and the sparks they fly, showering the fuel of the open fire. So this what make her the goddess of all orphans.

Elephant Woman take what Jack got and stuff it all under her clothes, she heave herself up and head back the way she came, underground towards the river through out-houses and annexes attached to Great General, the old laundry, the records office, the storage depots till she come up again at the old East London Hospital for Children on the Glamis Road, used to be there just over from St Mary's. This where she lives most of the time, hunkered down in a nursery lined with radiator pipes wrapped in asbestos, feeding her babies with lemon sherberts and milk powder till they fatten up enough to go to market and be sold.

You know there are all these old market-places in the area round here, well the one I'm real concerned with is the old fish market next to Shadwell Dock Stairs. It's been landscaped over as a recreation space, so now you've got this kiddie playground there, with swings and slides and little wooden dolphins rock back and forth. Yeah, you've got these tennis courts and lawns there, deserted at twilight, when the bowling green is royal blue and the flags snap in the air. Now this is the time its past come back to haunt it, some say it's when the ghost of the old sea monster Anu is sometime seen, crawling up the Stairs on his pale white belly or basking on the Thames National Path or swimming deep at the bottom of Shadwell Basin inland next to St Paul's church.

Anu connected to the fishing rackets from back in the day, when the Thames known as the River Isis, thousands of years ago in the Ancient English dream-time, when it was all fucked-up versions of the Afro-Atlantic deities ruled. So Anu used to slide round under the Atlantic Ocean, switching his crocodile tail from side to side and beating shoals of fish into the nets of the merchant seamen in their little wooden vessels, he finish his end of the deal and rear up out the foamy waves, raising his arms in a victory salute, he such a good looking boy from the waist on up.

Now the fisher folk gotta keep up their end when they haul their catch back home, they seen Anu bring down storms when he gets pissed off, lashing out at vessels bob like toys on the waves, he toss them in the air and rip them all up. So this is why every time at the winter solstice they offer up the most gorgeous of their girlies, stake her out on the ground at Shadwell Dock Stairs. Anu float on the Thames watching the ceremony, his cold eyes never even blink, he waiting for darkness to come on down, then he up on the bank and snatch that girl between his teeth, carry her back to his underwater Kingdom of Atlantis, way on down there miles and miles away, complete at the bottom of the deep blue sea.

I don't know what goes on down there but I hear tell Anu live with a bunch of real old gods originally from a distant star, twinkle in the evening with a mournful light, it's gotta be Sirius, this is millions and millions of years ago, these fishy aliens come on down and they live underwater with the sharks and the rays. Thing is they start to die out from all the in-breeding, they gotta replenish their thin gene pool. So this what Anu does with his stolen girlies, he treat them as his babymamas and fill them up with his seed, pretty soon they give birth to a new line of mutie creatures, half-human and half-fishy alien, submarine mammals that get to evolve, breathing liquid oxygen underwater is what they all do.

So that's Anu as far as I know, the god of kidnapping round these parts, he takes the young girls and he make them disappear, he take the boys too, he abduct children and work them to death in his Kingdom of Atlantis. Anu come back just the other century, with the press gangs and the slave traders, he not so far away. But now I guess, he forced to bide his time, under the ocean looking at the stars, some say he made a new deal with the old King in his space station above the Caribbean, but I don't know about that.

Well, that's about it for the deities round these parts, the ones I know about from way back when, there's new gods coming, you can bet that for sure. I guess it's time for me to ship out, get back to my wandering, track back along the trail past them good old Bengalis, them Jews, them Roman Christians, them pathfinding Afro-Atlanteans, connect with the traffic got no nation and got no name.

## Sado-masochistic lessons in magick

SETTING: DEMONOLOGY SCHOOL
*A concrete chamber with no windows.*

*The walls are racked with occult periodicals whose titles*—Journal of African History, Astronomy and Astrophysics, Experimental Neurology—*are barely visible. Taped above them are Polaroid photos of the sex parts of stupendous water-lilies in full bloom.*

*A ridged floor is littered with machine parts, tools, children's toys, dirty clothing and plastic dildoes. There are squares of carpet lying around. They are trade samples.*

*Enter the DOM and the SUB. The DOM is dressed in a leather jacket overlaid with a purple Oxford University surplice. She carries an open toolbox containing hacksaws, crowbars, blowtorch nozzles and electrotorture equipment. The SUB is shivering and naked.*

LESSON: SIRIUS LEYLINE
*The DOM wraps the SUB from head to toe in cling-film, leaving only a gap for the nose and mouth, and ties a knotted rope round her ankles. The rope runs on a pulley attached to the ceiling. The DOM hoists the SUB up so that her fingertips hover centimetres above the ground.*

*The DOM selects the electric wand from her toolbox. Sweat already leaks from the mummified victim.*

S: Holy Satan!

D: Whatever.

*Szzt!*

S: Ow!

D: Did you feel that?

S: Of course I fucking did. Maybe you wanna adjust the voltage on that wand…

D: Or maybe it's time to make you a little more sensitive to the vacuum polarisations which vary the sense ratio between pleasure and pain. Know what I'm saying, girlie girl?

*Szzzzzt!*

S: Ow! Fuck! Hey, are we back doing the scene? Mommy? Mommy dearest?

*Szzzzzzzzt!*

D: Phew! This is tough work. I hope you're grateful, you little cunt.

S: Yes, Mommy...

D: I hope you've learned your lessons. When I think of how many other little girls could be here. You don't know how privileged you are.

S: Yes.

D: So...time for your test. What did you learn from your last lesson? Can you remember?

S: I think so. It was something about the Sirus Leyline.

D: *I think so*? Not good enough.

S: Ouch! I'll tell, I'll tell.

D: Go on then...

S: Um...

D: Oh, for fuck's sake!

S: Aaaaaaaaagh!

D: That's better. Now try...

S: OK, OK, OK, Mom. OK, Mom. OK.

D: OK...come on then, darling. Tell it to Mommy.

S: The...the solutions to the equations of quantum physics do not necessarily occur in the real world. They can for example occur in the virtual world.

D: Yes, good...

S: The magician Einstein demonstrated that a working channel exists between twin particles which though separated in the fourth dimension of space-time are nonetheless linked by a state of quantum entanglement. The mathematicians Kaluza and Klein went on to show that this link operated across the fifth dimension of gravity according to a model of action-at-a-distance.

D: Not quite!

S: Urgh! P-p-passion-at-a-distance. Passion-at-a-distance.

D: Exactly! Now, what does this mean for the working of the Sirius Leyline?

S: Oh, that's easy. The Sirius Leyline defines an entangled quantum loop between our solar system and the triadic star system of Sirius.

D: Does it, you little fuck?

S: Um, yes. Isn't that why we're here? Garbage Disposal is where the Crown ships out cargo to Sirius. Although how anyone could want all that crap, I really don't know.

D: Never mind that! Stick to the lesson!

S: OK, OK! Oww! The magician Einstein tells us that the speed of light is always constant. A quantum loop will only work when it's grounded by an electromagnetic carrier wave connection.

D: Oh yeah? Explain in more detail.

S: Oh fuck! Aaagh! It's something to do with the collapse, the collapse...

D: Yes, yes! The collapse of a superposition at the instant of measurement!

S: Y-yeah. Quantum information needs to be combined with classical information both at our end and at the Sirian end of the Sirius Leyline. That's why those drones were sent out by the aliens...

D: And why were they sent out, you little toe-rag?

S: Ulp! To lay the fibre optic cable. It's cheaper than building star-ships, isn't it? A cheaper way to trade. Even if it's still slow...

D: Slow? It takes less than nine years! The drones have done their work. We're at the start of a glorious new era in the history of the Ukanian Combine!

S: Whatever. As long as the Sirians hold up their end of the deal and don't start diluting the Substance Negative E...

D: What do you know about Substance Negative E? That's classified information! *Crack!*

S: Ow. I think you've really done it this time...

D: Nonsense! What do you mean...?

S: I think you've broken something, you clumsy dolt. Holy Satan!

LESSON: QUANTUM ENTANGLEMENT CONSIDERED AS WORMHOLE CREATION

*The DOM checks the alignment of the bones in the legs of the SUB. She massages the soles of her victim's feet. Then goes back to her toolbox, selects a billy club and returns to work.*

S: Holy Satan! No, please!
   *Schloppp!*

D: Suck on this, you lying little cunt! Next time I *will* break your bones!

S: Ummmph!

D: Don't you dare look at me. Don't fucking look at me! Now, are you willing to be more respectful?

S: Gaaaak!

D: There, there, precious. It's OK. Look...do you want me to keep on looking after you?

S: Yes please, Mommy.

D: OK. Now that I have your attention...let's get back to passion-at-a-distance. Configure it according to Sir Edward's magical theory.

S: The quantum entanglement of a pair of particles corresponds to the creation of a pair of virtual particles from the quantum vacuum. It is this virtual pair which establishes a working channel between the real pair...

D: Continue.

S: Sir Edward's hypothesis is that this working channel is a wormhole. He is looking for the entrance black hole at Garbage Disposal which links to the exit black hole at Sirius C.

D: Once he finds it, what does that mean?

S: Faster-than-light connections between us and the Sirians!

D: Exactly! But, hold on...doesn't the magician Einstein tell us the speed of light is constant?

S: Sir Edward observes that a constant is not the same thing as an absolute. There are some equations which permit speed to be infinite.

D: Oh yes?

S: Yes! The alchemist Newton suggests that the speed of gravity is infinite.

D: *Exactly!*

S: Y-yeah. Sir Edward says that a wormhole is a working channel for a quantum space hop because its entangled pair of virtual particles consists of a graviton and an anti-graviton.

D: Define graviton.

S: Gravitons are the carrier particles of the gravitational waves predicted by the magician Einstein and discovered by our own Sir Edward. These waves appear in the fourth dimension as wrinkles in the curvature of space-time travelling at the speed of light. They are the embedded signs of fifth dimensional wormhole activity which always already will have occurred.

D: So?

S: Well, uh...

D: Instantaneous communication at the quantum level sidesteps the need for light tech.

S: Oh...

D: Sir Edward does not tangle with fibre optic cable.

S: OK.

D: Now that the Sirius Leyline has worked once, it doesn't need the fibre-optic cable any more. The universe can take over. Do you *get* it?
*Shzzzt!*

S: Ahhh! Yes! I get it! M-morphic resonance...

D: Whatever. The point is that Sir Edward says we can jump across the Sirius Leyline through quantum hyperspace. What do you think of that?

S: I don't think anything. You don't need a wormhole to travel down a leyline, do you?

D: Where did you hear that?

S: Where do you think?

D: Do you mean who I think you mean?

S: Doctor Dee.

D: Oooh! Don't even say the bastard's name.

S: Who? Doctor Dee?

D: Shut it!

S: I hear that the Antarctic Leyline guides his travel between Parliament Hill and Garbage Disposal here on the Ark of Old England.

D: You reckon? But he has no space vehicle...

S: I hear that he doesn't travel in person. He sends out his astral body.

D: Does he indeed?

S: Yes, he does.

D: So tell me about it.

S: What?

D: Tell me what you know.

S: Well, you know...

D: *Tell* me!

*Riiiiiip!*

S: Fuck! Oh dear, I think...

D: Yes? What do you think, you little worm?

S: I think that you've forgotten you've already taught me all about the White Lotus ascent.

D: Have I?

S: It was my first lesson.

D: Of course it was. Uh, well, how about the White Lotus ascent? Yes, the White Lotus ascent. How well do you remember your first lesson?

S: Oh that's piss easy. Astral travel I can do in my sleep.

D: Really?

S: Only last night I strung myself up to roam the astral pathways in spirit...

D: Hmmm, no wonder you look so tired.

S: Yeah, well...Ya-awwwn! Astral travel will do that to you every time.

D: I'm just wondering about Doctor Dee...

S: B-o-ring!

D: Shuttup! That Doctor Dee always spells trouble. His Royal Highness will not be amused.

S: Yep!

D: Right, you little piece of shit. Just for that we're going to switch.

S: Really? Hold it a minute. What you got there?

D: The bolt-cutters!

S: Huh?

D: Fingers and toes, girlie! Fingers and toes.

S: Holy Satan! Holy Satan!

LESSON: THE PINK LOTUS DESCENT
*The DOM frees the rope and lets the SUB drop. The SUB lands on a pile of old carpet squares. The DOM rolls her cocooned body aside with the toe of her boot. The SUB is spitting and cursing.*

    *The DOM begins to arrange the carpet squares—some light, some dark—into a checked pattern of intersecting lozenges. Together they form a very rough Penrose map of a rotating black hole. The DOM grunts with satisfaction and removes her clothes.*

    *The DOM peels the cling-film from the SUB's body. The two naked accomplices pause to kiss each other on the mouth. Then the SUB ties the DOM to the pulley by her ankles and hoists her over the Penrose map.*

D: OK.

S: Say it!

D: Say what?

S: Holy Satan!

D: Holy Satan.

S: You could put a little more effort into it!

D: *Holy Satan!*

S: That's better. Fuck! Can we stop? I'm exhausted!

D: Look! I'm going to teach you a very secret move.

S: How secret?

D: It's one of Sir Edward's moves.

S: Oh yeah?

D: Oh *yeah*. He taught it to me himself.

S: OK.

D: And now I'm going to pass it on to you.

S: What does this do? Owww!

D: Put that *down*!

S: OK. So what is this secret move?

D: The Pink Lotus descent.

S: Oh, I've heard of that. It's a technique for converting a quantum space hop into a quantum time hop. But it's only theoretical.

D: Not if you've found a wormhole that works!

S: Right, right. Of course.

D: Leave that tool box *alone*.

S: Calm down!

D: I give up. Why should I even *think* about showing you the Pink Lotus descent?

S: Because good mommies do that for the girlie girls in their care?

D: Harumph!

S: Oh please show me, Mommy. Please! Tell me all about it. Did Sir Edward find out about the Pink Lotus descent when he was with the Nazis in Old Egypt?

D: *No!* Look, you're getting it all confused with the Hollywood movies.

S: Oh!

D: I don't know how Sir Edward learned about it. Rumour has it that some passing desert Tuareg nabbed him when he was excavating the boundary ditches of an 11,000 year-old ancient kingdom in the Sahara. Maybe that was his initiation.

S: I see.

D: It doesn't really matter how Sir Eddie got his technique. The point is it works.

S: Have you done it?

D: I know *how* to do it.

S: Has anyone actually done it?

D: *Listen!*

S: OK, OK.

D: Now watch as I demonstrate how an astral body in free fall would use a wormhole to get from our universe, represented by this bit of carpet, to an adjoining parallel universe, represented by this other bit of carpet. OK?

S: OK.

D: Cross the event horizon of a black hole, skirt the singularity at its throat, then cross back over the event horizon of the black hole. Like this...
*Whup-whup! Whooosh! Whup-whup!*

S: OK. Simple enough.

D: OK. Now watch as I repeat the same move and get to another parallel universe still.
*Whup-whup-whoosh-whup-whup! Whup-whup-whoosh-whup-whup!*

S: OK. But where does your astral body actually end up?

D: It keeps occupying the next real body down the line in our stacked multiverse of parallel universes. It's an infinite cascade, yeah? You can keep on going like this all day and all night.

S: But somewhere down the line...

D: Bingo! Somewhere down the line, somebody has to pay. Eventually you run out of real bodies and there's a homeless astral body floating around.

S: The Pink Lotus descent sounds dangerous.

D: The Pink Lotus descent *is* dangerous. But I haven't shown it to you yet. The Pink Lotus descent is what breaks the chain of infinite parallel universes. It's a manipulation of the force of gravity. Or anti-gravity...

S: Uh huh.

D: Don't worry...you'll get it eventually.

S: Will I?

D: The important thing to remember is that the Pink Lotus descent requires a massive sacrificial input to make it work.

S: Huh?

D: Exactly! You need to discreate the universe you're leaving, create the universe you aim to get to *and* keep the karmic accounts balanced all at the same time.

S: Right.

D: A thousand units of psychic energy should do it.

S: Curse my soul! Well, I'll certainly have to remember that!

D: Lesson over. Untie me.

S: What? I was just...

D: It's time for you to figure out the Pink Lotus descent based on what I've just shown you. Just remember that this bit of carpet, here, represents the nearest anti-grav universe.

S: Well, I know *that*!

D: Untie me, you little freak!

S: Huh?

D: Holy Satan and all his angels! *Untie me!*

*The SUB frees the rope and the DOM drops to the ground. The DOM puts back on her leather jacket and surplice. The SUB stands there shivering*

　　*The DOM pulls on her leather boots, slaps the bare arse of the SUB and then strings her back up. This time they don't bother with the cling-film.*

　　*The DOM picks up a saw from the toolbox.*

D: OK.

S: Holy Satan!

D: *OK.*

S: Please don't make me wait...

D: Bleed yourself dry, cunt.

　　*Plip!*

S: Ho hum!

D: I see you are determined to vex me. So…take that!

S: Aargh!

D: Who the woman?

S: You! You!

D: Well done, girlie! You may kiss the toe of my boot.

S: Oh thankyou, Mommy dearest!

   *Smmmack!*

D: Now show me how an astral body in free fall whups sideways through a wormhole to the next parallel universe over.

S: Um…

D: Oh, for fuck's sake. I just *showed* you.

S: Yes, Mommy! Um…

D: Right, this time there will be no pissing about.

S: Ulp! Yes, Mommy!

D: This time we will have no mercy…

   *Slaa-a-ash!*

S: F-f-f-fuck!

D: Now we're receiving each other. No pain, no gain. Do you get it?

S: Y-y-yuh…yeah!

D: Well, you will have got it by the time I'm finished with you. This is your last
chance, fucker. My honour is resting on this one.

S: Mommy, yes Mommy!

D: I've given you my best material and what have you done with it?

   *Fwoosh!*

S: Gaah! Dunno. Dunno, dunno, dunno.

D: Fucked it up…You've fucked it all up. What have you done?

S: Fucked it all up.

D: Right.

S: Not really! I was just fooling…

   *Whup-whup! Whooosh! Whup-whup!*

D: Why you little rascal!

S: Ha ha!

D: I'm really going to have to punish you now. Get ready…

   *Shee-oo-k!*

S: What happened? I didn't feel anything. Fuck! I've gone numb.

D: Stop panicking! You've still got all your arms and legs. It's just the endogenous
opioids flooding your brainstem…

S: Yeah?

D: Backgrounds the pain. You're threatening to disappear.

S: Ummmm! It's nice!

D: Yeah, yeah, yeah! This is your rite-of-passage, girlie! It's time for you to rehearse the Pink Lotus descent. But first I'm gonna give you some more background...

S: Thanks, Mom.

D: Are you taking the piss?
*Squ-eaa-shh!*

S: Sorry! I'm sorry!

D: I hope you're gonna clean that up. Never mind...Look at me.

S: Huh?

D: Come on! I'm gonna give you the skinny on your astral body. It's now or never. Look me in the eye.

S: I'm scared...

D: This is the astral eye. Right here. This is your transmitter in the fifth dimension, OK? You cast out a gravitational wave and it bounces back to you off the positive voids and negative solids of the virtual zone. Gives you a read-out on the terrain.

S: I think I want to get down now, Mommy.

D: *Listen!*

S: I'm sorry. But didn't you feel that?

D: Hmm?

S: The hairs just stood up on the back of my neck. Like someone crept over my grave. You sure you didn't feel it?

D: That'll be your astral skin crawling. The pilose system is your receiver in the fifth dimension. OK?

S: Right. OK.

D: OK. Now show me how you'd do the Pink Lotus descent. You can figure it out.

S: I really *do* think I want to get down now.

D: Pathetic!

S: I've had *enough!*

D: Shhh! It's OK. I'll guide you through the Pink Lotus descent. Pretend you've made your sacrifice...

S: What?

D: The one thousand units...

S: OK.

D: You have to say a little prayer....

S: Huh?

D: You have to make your sacrifice to a deity.

S: Like Satan?

D: Good enough. Close your eyes and imagine the new universe you aim to reach.

S: No, no! Please! I'm getting some really bad deja vu.

D: What a lot of fuss! It's only a *practice*!

S: I don't *like* it, Mommy.

D: There, there! Mommies know how to do it right. Now I'm going to tickle you until you can't stop laughing.

S: Hee, hee! Mommy, stop!

D: OK. You ready?

S: Ha ha! I suppose so.

D: Show me how you get from our universe to the nearest anti-gravity universe. Come on. It's easy.

S: Cross…cross the event horizon…this time pass through the singularity… *Whup-whup!*

D: Careful! *Shooooom!*

S: …and disappear into the antigrav universe. Yes! Made it.

D: Well done! Now for the occult part of Pink Lotus descent.

S: Eh?

D: Once you're in the antigravity universe you have to collapse your superposition along the trajectory of your evil eye and propagate yourself as a virtual graviton. Or virtual antigraviton.

S: Huh?

D: Same difference. Look, this enables you to go to any parallel universe you want. An infinite number will open up to you like the planes of a giant crystal lattice. Pick your one out and uncollapse your superposition to re-emerge at the singularity, pass back through the wormhole and slide over the event horizon into your imagined universe. Got it?

S: Erm. How do I know which one to pick out?

D: It's just been made for you by your deity! You'll feel an immediate attraction for it.

S: Oh!

D: It all happens in the blink of an eye, you know…

S: It does? Of course it does!

D: You'll hardly know you've been away.

S: I see…

D: Come on then. Show me how you'd complete the Pink Lotus descent.

S: What was that bit about collapsing and uncollapsing your superthingy?

D: I was *hoping* you'd ask that. Let me show you a little of what it must feel like.

I'm gonna close you right down and push you past the limit of sensory dropout. Break the boundaries of your skin and flip you inside out…

S: You kill me, Mommy!

D: Remember your breath control!

S: Mmmppgh!

D: Try not to make too much of a mess.

*Flip! Flop!*

S: Holy Satan!

D: It's too late for safewords.

S: *Help!*

D: Come on. Pass back through the singularity…

S: Satan!

*Shooooom!*

D: …and crawl back over the event horizon to get home.

S: There!

*Whup-whup!*

D: I'll cut you down now. You might need some medical attention.


*The DOM clasps the SUB with one mighty arm and cuts her free with the other. They sink to the floor and lie together in a pool of vomit.*

S: I g-g-got g-g-goosebumps all over…

D: You're disorientated. Getting flipped inside out will do that to you.

S: I feel wasted! Satan knows what it must really feel like to collapse and uncollapse your superposition.

D: Don't worry. You're not quite ready for that yet.

S: Is anyone?

D: Noone has yet tried it. Not even Doctor Dee.

S: What about Sir Edward?

D: Eh?

S: Any chance of a meet-and-greet?

D: Oh, he's busy…conferences, shuttle missions, consultancies, you know…

S: Aww!

D: …but something might be arranged.

S: Really?

D: Really!

S: Ye-ahh!

D: I'll have a discreet word with an old girl I know from the Royal Institute.

S: Holy Satan for real!

## Game on

*Screen Message*
GAME MENU
- i. Installation
- ii. Story so far
- iii. Prologue
- iv. Introduction
- v. Mission
- vi. Entities
- vii. Resources
- viii. Overall Strategic World Index
- ix. Tactical Level Maps
- x. Terrain Peculiarities

*Screen Message*
I. GAME INSTALLATION

*Player Status*
Before installing game check subjectivity meets minimum technical requirements.

Minimum hardware requirements: crippled human body.

Minimum software requirements: fucked-up immune system.

Insert the *Secret Ukanian Combine* Disabled Exogenous Retrovirus into your drug drive. At the neurotransmitter prompt it will automatically select an Endogenous Provirus to model the game as a viral recombination. If the install programme does not automatically run then you need to get wasted. Got it?

*Screen Message*
II. GAME STORY SO FAR

*Real Audio Stream*
"There we were setting up the world's first truly multi-cultural rock'n'rave society, when the City of London moneymen did a deal with the Muslim monotheists and stabbed us in the back. Now look what's happened to all our ancient liberties! No

more Glastonbury Festival, no more Wicker Man, no more Beaufort Hunt! I was born in this country and I don't even recognize it any more."
—Doctor Double Oh No, Crown secret agent, occult cryptographer and head of Ukanian Stay-Behind rear-guard cellnet.


*Narrative Voiceover*
Previously, in *Rave Nation*, loads previously, it was 3000-2000 BCE in North West Europe. That's right. Before the Normans, before the Saxons, before the Romans—before even the Britons and the Celts—were the Afro-Atlanteans. Now these groovy little fuckers were the original technopagan vagabonds shipped into the Mediterranean trade network from Babylon via the Old Kingdom of Egypt. They were following their oracles towards the setting sun, in search of the precious incense ambergris which was reckoned an immortality drug.

So they're passing through Cornwall, Ireland and the west coasts of Wales and Scotland on their way to Lapland and they get busy throwing down all their sacred tech—their trackways, earthworks, stone circles and long barrows.

Their shot-caller is a big fat dyke called Gogmagog. She is initiated into the mysteries of Isis and can get an indirect line puts her through to Osiris, Lord of the Dead, and his crazy brother, Set. All the Old Egyptian deities move in the orbit of the Dog Star and are the zodiac avatars used by the Sirian breed of space aliens to communicate with their designated handlers on earth. All of this makes Gogmagog a real dab hand with proprietary Anubis interface code. The gal is a regular fucking demigoddess.

Anyway, years pass and all these Christian mainframes get dumped on the sacred sites of the Afro-Atlanteans by a bunch of monotheistic barbarians dressed in white sheets. The Crown/City duopoly gets going on the Thames. But old gods die hard and in 1582 true hacker and bisexual occultist Eddie Boy Krishna turns up on Doctor Double Oh No's doorstep in Mortlake with a test-tube of ambergris and an Anubis manual says he found in the ruins of Glastonbury. Soon the two of them are trip partners grooving with the dead as they set up the Afro-Atlantean zombie circuits of the Old Ukanian Combine. Eddie worms his way into the Old Egyptian extranet while the Doctor starts running the Sirians without paying them like they were his pet monsters or something.

So, things are building to a climax. It's 1988—the beginning of events covered in *Rave Nation*—and Eddie is chilling in the monotheistic state of Goa recovering from some really bad experiences in the 1960s. He's got his bare feet up on the beach at Vagator catching some of the new electronic vibes when word reaches him that his old partner in crime is back in operation...

*Full Motion Video*
Drug lord flying in from his offshore island haven with coked-out wannabe super-model in tow. He leans out from beneath the whirling blades: Hey, Eddie Boy, aincha heard? The Ibiza sound is the next big thing. Check out Clink Street.

*Narrative Voiceover*
So Eddie catches the next plane to Heathrow and barrels through the jet-lag to end up necking Substance E with a bunch of London wide boys suddenly eager to get oral on his bits. Damn! Where the fuck did this new drug come from? This is better than mandrake root. He has never partied so hard.

What do you know? Eddie grabs some Adidas shell-toes and starts running with the Inter City Firm snipping locks on empty warehouses in the East End and putting down the competition with machete attacks and Stanley blade rushes. It's real small-time stuff but it gives him back his edge. Pretty soon he's got the local constabulary in on his scams and he's the lord promoter of every dodgy rave between Plaistow, Stratford and Poplar. He's keyed himself into the local extranet and pulled down the Karma Twins to put the frighteners on the indigenes. Everything is pretty fucking sweet.

Inevitably, Eddie gets bored. He hears the Doctor is hanging at the Dungeons on the Lea Bridge Road and one night they meet at Mudchute Common opposite City of London outpost east Canary Wharf. Designated venue the Crossroads of Anubis deep now underground.

*Full Motion Video*
Two sad old English blokes sniffing ambergris and smoking dried leaves in a crib done up like one of the back-rooms at the Globe Theatre. It is earthy and damp.

Eddie: How's tricks, matey? You don't look so good.

Doctor: I assure you the news of my demise was most et cetera. As a matter of fact...I'm back.

Eddie: I dunno, man. You should lay off that kiddie porn.

Doctor: Very funny. Listen, Eddie, don't you realise what we're sitting on here?

Eddie: Please don't say a goldmine. That whole El Dorado thing really freaked me out.

Doctor: *Edward!* Look, my Crown rating is still good. With my intelligence contacts and your funny money connections, we can put together the act again.

Eddie: You want me back in the City of London?

Doctor: Not exactly. Have you seen the way the natives gobble down this Substance E?

Eddie: You want me to set up the bathtub lab, again.

Doctor: Bigger than that, Eddie. I'm thinking the old Raleigh network. Czech drug factories, MI6 spook runs, Caribbean money washes. The works.

Eddie: Off-shore accountability. It figures.

Doctor: Plus, I'm thinking pharmaceutically indentured sex labour. The groundlings are already hooked. All we have to do is manufacture a scarcity and line up a new supply.

Eddie: Brand name?

Doctor: Substance F.

Eddie: Ooh, Doctor. What a comeback!

Doctor: We'll do a test run. If it works, then we'll get the old devil in on the act.

Eddie: Gizza kiss, ya auld cunt.

*Narrative Voiceover*

So this is how the Second English Revolution kicked off. Eddie gets his chemical kitchens up and running with raw materials squeezed out of Latvia and finished product cooked up in phoney biomedical research labs in the Czech Republic. Substance F hits the scene. He's following the Benetton model with batch production runs and just-in-time delivery systems. The MI6 boys have their work cut out shipping the stuff into the country under the disapproving noses of Customs & Excise. Imports get so high it's embarrassing and the spooks have to keep cutting loose more and more bodies to keep their HM colleagues in the loop. Luckily, they've got the ICF and their newly loved-up ex-rival stadium gangs—the Bushwhackers in South London, fragments of the Highbury and White Hart Lane firms up north, the Headhunters out west—patched in on the ground as a dealership network and these guys are routinely expendable.

Pretty soon, Eddie is supplying all the orbital raves which have sprung up like weeds in the deregulated capital investment zones which rake the late industrial landscape outside the London ramparts of the M25. He's got bouncers, ex-squaddies and demobbed SAS guys on the payroll wielding shotguns, TAC key codes and CS gas. Things are getting so out of control that the national police net wants to take over his drug ring. The Doctor is running interference for him with wild cover stories about Sirian black ops and psychological warfare test programmes. But noone is buying his nuclear monotheism number and when the cops send out their HOLMES encryption guys he shrugs and fucks off to Glastonbury on the Hypnosis trail.

Meanwhile Eddie is coining it. He's opened an account in a snide name at an EC4 branch of Barings run by an old Oxford chum and finds himself on the receiving end of unlimited borrowing privileges. Time for the Church's brogues. He funds his whole thing out of Queer Street on a mobile phone and routes his profits through a nested hierarchy of shell companies on the forex markets until they pay out from the Transatlantic Corporation registered in a Virgin Islands tax haven. Then it's bags of cash flying back over the Atlantic pond in note form. A quick bung to Customs and the money's in his clip near fresh as the day it was minted.

Neat little scam, eh? Eddie lets it run on automatic pilot and rearranges his shoe closet. But then his bagman throws a wobbly at Terminal 4 and coughs him up. Suddenly the Inland Revenue sniffer dogs are wanting to go through his pockets and fucking Anubis cuts in to tell him the jig is up. Eddie siphons off his remaining assets into a Swiss holding account—no names, just numbers—and steps back to watch his entire operation go into meltdown.

Que se-fucking-ra. Looks like the scarcity economy has arrived. Eddie pulls in his remaining stash and starts cutting it with amphetamine, synthetic opiates, toilet cleaner, strychnine…any fucking shit he can find. So this is the really bad Substance G produces a void where there should be ecstasy. Eddie don't care. He spears 500 boys in a field in Buckinghamshire. He files his toe-nails. So what the fuck is happening in Glastonbury anyhow..?

*Full Motion Video*
The Doctor dropping science with a bunch of nomadic anarcho-occultist sound system jugglers sporting close crops and black combat gear. He is deep under cover.

Doctor: So did I ever tell you kids bout the time I worked for government intelligence rat-fucking the Algonquins..?

*Narrative Voiceover*
Eddie pulls on some 12-hole Docs with rainbow laces and slots in alongside his mentor. The pair receive their marching orders and fall in behind the Dogstar Tribe. These crazy jugglers are wandering the countryside hitting on all the old Afro-Atlantean sites in an effort to rouse the Afro-Celtic gods and challenge the powers of the Old Ukanian Combine. It seems to work. The tribe gets buzzed by Tornado jets as they dance up a storm in Cornwall while reports file in that Osiris is getting moody. The Doctor is in his element working both sides of the track. He boosts his Crown rating by calling in the scores to the HOLMES boys but then gets Eddie to throw the Sirians round the place keep the Dogstar folks on their toes. It gets so he starts handing out tips on the best domains to hack.

So this is how the Battle of Mudchute came down. The Dogstar Tribe are fronted by this charismatic turntablist called Mark 23. He travels the countryside with a band of merry people, their kids and their dogs. Mark 23 knows how to dig the crates of history as he pumps the wheels of steel. Eddie synchs him into the Raleigh network and pretty soon he's switching the pitch on European techno tracks and animating them with escaped Atlantic drum loops using Caribbean voodoo techniques. The beats are dark and fast.

Osiris is listening. He's trying to get past the lock Eddie has on his box:

*Real Audio Stream*
"Blown minds of screaming-dancing-tattooed-sorted-armed-feathered Dogstar People are only the sparks of a revolutionary implosion and devolutionary planetary regeneration."

*Narrative Voiceover*
Rightey-ho! The Doctor has evolved a strategy of tension and is mouthing off rumours of an insurrection led by Gogmagog. Mark 23 wants the showdown at a stone circle in Wiltshire but the Doctor has other plans. He uses HOLMES to cast an exclusion zone around the meeting place in Wiltshire and sneaks the Dogstar Tribe into Mudchute's green and pleasant land. Mark 23 throws down a mad groove with Eddie slipping him the vinyl. They throw a Stop the City party J21 as the planet turns around the sun. The people are doing a ghost dance and their dogs are going crazy.

The City of London cuts off the green with a secret police roadblock and hits back at the symbolic terror with black helicopters, FM rock and searchlights. The Dogstar folks are pinned down. Eddie has his finger on the page in the Anubis manual deals with the conjuring of spirits. He gets the nod from the Doctor. It's time to download Osiris. Bingo! All hell breaks loose from Mark 23's decks as Osiris fucks with the infrasound and takes out a building near the Canary Wharf tower.

There's pandaemonium on the Crown's black datanets. The Dogstar Tribe seize the day. They set their dogs on the coppers and swarm over the roadblocks into the City. Eddie wrestles with his Anubis Manual and gets Osiris back in his box. The Doctor hits Mark 23 with a chloroform pad and hauls him off the scene. He might need a hostage. Mudchute empties out.

Next day Mark 23 wanders Threadneedle Street in a daze. He is being led on a rope by this cute little devil dog knows which way is up. The Dogstar Tribe been celebrating with motion tactics in the City. Getting loaded and doing it in the road. Breaking finance house windows, spilling garbage, setting fire to cars...

*Full Motion Video*
The Doctor and Eddie hooked up on the sacred mound at Parliament Hill engaged in an emergency failsafe procedure. Lots of thunder and lightning.

Doctor: This is a recoverable situation.

*Screen Message*
III. GAME PROLOGUE

*Narrative Voiceover*
Events move fast. Riot leads to revolution and the symbolic order implodes. England resets the polarities of its chaotic equilibrium.

The Dogtar Tribe mass convert to Islam, take over the state apparatus and rename the country the Caliphate of New New England. They repunch the calling cards of all the Christian mainframes left to rot in the City and let the rest in the East End of London revert to paganism or go to hell. Mark 23 is ousted by a gang of fanatical Muslims and sent into exile where he gets into drug abuse and elective surgery.

Meanwhile, the Crown deterritorializes so far it ends up off-shore running its Caribbean island territories as a global leyline net from an orbital space ark. Calls itself the New Ukanian Combine and fronts its drug rackets with stadium rave operations. The Doctor elects to stay behind at his listening post and mount a rear-guard action from within the new Caliphate. Eddie is nowhere to be seen.

There is a stand-off. The Caliphate are establishing step-down programmes for demobilizing their vagabond armies now the war is over. The Crown is building carceral holiday resorts to attract the human flotsam of the Afro-Atlantean tourist circuits.

What could tip the balance is Operation Dogon. Seems the Crown with the support of its secret agents in America has detected the laying of fibre-optic cable between the star system Sirius and our home solar system. Trading circuits have opened and symbolic exchanges of sacred code are beginning to occur with the Sirian breed of space aliens. One result the Crown is now building up a menagerie of alien/human mutants on its orbital space ark. One of these creatures is exposed to gamma radiation and becomes a dangerous monster more powerful than all the rest combined. Her name is Anu and she known as the Chameleon Kid.

*Screen Message*
IV. GAME INTRODUCTION

*Player Status*
*Secret Ukanian Combine: Rave Nation 2* is the long-awaited sequel to the original action-adventure game from Orion Intraveinment.

In *Rave Nation* you became London rudeboy and ex-workingclass hero Mark 23 and with your band of merry Dogstar people you wandered the old trackways quickening the pulse of mana at strategic Afro-Atlantean sites in an effort to evict the Crown/City duopoly from your land and build a new society.

Now in *Secret Ukanian Combine* the bases have switched. You become Doctor Double Oh No and with your sidekick Eddie Boy Krishna you embark on a magical quest to rebuild a Secret Ukanian Combine. Anu the Chameleon Kid will do everything in her power to stop you. A deadly contest is in the offing.

*Screen Message*
V. GAME MISSION

*Player Status*
During the course of the game you are challenged to accumulate the tezma or cursing power necessary for Doctor Double Oh No to make the Pink Lotus descent. This dangerous procedure will launch a world-changing curse designed to restore to the Crown its lost English territories and deliver a Secret Ukanian Combine. It is not to be used lightly.

*Screen Message*
VI. GAME ENTITIES

Doctor Double Oh No
Crown secret agent, occult cryptographer and SIGINT analyst. The Doctor is an expert in black operations and psychological warfare. He has elected to remain at his radio listening post on Parliament Hill in an effort to destabilize the Caliphate as head of the Ukanian Stay-Behind cellnet. From here he directs the Crown's remote contacts with the aliens in the star system of Sirius. The Doctor is a radio veteran reluctant to involve himself in new methods of intelligence collection. He was born in Mortlake on the Thames but is always hyping up his Welsh ancestry. His extensive knowledge of Central Europe dates back to his Cambridge days.

Eddie Boy Krishna
Freelance drug alchemist, financial wizard and true hacker. Eddie has the gift allows him to check things out with his third eye. He has formed a temporary

partnership with the Doctor which sees him channelling the Sirians on his behalf. Eddie is a vagabond sport boy shuttles between the Muslim-occupied territory of London and the exiled Crown powers in orbit over the South Pole. When he is not doing anything else he is running the luxury Cathedron-a-Go-Go nightclub and casino complex in the Virgin Islands. Eddie is a West Country lad who dropped out of Oxford. His sexual orientation is as variable as his racial designation.

Anu the Chameleon Kid
Shape-shifting human/alien monster produced out of the contact zone between blacklisted Crown scientists and the Sirian breed of space aliens. Anu has escaped her pen on the Crown's orbital space ark and set her sights on returning to earth. She exists as a quasi-solid blob which occupies a trajectory rather than a fixed coordinate and is able to creep under locked doors and slide across walls. She is composed of millions of isomorphic hypersurfaces whose halos of attraction model a shape-shifting tectonics. Anu is singular and networked at the same time and able to introject other partial subject positions. She has twelve extra lives.

Professor Natasha Supanova
Mad ex-Soviet biotech scientist and deadly enemy of the Crown from long time ago now working for her old antagonist Doctor Double Oh No in a freelance capacity. Professor Supanova is prized for her gene-splicing skills and attends to the captive alien/human mutants in the orbital space ark extracting the prized Substance H from their blood cells. She is so dedicated to the creatures in her charge she administers the last rites for them once they reach the end of their short life-cycle. Professor Supanova's incipient schizophrenia makes her an easy hypnotic mark for the Doctor, who is able to use her as remote control agent Bad Nat over an astral link.

Jack the Mack
Stumblebum maniac and deranged visionary hacked together from stray bits of City of London interrupt code by Eddie and animated with the force of tezma or negative mana by the Doctor. Jack haunts the choked ditches and occult corridors of the East End and is a disgusted fan of the local crack whores. He is operated as a remote control agent by the Doctor and has limited powers of mobility around London. Eddie wrote his front end as an incarnation of the last prophet of Allah and gave him a mission to purge the land of the evil demon Ashtoreth. Jack's tragedy is that he believes his own cover story.

Karma Twins

Wooden mannequins built by original Afro-Atlantean mob boss Gogmagog in her own image as guardians of East London. Regina Karma is the soft one, the nice one, the femme one. Rhona Karma is the hard one, the nasty one, the butch one. The Karma Twins sleep underground in the ruins of the old Osiris billiard hall dressed in gorgeous double-breasted suits. Regina clasps a list of names and Rhona stands there with an open hand. They can be animated by anyone brave or foolhardy enough to fill Rhona's hand with the Kingsize Dildo she lost in the streets all those years ago. The Karma Twins are devoted servants of Isis and continue to be worshipped by those with long memories in East London.

Mark 23

Misanthropic ex-workingclass hero, ex-revolutionary turntablist and ex-Dogstar Tribe frontperson. Mark 23 is a lone vagabond permanently in search of the bonds of community which would grant him the fixed identity he craves. After quitting the Caliphate he travelled into voluntary exile in East London where he set up as a one-man pirate TV operator. In his self-appointed role as tele-arbiter of the nation's morals he prowls the streets with a vidcam and portable studio. Mark 23 grabs occult testimony for his reality TV show and remixes it through the received imagery of the day. He has developed an obsession with Jack the Mack.

*Screen Message*
VII. GAME RESOURCES

Mana

Mana exists as the sum total of partial subject positions projected on to a figure within a closed symbolic system. As the amount of mana possessed by a figure grows so their own subjectivity is eclipsed. They become the bearer of an empty sign which is all things to all persons.

Baraka

Positive mana or blessing power. Mana must be recycled through a symbolic system in order to function well. Expenditure of mana is beneficial.

Tezma

Negative mana or cursing power. When mana cannot be exchanged then it builds up to dangerously high levels. Accumulation of mana is potentially harmful.

*Screen Message*
VIII. GAME OVERALL STRATEGIC WORLD INDEX

*Real Audio Stream*
"I think the idea of equipping Jersey to serve as the HQ of a Crown government-in-exile only makes sense if you're a rabid devotee of open-air toilets."
—Doctor Double Oh No sipping claret in his glass closet underneath Parliament Hill.

*Player Status*
The overall strategic world index of the Crown's global leyline net is made available to you through a Very Small Aperture Terminal (VSAT) satellite system whose data scans operate to a high degree of resolution. Select the scan ratio required and the data will be displayed in anything from a long shot to an extreme close-up. The data is quantified in terms of the telematic alignments which exist between the most significant Ukanian island territories. It is available for view on seven world screens:

1 Europe world screen: Jersey in the English Channel between the North Atlantic Ocean and the North Sea; Gibraltar in the Strait of Gibraltar between the North Atlantic Ocean and the Mediterranean Sea.

2 Africa world screen: Ascension and St Helena in the South Atlantic Ocean.

3 North America world screen: Bermuda in the North Atlantic Ocean; Jersey in the English Channel between the North Atlantic Ocean and the North Sea.

4 Central America world screen: Cayman Islands, Turks and Caicos Islands, Royal Virgin Islands, Anguilla and Montserrat in the Caribbean Sea adjacent to the North Atlantic Ocean.

5 Antarctica and South America world screen: Pitcairn Islands in the South Pacific Ocean; Falkland Islands, South Georgia and South Sandwich Islands in the South Atlantic Ocean adjacent to the Weddell Sea; Tristan da Cunha and St Helena in the South Atlantic Ocean.

6 Asia world screen: Royal Indian Ocean Territory.

7 Australasia world screen: no data.

*Screen Message*
IX. GAME TACTICAL LEVEL MAPS

*Real Audio Stream*
"Every Londoner worth their salt knows that once you cross the river you're in limbo."
—Eddie Boy Krishna holed up in Lambeth after a done deal got badly undone.

*Player Status*
You will find that each of the overall strategic world index's seven screens delivers a menu of tactical level maps. The most habitually used of these maps is from the North America world screen and defines the leylines of the London double septagram in the Muslim-occupied territories of Ukania. The double septagram is accessed using the methods of a habitual psychogeography and distributed across thirteen nodal points. Each point designates an address code sacred to the Crown.

1.  Water Street on Manhattan Island
2.  Old Swallow Gardens in Whitechapel
3.  Pinchin Street in Whitechapel
4.  Old Castle Street in Whitechapel
5.  Gunthorpe Street in Whitechapel
6.  Henriques Street in Whitechapel
7.  Hanbury Street in Whitechapel
8.  Durward Street in Whitechapel
9.  Mitre Square in the City of London
10. Old Dorset Street in Whitechapel
11. White's Row in Whitechapel
12. Maidman Street in Mile End
13. Shadwell Dock Stairs in Shadwell

Note that an occult retro-strategic index of the Crown orbital space ark can be accessed via a remote viewing capability from significant terrain peculiarities designated by any of the tactical level maps. ·

*Screen Message*
X. GAME TERRAIN PECULIARITIES

*Real Audio Stream*
"I want to know where the Caliphate fibre optic cable is hidden. I want Eddie to go in and break it up and force them into the ether."
—Doctor Double Oh No, smarting from an accusation that his radio listening post is obsolete.

*Player Status*
The use of terrain peculiarities is one of the key elements of success in your struggle against the possibility of an alien invasion of the Crown leyline net. As Doctor Double Oh No you have shifted your home base in the Muslim-occupied

territories of Ukania from Glastonbury Tor to Parliament Hill on Hampstead Heath in London. The radio listening post at Parliament Hill functions as the root node of the Ukanian Stay-Behind cellnet.

1. Sacred hill: The station for a remote aerial radio antenna. The radio station is protected with an array of cut-out switches, booby traps and alarms and insured against Caliphate police raids by an emergency back-up antenna on top of nearby Primrose Hill.

2. Hermetic hole-in-the-hill: The site of a glass Faraday cage shielded against electromagnetic pollution by a coating of visually transparent but radio-opaque conductive ink. Doctor Double Oh No's bedroom cell.

3. Cosmic tree: The studio where Doctor Double Oh No uses Eddie Boy Krishna as a natural microwave antenna to bounce messages between himself and the radio aerial. These line-of-sight micro-links operate according to a psychic driving principle embodied in various sex magick techniques.

4. Zodiacal pond: The real-space Visual Display Unit (VDU) which guides Eddie Boy Krishna's spectre to the VSAT satellite window hooks the Ukanian Stay-Behind radio cellnet into the Crown's global leyline net. Eddie also has his own back-channel direct to the Sirians.

*Full Motion Video*
The Doctor squatting on the bank of the zodiacal pond. Looking past the stems of the water-lilies into the flowing depths. Something floats to the surface of the pond and disturbs the wide flat leaves. It is a ripe seed-pod bristling with defensive spines.

The seed-pod bobs on the pond. The Doctor leans out and poles the golden-skinned fruit towards him with a twisted wooden stick. He grapples with the seed-pod when it reaches the bank and hauls it out of the pond. Green pond water gushes over the edge of his long black coat.

The Doctor's finger nails are long, sharp and tough. He uses them to slice into the flesh of the seed-pod along one side. Juice spurts over his knees. He reaches deep into the seed-pod and pulls out handfuls of soft white pulpy fruit which he throws to the ground. Once he has completely scooped out the seed-pod, he is left with only its limp, sagging skin.

The Doctor stands up, sucking swollen black seeds from his fingers. He pulls a shiny silver Nikon from his pocket. Wipes his mouth with the back of his hand and takes a light reading.

*Player Status*

Once *Secret Ukanian Combine* has been installed, select the appropriate erogenous zone and initiate a state of arousal. You will then become Doctor Double Oh No and be ready to start the game.

*Screen Message*

START GAMEPLAY ?

START GAMEPLAY?

START GAMEPLAY?

## Confession of Professor Natasha Supanova

I Nastasha Supanova work a captive surgical monster drug bodily fluid taker here in the fully recycling self-contained environment of the space station ecosphere known as the Ark of Old England and depart every new moon on the causeway travelator used only by the unliving oh yes to keep my secret appointment in Garbage Disposal with the Spectre of my diseased giggling control the mad Doctor Death.

I sleep one night only in an overflow septic tank outside the zone where lifeless bodies of alien/human graft entities are dumped their bioplasmic energy tribute fading away slowly down fibre optic cables to the far side of a black hole. The microminiature psychotronic electrode implanted in the tympanic membrane of my ear I know it is there the property of Doctor Death my psychic driver he calls me Bad Natasha not Professor and activates me with post-hypnotic trigger commands to see the sights and hear the sounds recorded by my brain. He orders me to step out of the septic tank and move over to the lifeless bodies one by one I perform surgical caesarean sections unbelievable overnight. The slimy vicious English doctor leaves with his organic loot back there beside the septic tank full of scummy waters close enough for him to reach. On the floor I Professor Supanova find myself awake again no longer Bad Natasha this time alone and unsteady with a buzzing noise in my head.

All this is completely unknown whereas the abuse perpetrated by the Gangster Capitalist Oligarchy in the Royal Substance Lab of the Ark of Old England is a worldwide open secret.

Only I Professor Natasha Supanova PhD am survived to witness the alien/human graft slave dreaming pharms of the Royal Substance Lab with a PROPER SCIENTIFIC KNOWLEDGE of their deadly hangman rope connection to Garbage Disposal and all points beyond. That is because I still follow the methods of the great Soviet agrobiologist a star proletarian scientist Trofim Denisovich Lysenko as approved by Comrade Josef Stalin himself at the world historic 1948 convention of the Lenin Academy of Agricultural Sciences.

Please allow me O my Unknown Interlocutor to wax personal for a moment I was not always the shameful parasitic Methuselah who writes these saving words. Before I allowed myself to be captured by the Ukanian imperial spy his real name Doctor Death in the Socialist Republic of Czechoslovakia during the Great Patriotic Collapse of 1989 I was a Soviet biologist renowned for her work with Bioplasmic Technology.

Whatever poor successes I managed to achieve in the production of new forms of Artificial Life I owe to the green-fingered Ukrainian muzhik's son. Comrade Lysenko was a heroic member of the elite cadre of agricultural workers who inspired their fellow agronomists, zoo technicians and kolkhozniks across the state farms and breeding stations of the Soviet Union. He was truly a great man slandered by all the tame capitalist running dogs of Mendelism-Veysmanism-Morganism who made jokes about him breeding sheep from goats.

Pah! Comrade Lysenko was never a man to interest himself in the genetic breeding programmes of the worldwide impossible Neo-Imperialist Slave Trade. This is where his detractors cannot escape the limitations of their own neo-Malthusian ideology which insists that our great world of plenty is a berth of scarce resources which must be dominated by a master race.

Genetics is all a justification for racism, exploitation and genocide as any educated person can clearly see. Genetics is CAPITALIST MYSTIFICATION. It was the achievement of Comrade Lysenko to demonstrate that THERE IS NO SUCH THING AS A GENE. The gene is a metaphysical concept dreamt up by the pea-counting atomist Gregor Mendel who was insufficiently socialized. It is Menshevising Idealism pure and simple.

Bioplasmics is the really existing science of life. The simplest peasant knows this it is obvious all that is new under the sun is created from the fertile electromagnetic ether which wraps itself around our planet earth. The Heraclitan flux of energy into matter and back once again defines the bioplasmic continuum from which the fatal enemy of the entire human people namely the Gangster Capitalist Oligarchy constructs totemic entities like GENE and PARASITE and BOURGEOIS INDIVIDUAL.

How else O my Divine Human Interlocutor could Comrade Lysenko deliver sudden revolutionary leaps in the development of crops? By modifying the environment direct he varied temperature and humidity levels until the bioplasmic pressure exerted on wheat seeds induced them to mutate spontaneous into parallel cereal forms.

This is not Natural Selection it is not even Artificial Selection it is Directed Emergence. It has nothing to do with lines of descent pure or otherwise. It has everything to do with points of discontinuous variation on a bioplasmic spectrum extending in time as well as in space some might say the switching stations of the dead and unborn I call them simply projected Spectres.

Never mind the Lamarckists and the Darwinists closeting themselves away with perspectivalist arguments about whether genetic property is inherited direct or indirect from generation to generation. Remember instead Comrade Lysenko out there barefoot in Azerbaijan probing the nonlinear earth/light dynamics of the bioplasmic continuum along its chaotic air/water edge. He made the effort to generate new forms of life immediate.

All this is old news thankfully leaking out from the concoctions and manipulations of fabricated news media. So nowadays the lily-fingered propagandists of so-called genetics like to talk of TRANSPOSONS and JUMPING GENES in an effort to save their crippling diseased paradigm it is too late. When will they realize there is no difference between the genotype and the phenotype there is only the drifting adaptation of the bioplasmic continuum to the projected Spectres of its inhabitants?

Maybe never. Now you see why Comrade Lysenko's scientific enemies needed to be removed from positions of influence and stripped naked on the gulag operating table for instant corrective brain surgery. They were jeopardising the truly Stakhanovite improvements in grain yields which Comrade Lysenko's methods promised to safeguard. Inevitably only when all unbelievable sophisticated efforts at rehabilitation had failed was the humane method of termination preferred.

Now this is more than can be said for Doctor Death's slave dreaming pharms in the camouflaged green-and-oh-so-pleasant synthetic lands of the Ark of Old England. I should know because I am employed sorry creature that I am to tap the alien/human graft entities at the end of each lunar cycle and siphon off the neuromelanin-enriched cerebro-spinal fluid which the Gangster Capitalist Oligarchy intends to sell as the immortality drug Substance H to dope fiends worldwide.

I Professor Natasha Supanova PhD confess that I have injected myself with the secretions of my alien/human former future comrades and SHARE IN THE GUILT which is why I write this testimony. But I separate myself from the hopeless attempt to breed a worldwide population of slaves from the historic encounter between the Sirians our divine friends in the Universe and the surplus late-industrial humans lured by engineered dance crazes to a false consciousness of death in the Caribbean.

The insane criminal Endura cult run by faggot playboy con artist Eddie One Thousand is a digital version of the contagious peasant dance of St John which had manic German yokels leaping in and out of a showdown with the Black Death. It is a lifelong fatal machine plague scored to the mantra of repetitive beats.

Doctor Death's unprecedented patenting of the complete sequence of DNA found in the alien genome or cell nucleus is a felonious expropriation of the true gift offered by the Sirians our universal siblings to all human people. What is worse is that inside his sealed Caribbean anatomy theatre Doctor Death performs impossible genetic engineering operations overnight taking late-industrial female humans to experiment on their uterine glands.

He calls this cloning he is possessed by the insane alchemical desire to give birth to Sirians direct from the DNA code. But as a follower of Comrade Lysenko I know this is NUCLEAR TRANSPLANTATION only which results in instant deep stretch marks, scars, age spots, freckles, blemishes, pimples, skin rashes, fever, arthritis and inflammation of the sacro-iliac joints.

Other side-effects unpredicted include morbid growth of fibrous tissue in the uterine gland a function of noise on the line between the pineal gland emitting neuromelanin and the pituitary gland emitting reproductive hormones. Neuromelanin and repro-ductive hormones are mutually inhibiting a positive feedback loop for the uterine gland lasting nine months itself the total life cycle of the alien/human graft entities.

I Professor Natasha Supanova PhD must say at once that Doctor Death's monthly neuromelanin harvest results from the pharming of an auto-immune side-effect completely unintended. He presents the substance to his gangster boss Charles the guilt-ridden Termite King while secretly using me to clear away all incriminating evidence of uterine gland infection it must all be flushed away down the black hole in Garbage Disposal.

When the Termite King's secret police brought you here to me in Garbage Disposal I was kneeling at the foot of the overflow septic tank on the cold tiles released for a lunar period from the ministrations of Doctor Death's Spectre a mistake in the control circuits Bad Natasha was gone. I knew at once O my Infinite Precious Interlocutor that this was the beginning of a revolution and my chance to redeem myself.

What Doctor Death and his Neo-Imperialist Slave Traders have done to you is to remove the cell nucleus from one of your eggs and inject into the remaining cytoplasm a chemically synthesized version of the Sirian genome they think like a programme loaded into a surrogate workstation for rewriting.

Now Comrade Lysenko always understood the power of the egg cytoplasm which is the exclusive carrier of mitochondrial DNA and a lifeline back to the Ancient Free Lives of bacteria in the planetary bioplasmic membrane. Mitochondrial DNA incarcerated in the cytoplasmic power stations of multicellular life are the true pro-letariat of all Divine Human Becoming they produce neuromelanin in the shadow of cancer not alien homonculi once organized by the revolutionary avant-garde of Sirian DNA itself very close in chemical composition to the photosynthesizing cyanobacteria of blue-green algae plastids.

No alien/human graft surrogate mother has given birth to a Sirian hominid nor ever will they are a new creation entire in the history of the universe as solely I understand. What Doctor Death sees as a side-effect is the main event a mutation which it is necessary to accelerate in order for the Full Sirian Human to emerge. Neuromelanin is not ever an immortality drug this is a grandiose cosmetological fiction it is instead an alien/human superconductor transducing electromagnetic frequencies from the bioplasmic continuum making them available as spectral templates for Directed Emergence.

So far this has been exploited only as a showbusiness gimmick by the Gangster Capitalist Oligarchy with alien/human graft entities put on stage once a month prior to spinal tapping by me and made to shift into parallel monstrous forms. It is not understood these tetralogical entities are the result of projections from the bioplasmic continuum of the Ark of Old England it is thought instead they are holographic fluctuations merely the signs of a hormone imbalance itself the rationalisation for neuromelanin extraction.

Only I Professor Natasha Supanova PhD understand the real nature of the abuses at work in the bioplasmic field of the Ark of Old England. During a monster show what happens is one of the scum-on-top cronies of the Termite King the designated predator fashions a Spectre from guilt all unknowing and projects it on to one of the alien/human graft entities the designated prey seeking to discover a ragged hole in their bioplasmic field a pulsating wound and infect it with rage.

Inevitable gradualness of death. Except that the neuromelanin of the alien/human graft entity no longer the designated prey in a self-protective counter-offensive photocopies the incoming Spectre to create its uncanny double an Emanation. Situation reversed the Emanation tends to suppress the guilt Spectre of the would-be predator now shrinking back in fear. The alien/human graft entity the victor now adds this latest Emanation to their repertoire of multiple personalities some might say a symptom of dissociative identity disorder I say the index of successful bioplasmic conversion.

Eureka! Only one thing capable of interrupting this bioplasmic conversion process that is the activation of the resonant frequency of the Spectre photocopied into an Emanation once named it dissolves in a recognition event.

O my Nameless Interlocutor you are near to a scaly little spore from a benevolent star who lives on white light alone as I Professor Natasha Supanova PhD have divined through complete scientific understanding of Trofim Denisovich's methods themselves based on the successful hybridisation work performed by rehabilitated Russian aristocrat horticulturist I V Michurin on fruit tree grafts. Now no longer a captive drug dealer and vicious kosher butcher I have the chance to become a gardener who tends the adaptive mutation of an alien/human graft entity to the bioplasmic continuum as altered by Sirian contact.

This is a historic mission which solely I accept.

There is no need to fear O my Divine Human Interlocutor you were brought here to Garbage Disposal as a secret health example but I will redeem you safe from the surveillance system of the Termite King now showing placebo footage it was long ago planned. Thankyou for letting me repurpose the cutting tools of Doctor Death's Neo-Imperialist Slave Trade they have stained fingers red which should have been green.

That is why my tender little comrade I intend to grant you the gift of a hole in the head they say trepanation the surgical removal of a disc of bone from your skull to uncover your pineal gland. O my Divine Human Interlocutor know this you are about to receive what I Professor Natasha Supanova PhD have designed as a means for your neuromelanin to receive much stronger signals from the bioplasmic continuum especially prophetic radiation from Sirius.

When I have finished my work made necessary by the botched anti-abortions of Doctor Death I will release you into the bioplasmic continuum of an earth ruled by the Gangster Capitalist Oligarchy in the hope your merciless interventions will build UNIVERSAL COMMUNISM from its Heraclitan flux. Prepare your body to become the vehicle of an emergent intelligence directed from an alien planet code name Sirius C some say a fantasy I say our only hope for a future.

Did we not used to praise the example of our own leader and teacher overcoming setbacks the great friend and protagonist of science Comrade Stalin? Trofim Denisovich followed safe in his footsteps just as I track his own path to redeem my criminal errors the price of my survival here at Garbage Disposal in the Ark of Old England.

O my little Anuket I will shape you into a gorgeous body to swing like a shooting star from this pitiful canopy to our last bed down below. Do you know one word of prayer for me Professor Natasha Supanova PhD? If so then do not dare to repeat it for I have judged myself more exact than even Genghis Khan called up on the big telephone.

## Child abduction at Shadwell Dock Stairs

Eddie still sweating under the lights. He's got an idea his name's come up in some dodgy informant's file.

*A True and Faithful Relation of What Passed at Clarence House between Dr John Dee and the Devil.* Extract 2.1: The Juggler dismounted at the riverside, lighting up the sky with his crystalline water-craft.

EK Exegesis 2.1: You've got me bang to rights. That must have been me shooting back into Blighty from Atlantis. Now who else could it be?

The old man never used the Thames in later life. Said he'd had it up to here with river gods. Said they were all mad and stank of fish. He always flew upper class and he never had to pay. Connections, see.

So, yeah, it must have been me.

*A True and Faithful Relation…* Extract 2.2: The Morning Star drifted through the ruined park towards the surging water, drawn by the pull of the compulsive tide and the noxious smell of the faraway Atlantic Ocean. An age-worn flight of steps led down unto the bottomless river where water gently spanked the filthy stones. Never had she heard that noise before and she drifted into an awestruck trance.

The godless light changed.

And she looked and saw an amphibious wonder of shining glass that shimmered upon the seething water. Never before had she seen its like. It had a wide chassis of refulgent gold and a low iron running board. In its middle was an outer door and the door was marked by the sign of a gruesome fish-tailed woman. The Morning Star did recognise the alien sign but knew not what it meant.

The marvellous chariot sank mysteriously into the fathomless river until she could glimpse it no longer. Immature was she, and damaged, but for the first time in her mangled life she felt devastating awe and joy. It frightened her.

She looked back unto the spire indistinct of the Well of the Third Weird Sister near her abandoned home. With its noisome rankness and its pathetic children screaming in the overcrowded corridors, the desolate orphanage had left upon her a bone-revealing impression.

Her restless trance was broken by a croaking voice. "I have come for you."

She turned and saw a black man looking right through her. The Juggler had risen uncannily from the darkening river and was limping up the mossy steps.

"I was only looking," she said.

"Look you for someone I know?" he replied. "My chariot is here. Its entrance lies down in the river."

EK Exegesis 2.2: I'd parked the vehicle at Shadwell Dock Stairs, hadn't I? A very nifty pick-up spot, that. Sheltered little reach of the Thames used by Marty Frobisher and his sort when those mad fuckers were in the habit of jumping off after the North-West Passage or some other bleeding piece of fool's gold.

Found her moping about looking all wistful in this kiddies' playground right where the old fish market used to be. Allegra she said they called her. A scruffy little thing she was with red blotchy skin and tangled black hair. Now it was obvious to me that she was a wild one. In fact, she had all the signs of being another friendless runaway from the children's home back on Glamis Road near St Mary's church.

Now, in my own defence, I have to say there was no pressure. I left the gaffer tape well alone. Allegra could have told me to take a running jump at any time. But she didn't did she? She swallowed the old line about becoming a pop star. They always do.

She begged me to take her to Paradise Island and I took her out of the kindness of me heart. Couldn't bring meself to charge her, see? Let me tell you, there was barely room in the hold.

Well, this is what you get for charity.

*A True and Faithful Relation…* Extract 2.3: Grave coincidence did not escape the glorious one selected by the Devil Osiris. The unseen evil was directed against her in particular.

EK Exegesis 2.3: This all happened much later, didn't it? If I'd have known that Anubis was going to contact Allegra on behalf of Osiris, then I would never have gone near her with a barge pole.

Never flim-flam a flim-flammer, that what I say.

If you think about it, the mysterious end of the Doctor dates back to that pick-up in the East End.

## Transplantation

*You are being choppered into hospital. You are flying through the air over East London. You were picked up at Mile End. That's where you used to live. But now you are going to the big hospital in Whitechapel. You are going to land on the roof. You are inside a helicopter. It's the colour of blood. You've seen it whirling high above you like a tireless metal insect. But that was back when you were safe on the ground. Now there is blood in your throat. Someone is shouting beneath the noise of the blades. You close your eyes. They want to know your name. Someone wants to know your name. You are bleeding. You don't know your name.*

*What is your name? You don't know. You've forgotten your own name. Let it go. You let it go. You are losing it. Losing your own life. Let it go. You drift into a cold dark space. You are no longer yourself. You dream you are this dead girl. You dream you are no longer alive. What is your name? You don't have a name. You are Dead Girl.*

>>

Dead Girl was calling out to someone. She didn't have any clothes on. All she had on was this fanny-pack around her waist and she was calling out to her Fairy Sugadaddy. But he wasn't there.

It didn't matter. She could always look at all the stars rushing past in the darkness. They were pretty and she tried to catch them. But she was going too fast. She was falling. She was hurtling through outer space down towards Planet Earth.

It was cold.

<<

Dead Girl was travelling. She was crossing the Atlantic Ocean. She was going from a place in London Town to an island in the Caribbean Sea. She was hiding inside this ship. She had been put there.

It was cold. There was a massive amount of heat coming out of these engines. They were huge engines. They were big and fat and the colour of silver. There was this intense heat radiating out from the engines into a very cold space.

Dead Girl had her own little bed throughout the voyage. It had a little cabinet next to it. But she never used it. She didn't have the key.

The only thing that Dead Girl owned was her fanny-pack. It was a little purse on a belt made out of what they call mock crocodile skin. She always wore it round her waist with the purse at the front. She liked to unzip the purse to check her photo was still inside. It was a black and white photo. She kept it in one of the pockets so that its torn white border was always visible. It was the only thing inside her fanny-pack and she always wore her fanny-pack. That way she knew her photo was always there close to her. She found that very comforting.

Dead Girl wore her fanny-pack underneath this white hospital gown that tied up at the back. She didn't have any shoes or socks on. She wasn't wearing any knickers.

She had these sticking plasters on her arms. That must have been because she'd been cutting herself. They called it self-harming back at the children's home. But it wasn't that. It was because she couldn't stand it. That's why she'd run away. She'd run away from the Silver Birches because she couldn't stand it.

She was going to Paradise.

>>

Dead Girl was falling through the atmosphere. She was rushing like a meteorite towards London Town.

She didn't have any clothes on. She didn't have a home. She wanted to hear the voice of Fairy Sugadaddy. She wanted some comfort. But all she had was her fanny-pack.

Dead Girl screamed. She was burning up.

<<

Dead Girl arrived at this island in the Caribbean Sea. It was Paradise. She saw its name on a postcard when she got off the ship. The postcard showed these empty white beaches and shady golf-courses. It had a picture of the big honey-coloured casino where all the glamorous people went. The casino was called Atlantis.

Dead Girl stood on this red carpet inside Atlantis. It ran past rows and rows of slot machines lit up like television screens. There were all these empty chairs in front of the slot machines. They had these plush blue seats.

Dead Girl was wearing her white hospital gown and her fanny-pack. She was the only one in the casino. She walked down the red carpet in the warm silence. She called out but nobody answered. Even the slot machines were silent.

There was this bandstand in the middle of the casino. It had a domed roof held up by these thick white pillars. Running round the top edge of the bandstand were these pictures of dogs and birds and naked stick people. There was a red velvet rope surrounding the bandstand. Inside the bandstand there was this glass aquarium which went from the floor to the ceiling. It was all blue inside with little pieces of coral and shoals of fish that flashed from side to side. It was a very important place. The sign outside said it was a Beautiful Person Lounge.

Dead Girl touched the rope. Her hand was all sweaty. She could see how the rope was attached to the nearest pillar with a brass hook. She wanted to unhook the rope. She felt like she wasn't supposed to do it. But she wanted to go inside and get closer to the aquarium. She wanted to be a Beautiful Person. But she was dirty and smelly and her hair was a mess.

Suddenly she wasn't wearing her hospital gown anymore. The only thing she had on was her fanny-pack.

Dead Girl unzipped her purse and took out the photo. It had a torn edge. She only took out the photo when she was feeling very low. She didn't do it very often. She only did it now and again.

The photo was all dirty and creased. It was a black and white photo of a little baby wrapped in tissue paper. The baby was lying in a shoe-box.

Dead Girl stroked the image on the photo and then turned it over. On the back there was this logo showing two little animals standing up on their hind legs. It was what they call a Royal Crest.

>>

Dead Girl was falling naked through the air. Old River Thames was looping across London Town far down below.

Dead Girl was caught in a hail-storm or something. She kept twisting and turning, but it did no good. She kept getting jabbed and bombarded on all sides. She kept getting hurt.

She felt that she was splitting apart. She felt that there were pieces of her that were just shearing away. She was coming apart as she fell through the air.

What had happened to her Fairy Sugadaddy? She didn't know.

Dead Girl saw her arms and her legs and other pieces of herself raining down through the sky. She saw her head falling down with its eyes closed. They span away from her and disappeared.

Dead Girl was just this lump of flesh left over from herself. She was what they call a torso. She still had her fanny-pack. She was falling.

All this brown water came up to meet her. Dead Girl splashed down in Old River Thames.

<<

Dead Girl was inside the Beautiful Person Lounge. She was lying on this bed made out of coral and there were these Silly Bitches fussing over her. They were dressed in short white skirts and looked like nurses. They had mean little eyes and long rows of sharp white teeth.

Dead Girl was nervous. She held tightly on to her fanny-pack under the white linen sheet that covered her body. There was a light shining down on her. It was a light like the ones they have in operating theatres. It had all these bulbs arranged in a circle under an umbrella of mirrored glass. Dead Girl felt very hot.

One of the Silly Bitches smiled at her and said something about how she was going to be made into a Beautiful Person. She was going to get what they call a makeover. Witch Doctor was coming to treat her himself. Didn't she know how lucky she was? That was why she was here.

Witch Doctor. Who was that? Dead Girl became excited. She felt embarrassed and looked down at the carpet. It was handwoven and showed the Atlantic Ocean floating in a cosmos with little stars and a big sun and a moon on either side. The sun and the moon had these smiling faces.

The walls of the Beautiful Person Lounge were dark and made of glass. There were these lovely drapes hanging down on one side. They were made of velvet and they were the colour of champagne.

One of the Silly Bitches said Dead Girl had to put her feet in the stirrups hanging either side of her. She told her to be a good girl. Dead Girl lifted up her legs so that the sheet was in her face and her bare bottom was exposed. She was cold now. She could feel the cold air on her bottom.

One of the Silly Bitches she couldn't see made a joke and all the others laughed. Dead Girl looked out to see the reflections of the Silly Bitches in the glass walls. They were like ghosts. They were busy tending to all this glinting machinery. One of them put a cassette tape into a machine and all this soothing ambient music came out. Another one inspected a glass box full of flying blue sparks.

Dead Girl looked closer. She saw that the glass box had a long twisted flex coming out of it that connected it up to a glass wand. The wand was as long as a sword and hollow like the barrel of a gun. It had a hand-guard at one end and at the other it twisted round and round on itself in a spiral until it tapered to an open nozzle. It lay on a trolley next to a box of tissues.

Dead Girl saw the drapes twitch. She tensed.

The Silly Bitches came back to Dead Girl. One of them pulled the sheet away from her face and gave her a round plastic box with two little brown seeds inside. She was told to take them to make her feel better. She was given a glass of water and she drank them down. It was like taking headache tablets or something.

Dead Girl looked at the drapes from the corner of her eye. She saw first one foot and then another move out from under the drapes. They were bare and dirty with very long toe-nails. There was somebody standing behind the drapes.

One of the Silly Bitches was busy with a big magnifying glass. She swivelled it over Dead Girl's bottom. She was looking down at Dead Girl's thing. She was looking at what they call a vagina.

Dead Girl looked at the drapes again. There was nobody there.

Another one of the Silly Bitches was smearing something cold on the fleshy lips around Dead Girl's vagina. She was getting it from this tub of ointment and smearing it on with her fingers. She said something about a Magic Wand. She said it was so the Magic Wand wouldn't slip.

Dead Girl wanted to get up and leave but she found she couldn't move. She couldn't control her arms or legs. It was like they were stuck.

The Silly Bitches backed away from her. They started giggling and curtseying. Someone was coming. There was someone moving into the light. It was this thin old man. He had these grey whiskers tufting out of his ears. His pink lips were very thin like a slit in his face. He had all this wild hair like white candyfloss. His clear blue eyes had this blank expression. It was like they weren't taking anything in.

Dead Girl couldn't stop looking at him. The Silly Bitches called him Witch Doctor. He began to caper in his long black coat. He jabbered and sang snatches of a Gary Glitter song. The Silly Bitches gave him tweezers and scissors and scalpels and he dropped them all over the floor. He was making these deep barking noises.

Dead Girl was hypnotised. It was madness. She wanted to kiss Witch Doctor all over. She wanted to stroke his lovely hair. But she couldn't move. She could only watch. It was so sensual. Her eyes caressed Witch Doctor. It was like eating chocolate.

Witch Doctor picked up the Magic Wand in his right hand. He began to feint and parry with it in the air. One of the Silly Bitches pressed a switch on the side of the glass box. The blue sparks inside the box started to move faster. Witch Doctor said something Dead Girl couldn't hear and the Silly Bitches all laughed in one go.

Now there were blue sparks moving through the spiralling glass barrel of the Magic Wand. They surged towards the open nozzle and sprang out in a shower. Witch Doctor giggled and waved the Magic Wand in the air. He began to form patterns with the blue sparks. The Silly Bitches gasped and clapped.

Dead Girl broke out into a sweat. The sweat poured off her. First it was hot and then it was cold. It soaked through this bit of paper between her and the bed of coral. The bit of paper was dripping wet.

Witch Doctor was there between her legs. His eyes were wild. He told her it wouldn't hurt and she believed him. The Silly Bitches were still talking about a makeover.

The moment Witch Doctor touched her with the wand she started laughing hysterically because of the shock. She was crying with laughter. There were these tears running down her face.

Dead Girl turned her head to shield her bright red face from Witch Doctor. She was shaking.

Witch Doctor was shoving his Magic Wand in and out of her vagina. He kept on doing it. He did it for about an hour until he got tired. Dead Girl was so wet with sweat that eventually the nozzle slipped and touched her skin where the ointment was. Dead Girl screamed when that happened. She screamed and leapt up into the air. Witch Doctor had burned her with his Magic Wand. She wanted to push him away but banged her head against a tray of tweezers and scissors and scalpels held by one of the Silly Bitches. The Silly Bitch cried out in alarm. Dead Girl collapsed back on the bed. She leaned over and was sick on the floor.

She was ashamed. There were the two little brown seeds in the middle of all the vomit. One of the Silly Bitches immediately rushed over to clean up the mess. She knelt down with a tissue. She didn't notice the seeds.

Dead Girl was still leaning over the side of the bed. She had her head upside down. She could see what was happening through the gap under the bed. The Silly Bitches were turning off all the equipment and putting it away. They were moving around on their long white legs. Witch Doctor stood alone in his long black coat. He was panting. She could see only the lower half of his body. He didn't have any shoes on. She stared at his feet. They were covered in mud and his toe-nails were all long and twisted.

>>

Dead Girl was floating in the Old River Thames. She was very badly cut up. It felt like there were pieces of her missing. She didn't know where they were.

Dead Girl was aching all over. She hurt on the inside. She was just this torso now. How did she know that? It was a philosophical question.

She drifted in the water. She felt she had to find the missing pieces of herself. But she didn't know how. All she had was this old fanny-pack. It was strapped round her waist. It was the only thing she owned.

Then she remembered what Fairy Sugadaddy had said. He had told her she had got this blue light deep inside of her. She could take control of it. She could use it to make these images and project them on her skin. He said that she had got these Extra Special Powers. Could it really be true?

Dead Girl reached deep inside of herself and found the blue light. It was warm and wet and faint like quicksilver. It was hard to catch. Dead Girl knew what she wanted. She needed something to keep her going for the time being. She grew some spare body parts from the blue light deep inside her. It was like creating something in a hot blue forge. She had these new arms and legs. She made herself a new replica head. They glowed like holograms as she put them on. So now it was just her torso that was made out of flesh and blood and bone and marrow. The rest of her was made out of the blue light.

Dead Girl blinked and checked how her new eyes worked. She gazed at the stars high above her in the night sky. It was like seeing the world through a blue filter.

She drifted some more. She let herself be carried along by Old River Thames.

<<

It was not until Fairy Sugadaddy contacted her some time later that Dead Girl understood what had happened to her in the Beautiful Person Lounge.

Witch Doctor had injected these blue sparks into her belly and they had grown into a ball of blue light. She could use the blue light to make creatures and project them outside her skin. That was one part of her Extra Special Powers. The other part was that she could make herself look like whatever secret guilty things other people wanted her to be. She could change shape just like that.

Except the one thing she could never change was the place where Witch Doctor had burned her. His Magic Wand had left a big red lump on the outer lip of her vagina. It was incredibly painful and swollen for a day and a half after her makeover. It left a scar that never went away.

## Royal assassination in Paris road tunnel

Eddie with his feet up under the lights. He figures his captors are English Muslims. Decides to treat them as just one more tough crowd.

*A True and Faithful Relation of What Passed at Clarence House between Dr John Dee and the Devil.* Extract 3.1: The Little Devil delivered from the frantic scene of occult murder was a canard first emanating from the secret Osiris Club.

Now the Osiris was the most exclusive private gentlemen's club in London. It hosted a loathsome coterie of members, all of whom were rich, successful and powerful. Involvement in state murder being the main qualification for referral, its membership list included snarling police chiefs, grinning barristers and slavering criminologists.

And the Doctor did conspire with a Six duty officer after a lunch invitation was given to pay off outstanding secret obligations. As one of the most deadly and accurate magicians in London, the Doctor had often been useful to Six. The capacious use each made of the other was an unknown fact that needed neither apology nor excuse. Both did belong to this mysterious all-male cabal of the privileged few.

The lunch date indicated was convenient with the Doctor's phantasmal diary. Summoned he was to circumvent a cataclysmic risk that needed to be promptly countered. The cabal had recently been in danger supreme.

On this undetermined occasion, the canard was received.

The vaporous cover-up that followed was willed by this small and select rayless club under Eric Street where the original unhinged conspiracy was hatched.

The canard was writ in ancient lore.

EK Exegesis 3.1: (*Groan!*) Oh no! Let me guess: *Di had given birth to Dodi Al Fayed's child and the little bastard is the popular choice for the throne...*

Not that hoary old legend. The old man dredged that one up from the knacker's yard of the intelligence world. Figured it still had some legs. I think it was originally put together to smear Wills when he was investigating the death of his old ma in that bloody car crash in Paris. The bane of all our lives!

Anyway, the old man resurrected it as a cover story when he was on that secret mission hunting down the escaped Royal zoological specimen in London. Said it was a mission to discover the illegitimate girl pretender born in the ambulance on its way to Pitie-Salpetriere. What was the code name for the quarry? Analise? Some stupid nickname like that. Brought up in hospitals and children's homes, so one version of the story goes. Another says the kid was killed and dumped in the river.

You don't still believe it, do you? That photo was an obvious fake.

*A True and Faithful Relation…* Extract 3.2: The unvisited inquest said the Whore died from natural causes. This ultimate word concerning the scattered evidence seemed to satisfy her brooding husband. Her sudden death was an accident. Freakish and unlucky it may have been; murderous it was not.

And yet still the Old King was eaten up with a hypocritical guilt. He knew not who first spake of it: calling in the ghoulish K Team to deal with the nightmarish dilemma posed by the infinite investigations of his wife's perplexing death.

For in truth her death was no accident. Someone nefarious did interfere with the Egyptian's Merc.

Did the Old King really believe that his wife's anonymous note would be taken seriously when the Sun Prince looked at her disintegrating papers?

EK Exegesis 3.2: Like I said, the bane of all our lives. Whoever came up with the idea of forging a suicide note deserves to be hanged. That opened up a whole can of worms.

The K-Team operated out of Geneva, didn't they? Bunch of fucking amateurs! It was them executed the plan in the first place. Only originally it was some Serbian mobster they wanted to take out: *Let's shoot the driver with a strobe-gun in a road tunnel…*

For fuck's sake! It's up there with exploding cigars in the Caribbean, ain't it? But you know all this.

*A True and Faithful Relation…* Extract 3.3: Intended it was at first that the Whore should retire to a vacuous life having had an abortion unspeakable in an isolated private nursing home in Paris.

But she expressed a stunning preference for having the abominable child.

The phobic black ball was secretly placed in the formless muffle bag. And then it was unconcealed. Last words uttered were there none for the condemned child.

In response to this cryptic signal came the Doctor. He had a calling for the substantiation obscene of unholy communion flesh. A satanic midwife, an impossible anti-nurse, he appeared at the faintest smell of hot diabolical blood.

EK Exegesis 3.3: I don't think we should go into this one too deeply.

It's the missing link, ain't it?

The Old Ukanian Combine was saved by its dirty little *teoqualo* ritual at the end of the nineteenth century, wasn't it? Just like it has been every hundred years since the old man first cut his deal with Osiris. Only, fuck me, we didn't have the penny dreadfuls to contend with back in the days of Gloriana, did we?

The old man only just got away with covering it up that time in the foggy back-alleys of London. And what a nightmare that was! How could he possibly be expected to cope with the bleeding mass media at the end of the twentieth century? On a public highway! In the middle of the City of Light!

Let's face it. Some cover stories are true.

I mean, the motorized snappers caught the old man virtually red-handed. They photographed the birth. You know they did. We tried to pull the pictures. But it was too late.

The whole thing was a complete and utter shambles. We missed the opening of the Sirian window didn't we? The conjunction of stars in the sky passed. Least, that's what the old man says. There are other stories, of course. Stories of betrayal and double-dealing.

I make no judgement. Cos it's all the same result at the end of the day, ain't it? The Old Ukanian Combine got kicked out of its own bloody country and ended up all at sea.

*A True and Faithful Relation...* Extract 3.4: Something mortal was pink and moist and rare enough to be a communal meal.

There was the shuddering tribute of a few minutes silence.

The first time was it not that a shrieking infant had been sacrificed in London for a blasphemous treat.

EK Exegesis 3.4: The Osiris is a dining club, ain't it?

The old man started it up again in 1587. The usual moody revivalism. Its origins actually go way back.

London never really took to the Jesus cult, did it? Personally, I never could stomach the sight of a Jew nailed to a cross. Plus, it's only your real bumpkins who are actually gonna believe that a loaf of bread can turn into a hunk of steaming divine flesh just cos some bloke in a white sheet says it has. Go down to the East End and try that one on. I dare you! The real mystery of the Holy Roman Empire is how they got away with that cobblers for as long as they did.

Now your Londoner, he always demands the real thing.

*A True and Faithful Relation...* Extract 3.5: In a gloomy courtyard bounded by ten-foot pagan stones of various rough-hewn shapes the repugnant cadaver was named after the Devil Osiris. Only then did it become proper immortal food. Such poisonous gifts always made an agreeable diabolical supper.

The decadent members of the infernal club were addicted to dining in the huge pitchy cellar of the Second Weird Sister. Tempted they were to this monstrous luxury by the time-worn spell of a supernatural English custom.

Banished outside to a narrow ivied ditch was the First Weird Sister who was the Devil's battered wife. Her illegibly blood-stained walls were hung with rotting displays of the inedible part of the cadaver deemed worthy only of the Devil Osiris.

EK Exegesis 3.5: All this is a bit before my time, know what I mean? But if I rack me brains and go back to me Wallis Budge, then I think I can make sense of it for you.

Osiris is the old Egyptian god from the star system of Sirius while the grub in the stone circle is his baby boy Horus. Horus resurrects as Osiris, see? It's only the oldest story in creation.

Strewth! What you used to get in the old days was an infant dedicated to Horus-Osiris and sacrificed for a communion feast. Course, he had to be consecrated before he was shared out. That's where the pink lotus comes in. The flower was reckoned to be sacred to Horus-Osiris, weren't it? So it was only after the seed of the flower was placed under the tongue of the infant that he actually transubstantiated, if you know what I mean.

The holy communion was consumed by celebrants in the basement caff run by Nephthys. She was Osiris's bit on the side.

It was Osiris's missus Isis who made sure he got his portion. She worked in the ditch at the bottom of the altar. Them little baby torsos strung up on the embankment behind her were a definite sight to see!

## New Deal

ANUBIS: Isis, we have a problem.

NEPHTHYS: Isis aint here, sweetie. Whyncha let me handle it?

SATIS: Jagobat! Disregard, Anubis. Isis is most definitely in da house. I say again, Isis know what o clock it is. Break. *Jack yoself up, Nephthys!*

NEPHTHYS: Whatever. Cant blame a girl fe tryin to get a piece of de action round here.

ANUBIS: Ladies, ladies. What is Miss Ross without the Supremes? Please expedite my call.

NEPHTHYS: Hmph! Stupid-ass little jackal always runnin round de place flappin his mouth.

SATIS: Nephthys! You know Anubis is only taking messages for Isis. He really carry-go-bring-come.

ISIS: Hello, hello, hello. How are my two favourite sisters? Break. And how is my precious little pup?

SATIS & NEPHTHYS: *(Together)* We at uniform frequency!

ANUBIS: I say again, we have a problem.

ISIS: No need to skin up your mouth. Out with it, jackal!

ANUBIS: There is a short-fall in one of the accounts.

ISIS: Uh huh. Which account is that?

ANUBIS: The New Ukanian Combine account.

ISIS: Who is the radio contact?

ANUBIS: Doctor Dee.

ISIS: That wicked English scientist! Do you think he is still begrudgeful over the Pont de la Alma ting?

ANUBIS: I reckon so, mistress.

SATIS: The Lord of the Dead kicked Dee's Old Ukanian Combine off the edge of da world once they eye-pass him fifth time round and not give his twin bro Set a lickle pure baby of dey very own own fe end of century backsheesh.

NEPHTHYS: Osiris rules!

ISIS: You are cleared to pass your message, Anubis.

ANUBIS: Roger. According to the revised terms of Doctor Dee's New Deal he is due to bring down ya one thousand baby Horuses in return fe onliest use of the Lord of the Dead's Jizzum Stick.

NEPHTHYS: Pshaw! So few? Before-time it was millions.

SATIS: Times are harder now.

ANUBIS: The Dread Commander issued me his Jizzum Stick and I requested Satis carry it to Doctor Dee's own see-far man, Mister Kelley, at de old bram hall in Shadwell. But he back-squeeze the payment.

ISIS: How many Horuses has he bring down ya?

ANUBIS: So far? Acknowledge.

ISIS: So far. Affirm.

ANUBIS: Um, nutten, really.

ISIS: Nothing at all? Confirm.

ANUBIS: No babas, anyways. Correct.

SATIS: Cho! Such terrible bad-johnism! He is a hard-mouthed bag-blind skanker that Doctor Dee.

NEPHTHYS: Osiris will go aajay! He will dash a lash in dat rass-clate!

ISIS: So what *have* you collected? How do you read?

ANUBIS: I read good. Mister Kelley has bring nine hundred and ninety nine embalmed husks and come ya direct.

SATIS: Shocking news! Doctor Dee gives the Lord of the Dead belly-bottoms only and is keeping all de fine baby Horuses fe hisself.

NEPHTHYS: A haul-and-run bandit!

SATIS: The first of the pharaohs in the Old Kingdom were never so backanahand.

ISIS: I read you, Anubis. I read you, little creature.

ANUBIS: How could Isis not read her jackal?

NEPHTHYS: Osiris chop out too much credit to Doctor Dee. He grant him da full eight point six light years, mon! Set would never have been so slack.

SATIS: Set has gone agwasa. He got nutten to do with the New Deal. He has not been seen since da bacchanal at Mudchute.

ISIS: Never mind Set. Where is Doctor Dee?

ANUBIS: I have him last sighted inside Ukanian airspace…

NEPHTHYS: When Osiris hears of dat trickified Englishman's anancyism he will get vex and lock off his neck.

SATIS: He will mash him up!

ISIS: Request Doctor Dee's exact coordinates. Anubis?

ANUBIS: Confess I have no recent sighting, my lady. Doctor Dee is off-radar.

SATIS: He has gone agwasa!

NEPHTHYS: Just like Set. Dya tink they run bobol?

ISIS: No need to be so fast and forward! Let us tell the Lord of the Dead. He will know what to do.

OSIRIS: He will know how to handle his moko kid brother, you mean?

ISIS: My lord! You walk on your name.

SATIS & NEPHTHYS: *(Together)* We at victor frequency!

OSIRIS: Stand down, stand down. Sweet ladies!

ANUBIS: Osiris is faithful to Isis alone. Who could forget Marvin Gaye duetting with Tammi Terrell that night in Virginia?

OSIRIS: Anubis, kicksy protector of my heart's delight. How do you read?

ANUBIS: I read good, my lord.

OSIRIS: O little jackal, am I a kouyon?

ANUBIS: My lord..?

OSIRIS: To give Doctor Dee a second chance. He bad-play me on the Old Deal and now he bad-play me on da New Deal. I *must* be a kouyon.

ISIS: Nothing so, my lord. Nothing so!

OSIRIS: When I get hold of that kangalang, I will do such things. I will send

Doctor Dee's heart through his mouth!

ISIS: We must find him first. Doctor Dee is in hiding.

NEPHTHYS: Most likely in da same place as dem missing Horuses.

SATIS: Find Doctor Dee, find the Horuses.

ISIS: Anubis, get me a fix on Doctor Dee's babymama one thousand after she be touched by the Jizzum Stick.

SATIS: Such boldness! Isis jooks her mouth in business proper to the Lord of the Dead!

NEPHTHYS: She always was a gravelicious little keep-miss.

ANUBIS: In real time, now?

OSIRIS: In real time. Do as my lady says.

ANUBIS: Wilco. I have a fair-maid with her evil eye open at Garbage Disposal on the Ark of Old Innglan.

ISIS: Identity?

ANUBIS: Allegra One Zero Zero Zero.

ISIS: Request clearing of mesmeric airway.

ANUBIS: Wilco. Please maintain a level.

ISIS: My lord? What say you to letting me speak the message?

SATIS: What he gonna say?

NEPHTHYS: He can always seh no!

OSIRIS: I say, you are authorised to speak.

ISIS: Thankyou my lord. Anubis?

ANUBIS: Proceed. Words twice for message envelope.

ISIS: Allegra-Allegra One-One Zero-Zero Zero-Zero Zero-Zero, this-this is-is a-a message-message from-from yuh-yuh Dread-Dread Commander-Commander Osiris-Osiris. Find Doctor Dee and report back on this frequency. Osiris will grant you three wishes.

ANUBIS: Over and out?

OSIRIS: Over and out.

ANUBIS: Message transmitted.

NEPHTHYS: *Tree* whole wishes!

SATIS: Its really quite usual.

## **Trepanation**

>>

Dead Girl was floating. She was floating in Old River Thames. She was crying out for her Fairy Sugadaddy. Where was he? He must have gone away.

The water was very cold. Dead Girl shivered. She had all these goose-bumps on her skin. But the only place she had skin was on her torso. The rest of her was made from blue light.

There was this rash on her belly from her fanny-pack. It was chafing her. Maybe it was strapped on too tight.

<<

Dead Girl was on this Old Royal Spaceship in orbit high above Planet Earth. She was trapped inside. She had been taken there from Atlantis to work on a farm but it had all gone wrong after she had done something bad at the Royal Harvest Festival or whatever it was. Her memory was all fuzzy.

Dead Girl had used her Extra Special Powers on the Old King. That was the thing. It was the very first time she had used her Extra Special Powers. She didn't even know what they were at that point. She was just playing. She surprised herself. Dead Girl had used the blue light inside her and made herself into the Old King's guilty love. She had pretended to be his Lost Princess. But he hadn't got it. He hadn't got it at all. He was angry. He shouted at her but she only laughed at him in contempt. So they took her away.

So now she was being taken to where they threw away all the waste and the dead bodies on the Old Royal Spaceship. She was strapped down on this trolley with a sheet thrown over her. They had let her keep her fanny-pack. She kept touching it as the trolley was pushed down a long corridor.

The corridor was made of glass on all sides. Dead Girl could see the green and blue swirl of Planet Earth outside. She could see her own reflection. The steel columns set in the walls supported this railway running directly above. Dead Girl could hear the rumble of the tube trains as they went backwards and forwards. She could feel the air whoosh as they passed.

She got pushed down the corridor for a long time. There was this old blue carpet which seemed to go on for miles. Dead Girl was drowsy. She closed her eyes. She dreamt of the trains. She saw all these young girls sitting inside. They had bashed-in faces and missing limbs. They didn't look very well. They looked like broken dollies. That made Dead Girl sad.

She woke up when the trolley got pushed through these double doors. They swung open and swung back closed behind her. One door said GARBAGE and the other said DISPOSAL. So that's how she knew where she was. She was inside Garbage Disposal. She was alone.

The place was deep underneath this train station. Dead Girl could hear the trains pulling in overhead. The metal struts in the ceiling shook from all the busy movement. But down below with her it was dark and empty.

There was a curved window at the edge of Garbage Disposal. The glass was scored by these thin steel beams. The stars outside were cold and blank. They made it like twilight inside Garbage Disposal. The floor was paved with black and white ceramic tiles. The tiles were an oblong shape. There was water on the sloping floor. It ran off into a gutter which followed the curve of the window.

Dead Girl could hear her own breathing in the intervals between the trains pulling in and out overhead. She couldn't get off the trolley. She couldn't move.

At the centre of Garbage Disposal was this tall round building. It rose all the way up to the top of the ceiling. Dead Girl guessed it extended to the train station above. So that meant she was looking at just the underground part of the building.

The building was lined with thick white marble streaked with heavy blue veins. It looked like it was made of Italian ice-cream. There was this riveted metal door in the middle. It had these yellow and black chevrons around the side.

At the edge of Garbage Disposal next to the gutter was an old white ceramic bath with all this electrical equipment. The bath rested on these iron feet made to look like lion's paws. They were flaking with gold paint. The bath was very big and must have been quite nice once. But now it was stained with deep brown marks. There was a wooden board over the top of the bath. Dead Girl could hear this water slopping around underneath.

There were cigarette stubs and what looked like pieces of old orange peel blocking the drain under the bath. Dead Girl squirmed on the trolley and it moved towards the bath. It bumped against it and disturbed the lid. Dead Girl was hit by this vile smell of dung and chlorine all mixed together. She felt sick but couldn't move.

This shadow fell across her. Dead Girl tensed up. She could hear someone moving across the wet floor tiles behind her. Someone else had come into Garbage Disposal.

>>

Dead Girl was being nudged by the tide. She was getting washed up on the shore of Old River Thames.

There were all these pieces of brilliant rubbish in the shallow water. There was an empty glass bottle of perfume, a winding stretch of red cloth stitched with oblong glass slides and also a six foot long ostrich feather. These things were there bobbing in the water next to her. They kept touching her stumps.

Dead Girl was glad she had the blue light growing out of her. She checked her fanny-pack with glowing blue fingers. It was still tied to her waist. She didn't have to worry.

She let herself get washed up on the shore.

<<

Dead Girl was in this place called Garbage Disposal on the Old Royal Spaceship. She wasn't on the trolley anymore. She had been moved. Now she was lying on the board over the bath.

Someone had taken the sheet away. Dead Girl didn't have any clothes on. But she still had her fanny-pack. She fiddled with it. She kept moving the zip up and down. She felt bad. She wanted to get up and leave. Nothing stopped her. She wasn't tied down anymore. But maybe if she got up she would only make things worse. Maybe it was better to stay where she was. She stayed where she was.

Someone was behind her. Dead Girl could hear them moving in between the noise of the trains rumbling overhead. They were talking to themselves. They were making these humming noises. Dead Girl hoped that everything was going to be all right.

There was this little black and white CCTV screen on a jointed arm right next to her. Dead Girl could see everything that was happening to her. She had an overhead view. She could see everything on the little screen.

There she was lying on top of the bath looking very small and frightened and there was this Crazy Lady standing over her. It was the Crazy Lady who was making the humming noises. Her head was covered by this white swimming cap and she had this white coat on with brown stains all over it. Her legs were bare and she was wearing these green Wellington boots.

Crazy Lady snapped on these white surgical gloves. She started to talk into this microphone next to her lips. She had this guttural tone. Dead Girl thought she must be from Central Europe or somewhere. When Crazy Lady looked up into the CCTV camera that was in the roof Dead Girl could see how old she really was. Her face was all pulled back and taut and her eyes were covered in a little pair of blue goggles. She was wearing this blue one-piece swimming costume under her white coat.

Crazy Lady began to brush Dead Girl's hair. She brushed it with a gold plated brush. Dead Girl's hair was made of lots of different colours and thick as fuse wire. Crazy Lady talked as she brushed. She talked about how she was a Professor who knew about strange drugs and hidden space aliens and lots of other secret stuff. Dead Girl didn't understand it at all. But it didn't matter. Crazy Lady brushed her hair so it shined.

Crazy Lady ran her fingers through Dead Girl's hair. She massaged the scalp. Dead Girl allowed herself to feel safe. She shivered with pleasure.

The Crazy Lady was interested in the bit of Dead Girl's head at the front just above the hairline. She dabbed at it with shaving foam and scraped off the hair with this cut-throat razor. Soon Dead Girl had a bald patch high up in the middle of her forehead. She didn't cry or anything. Even when the Crazy Lady jabbed her with a hypodermic needle and her skin went all cold.

Then the Crazy Lady picked up this scalpel and cut the skin on Dead Girl's forehead. She pressed into the flesh and this blood came out. It didn't hurt. The Crazy Lady made lots of little cuts and none of them hurt. They intersected to form a sign like a cross.

The Crazy Lady wiped the scalpel clean and picked up this weird instrument made of rusted metal. It was very old, like it had just been dug out of the earth somewhere. It was shaped a bit like a corkscrew with a wooden bar across the top. There was a spike at the end which the Crazy Lady drove into Dead Girl's skull by pressing a button in the handle.

Dead Girl felt the jolt even through the anaesthetic. She gritted her teeth as this blood started to trickle down over her ears. Now she could feel this headache from very far away. There was this barrel round the shaft of the corkscrew thing which had sharp saw teeth set in a ring at the bottom. She watched as the Crazy Lady twisted the handle and the revolving saw started to cut into her forehead.

Dead Girl stopped looking at the TV monitor after that. She looked at the stars outside the window instead.

She guessed the operation went on for half an hour. There was all this white dust flying around. Dead Girl got it between her teeth and it was gritty. After a while she realised it was powdered bits of her own bone.

At one point she used her Extra Special Powers on the Crazy Lady. She didn't really know what she was doing. She was just trying to escape from the situation. That was why she pretended to be what the Crazy Lady wanted deep down inside. She pretended to be a Space Alien. But it didn't do any good. It was obviously a feeble imitation. Crazy Lady laughed and kept calling her this name that Dead Girl didn't recognise. She must have looked stupid. Crazy Lady could see right through her act. It wasn't like with the Old King. The Crazy Lady wasn't fooled. She knew what was going on.

When Dead Girl felt this cold air inside her head and had all this blood in her eyes, she wanted to scream. She couldn't use her Extra Special Powers on the Crazy Lady any more. She couldn't do much of anything. She opened her mouth and closed her eyes and she tried to yell at the top of her voice. But no sounds came out. All she could hear was this slurping noise from the blood that was spilling out of her head.

She opened her eyes again and looked back at the TV screen. The Crazy Lady had pulled the corkscrew thing out of her forehead and there was a solid chunk of bone inside the barrel at the end. It was at least an inch thick. The Crazy Lady was chuckling now as she dabbed at the edges of the hole in Dead Girl's forehead.

>>

Dead Girl was beached on the shore of Old River Thames. There were these cosmetic jewels lying on the tide-line. They were made of cut glass. She felt them digging into her side just below where she had the strap of her fanny-pack. Dead Girl was what they call a torso. Except now she had this head and these limbs made out of blue light. She had this faint glow.

The strand was covered in all this fine sand and silver glitter. The bank of the river was lined with a red-brick wall. On the strand between the river and the wall was this open square tent. Its frame was made of red painted wood and it had these open sides with long white gauze curtains pulled in at the four corners. Fluttering from the top of the pitched roof was this triangular flag with an emblem on it. The emblem had these little animals standing up on their hind legs. It was what they call a Royal Crest.

Next to the tent was this wrought iron spiral staircase. It led up from the strand to the top of the river bank. The lower steps were covered in green sludge.

Dead Girl saw something coming down the steps. It was moving fast. It was leaping down the steps. It was a bundle of rushing black energy.

<<

Dead Girl was in Garbage Disposal on the Old Royal Spaceship high above Planet Earth. She was inside the bath now. The wooden board had been slotted into place on top of her. It was like she was in a coffin. It was dark and she was lying in two inches of cold smelly water.

Crazy Lady had tried to be gentle. She had dried the blood from her ears with a rough towel and brushed the pieces of bone from her fanny-pack. She had wrapped a bandage round her head to cover the wound. She had done all this before she had put her in the bath.

Dead Girl tried to push the lid off but it was no good. It was locked down tight. She felt this panic in the back of her throat. Her head hurt from where Crazy Lady had drilled this hole in her forehead. She didn't know what to do.

That was when Fairy Sugadaddy first spoke to her. He spoke to her inside her head. He had a lovely musical voice that faded in and out. It was difficult to catch. It was like listening to something off the radio late at night. It was full of these clicks and whistles. Dead Girl guessed the voice must be coming through the hole in her head. She guessed it was coming from very far away. She thought Fairy Sugadaddy must live on a distant star.

Dead Girl closed her eyes. Fairy Sugadaddy said he would grant Dead Girl a wish. Dead Girl's fear ebbed away. She was calm. She listened to Fairy Sugadaddy. He said he would make her wish come true. But she had to do one thing. Would she do this one thing? Dead Girl nodded. She would have to find Witch Doctor and point him out to Fairy Sugadaddy.

Dead Girl understood. Fairy Sugadaddy wanted Witch Doctor but he was hiding. She had been given a very important job. Fairy Sugadaddy said he believed she could find Witch Doctor. That's when he told her about her Extra Special Powers. They would help her. All she had to do was reach inside for the blue light. It was like her own special power supply.

Dead Girl nodded again. Fairy Sugadaddy flashed this picture up inside her mind's eye. It was like something off an old videotape. It had these bright colour bands floating away from the outlines and it was all fuzzy and grey at the edges. It was a surveillance image of Witch Doctor leaving this building late at night. Dead Girl recognised him by his white candyfloss hair and his bare feet all covered in leaves and dirt. He was coming out of a door which was all painted black and he was stepping down into the street. The door had a bell with broken wires sticking out of it. The street was silent and empty.

Dead Girl thought Fairy Sugadaddy must be showing her quite an old picture of Witch Doctor because he didn't look mad or confused. His eyes were like shining blue sparks in the night. But they were taking everything in. They were alert and focussed. Witch Doctor was wearing his black coat with the collar turned up around his neck. He was looking good. He stood on the street and lit a cigarette. He smiled a secret smile.

Dead Girl tried to hold on to the image of Witch Doctor as it faded in her mind's eye. She tried to pull it back. She was excited. She wanted to grab Witch

Doctor and take him deep down inside her. She wanted him. He had burned her with his Magic Wand. She was angry with him. He didn't even know what he had done to her. She would show him. She would track him down and point him out to Fairy Sugadaddy. She would get a wish come true.

Dead Girl was sinking. She opened her eyes. It was cold and dark but she wasn't in the bath anymore. She was falling through space.

The Old Royal Spaceship got smaller and smaller above her. She had been dumped out of Garbage Disposal. The Old Royal Spaceship was a shadow in the sun.

## Five century pattern killing in East London

Eddie is smoking his captors' fags. He signals for more coffee. Figures he may as well make the most of this.

*A True and Faithful Relation of What Passed at Clarence House between Dr John Dee and the Devil*. Extract 4.1: So struck had been the Juggler, that infamous scholar of night, by the Temple of Stars at Glastonbury, that he was touched with the fevered idea of building his own weird astral station at the lonely source of the Fleet.

Shame it was that he channelled the White Devil as his whirring spirit guide. So distracted was he by that traitorous demon that he betrayed the vital interests of the queer man who employed him.

The Doctor used to hang upside down over the deserted moving waters of the Fleet. He squeezed his deformed neck with a strangling cord the better to hear the murmuring voice of his Crazy Lady. Visible always was her malign star. She was an infallible guide to the fishing out of the Little Devils clad in gold.

It is said that the Doctor went mad in his old age. But the bizarre suicide story is untrue. He threw himself from the outermost misshaped bough and was instantly gone from this world. The Morning Star crept up on him to see to his final wretched disappearance. So disenchanted was she with the Little Devil he forced upon her that she had returned it as an intangible dud.

So it was that the distorted sound of the Doctor's last piercing cry died slowly in the twilit air.

Alone at night when he is trying to call up his fantastic spirit guide, the Juggler does profess to hear that hysterical cry still. There are some eldritch watermen who like drifting too close unto the noiseless edge.

EK Exegesis 4.1: If you're trying to imply that I had something to do with the old man's disappearance, then I categorically deny it! It was my idea to build the listening post on Parliament Hill, I grant you. But the old man completely took it over.

I mean, he exploited my very intimate relationship with the god Set for his own ends, didn't he? I was just the bloody medium! He was the driving force.

And for another thing, he liked to keep himself to himself. What could I do?

The old bastard always was very paranoid. It wasn't enough that he'd done a new deal with Osiris on behalf of the New Ukanian Combine, once the bad feeling over the Pont de l'Alma thing had died down. Oh no! He also had to have a back-channel open to Osiris's twin brother Set to set up some secret deal of his own.

Don't ask me what he was thinking of.

Course, he couldn't actually communicate direct like me, could he? Didn't have god's gift, you might say. As a result, he was always using Hampstead Pond as one of them scrying pools, twisting and turning over the edge of the water while listening to the sound of the wind. Talk about a sad old bastard.

The thing is, he just refused to move with the times, didn't he? Still messing about with divination techniques that were out of date in the time of Gloriana. What was he thinking of? I kept telling him, that horrible auto-asphyxiation trick is unsafe. But I think he got a kick out of it.

As for this rumour about his private collection of dead alien babies. Well, it's too good to deny, ain't it?

*A True and Faithful Relation*... Extract 4.2: Who is the Clown Jack? He has always been there in East London. He keeps on coming back.

The last time before he went away at the end of the grim nineteenth century, the Clown had bequeathed his leprous memory unto his partner in ruin, the Doctor. The two sinister men had had their singular moment together in the last delirious installment of the great work most obscure. One was a secret Royal surgical doctor and the other a ghastly slaughterman in East London.

Rumour has it that the Clown's diseased memory was transferred unto the Isle of Dogs.

The Doctor was always the Clown's hidden projector. Well over four hundred years old was he at the end; but still had he done nothing mentionable since leaving Cambridge. Always had he belonged unto the primitive Royals; not unto the decadent family but unto their perverse staff. He dragged down their significant enemies to ward off trouble indescribable.

The Doctor called the Clown back. There was a new candidate for his septic memory lurking in the dark.

And so the Clown was abroad once more. Liable was he to see the most colossal angels and devils all the time; but only ever with the Doctor's furtive permission.

The Clown's gibbering passion for unnatural murder placed him inside the boundaries avoided of uncommon life. The Doctor it was who had an obsession with the innocent.

EK Exegesis 4.2: Jack was the old man's bodyguard from way back. Left for dead in the East End at the end of the whole sorry business time before last.

I found what was left of him propped against a wall underground. His various bits were too far gone to reanimate. Luckily, the Doctor found a new host for his good old bad old Jack thing. He set him up and running and cut him loose to terrorise the crack whores down Quaker Street. This worked like a charm for a while. A very handy little diversion while I was spiriting the girlies away across the Atlantic pond to Paradise Island.

The old man certainly liked them young. I cannot deny it.

*A True and Faithful Relation...* Extract 4.3: There were two phenomenal events separated by extra-cosmic light years.

The Doctor was destroyed by a nightmarish psychic attack. He had not produced the ultimate Little Devil. This was neither his innermost fault, nor was it a grotesque accident. It was wrought by the Weird Sister.

The Oracle dragged up an indescribable live birth as a makeweight transcendent.

EK Exegesis 4.3: I kept telling the old man, don't you mess with Anubis. But would he listen? Thought he could start up his own land of the dead and spend it on his own baby universe.

His curses all backfired on him in the end. That Pink Lotus descent will screw you every time.

## Wet sari number

'BOLLYWOOD' EPISODE

MARK 23: *(Voiceover)*    Assalamu alaikum, godly people. Here's your host Mark 23, ancient soul rebel and reality TV signifier, crawling the streets of East London with a hidden camera. My self-appointed mission—to unmask the legendary knife-wielding enforcer of the Saxe-Coburg-Gotha mob known as Jack the Mack. Who the hell was Jack? That, my dears, was the question.

*Cue titles and music*

A HOLY FOOL AND HIS ANIMAL COMPANION

*Fade up on a daytime riverside scene in Shadwell. An old park with a bowling green, tennis courts, empty bandstand and locked children's playground is hemmed in by Ratcliff Highway to the north and Glamis Road to the west. Screened from the southern edge of the park by a stone balustrade is a flight of stone stairs leading down into the Thames. This is Shadwell Dock Stairs.*

*MARK 23 enters the park from the north in a motorised wheelchair. He wears a bright saffron robe over an old Shoom T-shirt and baggy denim jeans. His feet rest on the drive platform of his wheelchair. They are clad in blue Adidas Gazelles which are scuffed, dirty and worn. His head is totally shaved except for a narrow fin of hair running down the back of the skull. There are two white horizontal markings on his brow.*

*Move in on the basket in front of the steering column of MARK 23's vehicle. It holds an aluminium flight case pasted with various promotional record label stickers—Reinforced, Suburban Base, Moving Shadow.*

*Accompanying MARK 23 is his djin. The djin is big and black and muscular with very sharp claws. It is covered in hair and has fiery red eyes. It runs on all fours and sports a head-dress of horns. The djin answers to the name SHETAN.*

*Track MARK 23 and SHETAN as they move past the flower beds, potted ferns and palm trees of the park towards the river. MARK 23 halts at the quayside. He throws open the gate in the balustrade and motors on to the slipway directly next to the top of the stairs. SHETAN runs down to the mossy stones below.*

*Close in on MARK 23 as he sits hunched in his chair looking out over the River Thames towards the corporate temples of the Isle of Dogs. His Sikkimese features are broad, flat and strong. Blood jets from a nostril and stains his upper lip. He blinks and looks for his djin.*

*Cut to SHETAN at the edge of the river worrying at a package which has been washed up by the Thames. It seems to be the carcass of a partially decomposed fish. The djin is snarling and growling and splashing in the shallow scummy water.*

*Cut back to MARK 23 as he calls off his djin and strains to see what he has found. He levers himself out of his wheelchair with powerful arms, holds on to a hand-rail attached to the side of the wall and bumps himself down the stairs one step at a time.*

MARK 23: *(Voiceover)*     It would not be the first time that the torso of a young girl had been sunk in the Thames. This was a crime that bore the signs of being the handiwork of Jack.

## FLASHBACK TO A BOTCHED SACRIFICE

*Exterior night-time shot of Shadwell Dock Stairs leading up from the Thames in a wide sweep of veined black marble. The balustrade at the top of the steps is silhouetted against the faint glow of the moon. Dry ice churns around the bottom of the steps next to a massive stone bust of Queen Victoria. Her blind aged face is as impassive as the Buddha.*

*Close in on JACK THE MACK crouched on the bottom step surrounded by rolling wisps of dry ice. His hunched figure is a video blur. His black bag rests at his feet with the clasp undone. He holds a bird-cage in his hand made of delicately wrought metal. There is a package inside.*

MARK 23: *(Voiceover)*     I had been hunting Jack for a long time. But he always seemed to be one step ahead of me.

## A FORENSIC SCENE

*Exterior daytime shot of Shadwell Dock Stairs leading up from the Thames in a flight of stone. A motorised wheelchair sits abandoned inside an open gate at the top of the steps.*

*Close in on MARK 23 kneeling at the edge of the River Thames. He bats away his djin from a fish-like package in the water of the Thames. He picks it up and discovers a belt wrapped round its scaly belly.*

*Cut to an exterior close-up shot of MARK 23's fingers scrabbling at the belt. Close inspection reveals it to be a Mulberry mock-crocodile skin Full Flap Waistpack. As the zip in the flap of the pack is undone, the torn edge of a little black* and white photograph is revealed.

MARK 23: *(Voiceover)*    I had always wanted to fall in love with a mermaid. It
was a secret wish of mine.


## VISION OF AN EXTRA-TERRESTRIAL ENTITY

*Exterior daytime shot of the strand of the Thames at the bottom of Shadwell Dock
Stairs. The back of MARK 23 is visible as he kneels at the edge of the water
wrapped in his saffron robe. His djin SHETAN gambols among plastic bottles and
polystyrene cartons.*

*Cut to a wide shot of the Thames. A light squall ruffles the surface of the water
and rain begins to fall.*

*Cut back to MARK 23 caught in the downpour. A MERMAID stands beside
him in the rain. The figure is a digital composite. She is dressed in a wet sari which
clings to her full over-fed figure. She sports a head-dress of lotus flowers with a
chain of golden fish scales around her bare midriff. The backs of her hands and
sides of her feet are tattooed with henna. She has webbed fingers and toes. Her
moon face is defiant and her mouth is crowded with sharp little teeth. There is a
red bindi dot in the middle of her forehead.*

*Close in on MARK 23 and the MERMAID. His head is bowed and he holds a
photograph in his hands. She stands over him with one hand on her hip and the
other holding finger cymbals. The cymbals make a sound like a tuning fork.*

MARK 23: *(Voiceover)*    I had heard of these shape-shifting mutants. They were
the totem creatures of the Saxe-Coburg-Gotha mob,
who lived in a Royal Spaceship far away in the sky.


## THE PHOTOGRAPHIC EVIDENCE

*Exterior daytime shot of the strand of the Thames at the bottom of Shadwell
Dock Stairs. MARK 23 scuttles back from the water on withered legs. A fish leaps
from the Thames and disappears in a splash of water. MARK 23 shouts in alarm.
SHETAN turns his head to look and growls.*

*Close in on MARK 23 with the photograph still in one hand. He places the
other hand to the side of his head and then reaches for the Solpadine in the back-
pocket of his jeans.*

*Close in on the photo. A black and white mug-shot of a baby in a white shoe-
box. The baby has dark hair and dark skin and is swaddled in bubble-wrap. The
photo is flipped over. Move in on an institutional admissions stamp—SILVER
BIRCHES ORPHANAGE—and an inked logo of a bare-breasted mermaid holding
a net and trident. Only the first letter of a smudged name is legible. It is an 'A'.*

MARK 23: *(Voiceover)*    It seemed that the Silver Birches orphanage was somehow involved with the Saxe-Coburg-Gotha mob. What was the connection? I had to find out.

TO BE CONTINUED…
*Roll credits*

## Assault

>>

Dead Girl was all alone on the Heath of London. She was wandering through the forest. The earth was parched and the grass was dry and yellow.

Dead Girl was sweating. The sun was high in the sky and it was hot. She had her white hospital gown back on. She kept checking her fanny-pack was still there underneath it. Her hands were not made of blue light any more. They contained veins and nerves. They were made of flesh.

Dead Girl could feel this cool breeze on her face. She had all this lovely new skin. She touched herself all over. The only parts of her that were still made out of the blue light were her legs. She still didn't have her real legs.

She was carrying this Magic Wand in her hand. She looked at it. It was a long spiralling tube made of glass.

Dead Girl had found Witch Doctor. She knew where he was hiding. She smiled to herself. She had stolen his Magic Wand.

<<

Dead Girl was lying on the strand of Old River Thames. There were all these cut glass stones next to her. There was this empty bottle of perfume. She could smell the Chanel Gardenia.

Dead Girl was this grey slab of meat in a rotting fanny-pack. The rest of her outside her torso was just this flickering blue light. She had a ghost head. That was what it was. She had a ghost head and she had these ghost arms and legs.

Dead Girl itched all over. She wanted to scratch herself but she couldn't move. She wanted to put herself back together but she didn't know how. She wanted to howl.

There was something rushing towards her. It was moving fast. It had raced down this spiral staircase on to the strand. It was big and black and angry. It had all this matted fur and its breath smelt of urine. It was a Black Dog.

Black Dog skidded to a halt before her and cocked his head. He was looking down at her with these red eyes that were ever so intelligent. It looked like he was grinning but it was just that he had all these sharp yellow teeth crowded into his lower jaw. The saliva kept dropping down from his gums.

Black Dog's nose was all wet and black and wrinkled. He was sniffing her from close up. He was investigating her scent. Dead Girl tried to shrink back but she couldn't move. Black Dog finally touched Dead Girl. He nosed her shoulder gently and backed away. Then he came in again and started to lick her neck. He was very hairy. He had this long matted hair down his back and he had these fine little hairs on his belly. His paws were all dirty and his claws were sharp.

Black Dog was all over her. He was licking her bruised skin and biting her sore nipples. He was slavering over her. She used her Extra Special Powers on him but it was no good. He ignored the blue ghostly parts of her. He wasn't interested in them. It looked like a human torso was already exactly what he wanted. Black Dog simply kept going and she went along with it. There was nothing else she could do.

Black Dog had this stiff black penis. It was growing out of this dirty bush of hair between his hind legs and it had all these veins on it. The glans of it was pink and glistening. Black Dog kept rubbing it against her and whimpering. He had his eyes closed.

He kept putting his penis inside the cuts and holes in her flesh. He was opening up the old wounds. They were starting to leak all over the place. He bit her neck until the old scabs came away and he found the soft wet channel of her open throat. He shifted his weight back on his haunches and moved his penis in and out of this newly discovered hole.

Black Dog was panting. He was building up a rhythm. Dead Girl could feel him moving in and out of her. She could feel his tiny sharp claws digging into her belly. There was fresh blood on his gums. He opened his fiery red eyes so they were just these narrow slits. He went into this spasm and whimpered.

Black Dog was squirting all this semen inside her open bloodied neck. He was leaning over her and his legs were shaking and wobbling. It was like he could hardly stand. There was all this spit bubbling out of his jaws and dropping down on top of her. She was all sticky and wet on her shoulders. She didn't like it. She wanted him to stop.

There was this whistling sound from the top of the river bank. There was this clapping sound and the shouting of a name. Black Dog cocked his ears. He looked up to the top of the spiral staircase. He backed off from Dead Girl. He turned round and raced back over the sand.

Someone was coming down the spiral staircase. Dead Girl couldn't quite see who it was. They were breathing hard and moving very slowly. They were coming down one step at a time. They were bumping themselves down on their arse.

Black Dog stopped when he got to the tent. He slumped down with his head on his paws.

>>

Dead Girl was wandering on the Heath of London with the sun going down. She came to this old silver birch tree growing by a lake. The lake was covered with the green flat leaves of all these water lilies.

Dead Girl sat down under the tree. Her legs were made of this blue light. They fizzled and glowed under her waist. It was like she was propped up. She was tired. She just didn't care.

The branches of the tree stretched out over the water. One of them had these chrome rings attached to it next to the leaves. They were clinking in the breeze.

Dead Girl adjusted her fanny-pack under her hospital gown to get comfortable. She still had the Magic Wand. She ran her fingers along the smooth spiralling surface of the blown glass.

<<

Dead Girl was lying on a soft bed of sand next to the Old River Thames. She was just this torso with fuzzy blue extensions. All she had was her fanny-pack. She was surrounded by glitter and shiny beads of glass.

There was this tent on the strand with a crisp red and white pennant fluttering in the breeze. It was guarded by this sullen Black Dog. He was lying on the sand licking the blood from his paws.

Someone was coming towards her. It was this Freak Boy. He was crawling along the ground. He was dragging himself along on his knuckles. Dead Girl could see from the way his Joe Bloggs jeans trailed flat along the ground that he had these withered legs. Freak Boy was breathing hard. He had this barrel chest and these big powerful shoulders. He was wearing this hooded grey top that partly covered his face.

Freak Boy loomed over her. He had this gaunt face with pink little eyes. He had all these pimples on his cheeks and fluffy white hairs on his chin.

Dead Girl dug deep inside and found the blue light. It was growing there where she hurt the most. It grew out of her shame at even being alive. She wasn't going to let Freak Boy do anything to her. She didn't care that her Extra Special Powers hadn't worked on Black Dog. He was just an animal. Freak Boy was human. Things would be different.

Freak Boy reached out to touch her fanny-pack. Dead Girl sparkled with a furious blue light.

>>

Dead Girl was sitting next to this lake on the Heath of London with her back against an old silver birch tree. She was wearing her old white hospital gown with her fanny-pack on underneath. Her thin little legs glowed blue.

It was a cool night. The stars were laid out on the purple sky above her. The moon shone down on the lake.

The flowers of the water lilies were opening. Their petals were big and white and square. They opened right up under the moon.

Dead Girl brought the end of the Magic Wand up to her lips. She blew down the open glass nozzle. The musical sound of her breath reverberated over the Heath of London.

It was time for her to tell Fairy Sugadaddy she had found Witch Doctor. She knew where he was hiding. It was time for Witch Doctor to pay for what he had done.

## Kiddie brothel exposé

'SCIENCE FICTION COP SHOW' EPISODE

MARK 23: *(Voiceover)* Assalamu alaikum, godly people. Here's your host Mark 23, cheesy bring-down clown and reality TV signifier, hopping along the streets of East London with a hidden camera. My hunt for legendary Saxe-Coburg-Gotha knifeman Jack the Mack had taken me to an orphanage called the Silver Birches. It had once been the home of a strange creature known to me only as A.

*Cue titles and music*

THE KIDDIE BROTHEL

*Fade up on the daytime exterior of the Silver Birches orphanage in Shadwell. A four-storey building supported by scaffolding is set back from the Glamis Road between St Mary's church in the north and an old park in the south. Each storey of the building contains four chambers and is windowed by a sheet of transparent plastic. The chambers are each large enough to hold a child actor. They are silent, dark and empty.*

*At the base of the orphanage is a large hinged door. It is decorated with an embossed polystyrene logo of a bare-breasted mermaid holding a net and trident. Above it is a red light.*

*MARK 23 draws up to the orphanage in his motorised wheelchair. He wears a black Edwardian frock coat over an old Shoom T-shirt and baggy jeans. His blue Adidas Gazelles are water-logged. He sports a carefully sculpted quiff. In the basket at the front of his wheelchair is an aluminium flight case covered in stickers.*

*Loping alongside MARK 23 is his dog SATAN. It is big and black and powerful. It has mean red eyes and slavering jaws. A rope trails from its spiked collar.*

*MARK 23 ties SATAN to the phone bracket inside an empty telephone box and knocks on the door of the orphanage.*

MARK 23: *(Voiceover)* I infiltrated the Silver Birches orphanage by posing as a customer.

## FLASHBACK TO AN EARLIER DEPOSIT

*Exterior nighttime shot of the Silver Birches orphanage on the Glamis Road in Shadwell. Image distorted by howl around feedback effects. Swooping white noise on the soundtrack.*

*Move in on the telephone box outside the orphanage. It is a big dark structure made of square panels of Burmese teak. There are two narrow windows set high in the front door. On the roof of the box is a light bulb.*

*Close in on JACK THE MACK on the street. His moving figure is a video blur. He draws up to the phone box, opens the door and places a package inside. The package is visible as a white shoe box with air-holes drilled in the top of the lid.*

MARK 23: *(Voiceover)*    Jack was a figure who haunted my dreams.

## A CHOICE OF WARES

*Exterior daytime shot of the Silver Birches orphanage in Shadwell. Dusk is gathering and the lights in the chamber windows go on one by one.*

*MARK 23 sits outside the front door of the orphanage in his motorised wheelchair. He restrains the barking and leaping SATAN with a strong right hand on the rope attached to his collar. He looks up at the windows.*

MARK 23: *(Voiceover)*    The Silver Birches rented chambers by the hour.

## FIRST CHAMBER WINDOW

*Fade up on the lit interior of an industrial corridor ridged with hexagonal metal arches bolted into place with rivets and painted in yellow and black threat colours. Slatted metal pull-down blinds are set in the walls. Strip lights line the ceiling.*

*Move in on an orphan girl on her hands and knees in the corridor. She wears a black short-sleeved mini-dress and decaying white plimsolls. Her red hair is up in a bun. She dips a tooth-brush in a pail of dirty water and scrubs the metal floor. There are dried spots of blood on the backs of her legs.*

MARK 23: *(Voiceover)*    The children of the Silver Birches were awarded points for good behaviour.

## SECOND CHAMBER WINDOW

*Fade up on the lit interior of a canteen lined with tables made from pieces of chip-board set over wooden benches. The windows are curtained with torn sheets. There are two bars of an electric fire set in the far wall behind a metal guard.*

*Move in on an orphan girl sat at one of the tables. She wears a long blue denim dress over a stained white T-shirt and knee-high white socks. Her black hair is piled in tresses on her head. She pushes the food around her plate. Close in on slimy overcooked vegetables, soft black mince, potato peelings and vomit.*

MARK 23: *(Voiceover)*    The children of the Silver Birches were made to feel thankful for anything they could get.

### THIRD CHAMBER WINDOW

*Fade up on the lit interior of a dormitory room containing a single bed made up from thin white sheets and a coarse grey blanket. A slatted metal blind is pulled down over the window and there is a solitary electric lamp on a corner table. The door opposite the bed is shut.*

*Move in on an orphan girl strapped to the bed by a leather belt. She is wrapped from head to foot in a blue striped Terylene towel. Her nappy hair is growing out of a crop. She thrashes her head from side to side. There are urine-stained sheets stuffed in her mouth.*

MARK 23: *(Voiceover)*    The children of the Silver Birches were always pinned down after an outburst.

### FOURTH CHAMBER WINDOW

*Fade up on the lit interior of a lounge dominated by a television installed in the centre of a plastic dais set with knobs and switches. The plastic walls are recessed with circles and the lino floor is bare. There is a massive hexagonal flood-light set in the ceiling.*

*Move in on an orphan girl sitting on a canvas chair next to a wooden table. She is dressed in a tailored shorts and jacket combo made of white figure-hugging plastic. Her blonde hair falls over her shoulders. She wipes the snot from her running nose as she sorts through the material on the table—children's ABC books, soft porn mags, individually wrapped multi-coloured condoms.*

MARK 23: *(Voiceover)*    The children of the Silver Birches were exposed to an atmosphere of generalised sexuality.

### A VIOLENT CONFRONTATION

*Fade up on the nighttime exterior of the Silver Birches orphanage on Glamis Road in Shadwell. The lights from the building's occupied chambers flood the street. The telephone box outside is distinguished by the blue light that revolves on its roof. From inside its sealed wooden panels comes the furious sound of a barking dog. This is SATAN.*

*Pan from the telephone box to the open door of the orphanage. Dolly through into a long dark tunnel which slopes downwards. Slime gleams from the floor.*

*Cut to the reception area of the Silver Birches orphanage. Geodesic metal scaffolding is suspended in darkness. Supported high up within this metal frame is a massively fat old woman wrapped in a chador made from yards of black silk. Her mean little eyes are set in a mound of flesh above a black veil. This is ELEPHANT WOMAN.*

*Move in on ELEPHANT WOMAN. Long rubber hoses sprout from her body and loop through the metal scaffolding to connect with sockets and port-holes in the walls. There is the sound of laboured breathing.*

*MARK 23 enters the reception area from a tunnel mouth in the wall. He motors up to ELEPHANT WOMAN and pulls one of her support cables from its socket. She sags inside her metal exoskeleton.*

*Close in on MARK 23 as he grabs more cables and winds them round his hand. He threatens to pull them out with an aggressive gesture. With his other hand he waves an old black and white photograph.*

*Cut to the face of ELEPHANT WOMAN. Her veil has been dislodged, revealing a soft wet pouting mouth.*

MARK 23: *(Voiceover)*    The Silver Birches catered for paedophiles. That much was clear. But how did that connect with the Saxe-Coburg-Gotha mob and their offworld menagerie of weird creatures? When I questioned the madame at the Silver Birches, she said that I needed to know the story of A. and gave me a Psychic Image Reader.

TO BE CONTINUED…
*Roll credits*

## White Lotus ascent

*Screen Message*
GAMEPLAY STARTING...

*Real Audio Stream*
"You want a near-death experience? Well, how near is near? Gotta learn to yank your own chain."
—Doctor Double Oh No carving his initials in the cosmic tree.

*Player Status*
You are Doctor Double Oh No, Crown agent, chaos magician and remote master of schizoid knife-wielding alter ego Bad Nat. She is the celebrated physician to hundreds of human/alien mutants on the Crown's orbital space ark.

You have programmmed Bad Nat to attend closely to the corpse of each mutant and retrieve the mana in its belly. You then draw this mana down to your glass closet on Parliament Hill and add it to your hoard of tezma. You call it Substance H.

You keep score of how much tezma you have accumulated by carving notches on your Tally Stick.

*Narrative Voiceover*
Bad Nat's posthumous operations. The belly cut open with a left-handed stroke. The cord severed. The trophy delivered in a rush of blood.

This is how Bad Nat collects the mana from the just dead mutants dumped in Garbage Disposal. Wraps the offering in the cut-open seed-pod of the White Lotus and packs it with amniotic fluid. Stitches the seed-pod back together. So now Bad Nat's got a big round golden globe on her hands.

It's a smuggling operation.

*Screen Message*
WHITE LOTUS ASCENT: LOADING...

*Player Status*
Location: Parliament Hill@North America screen

Pull down navigational menu from North America screen and access occult retro-strategic index of the Crown orbital space ark from designated terrain peculiarities. Bingo!

*Screen Message*
TEZMA HOARD: 0

*Narrative Voiceover*
So this is the good Doctor doing his White Lotus routine at night over the Antarctic Leyline between the zodiacal pond at Parliament Hill and the Crown orbital space ark. You got it?

It's simple, really. Here is the Doctor on the bank of the zodiacal pond next to the cosmic tree. He shrugs off his coat and buckles his naked body into a wide fleece-lined leather belt with chrome studs. Ties his feet together with a rope attached to a pulley on a branch, loops the other end through the D-rings fitted to his belt and then hauls himself up. So now he's hanging upside down over the water.

He's got his Nikon quantum teleport camera tied to the branch. Its aperture trained down on his suspended form. There's an infrared switch on his big toe tuned to the send button. One tug and it's time to go for designated inanimate object within camera's field of vision. Exact calibration required.

So now he's swaying in the hot dry breeze, blinking under the moon and stars. The Doctor is a control queen into sensory deprivation. He screws in the soft earplugs, also the noseplugs, wraps a soft velvety dressing-gown cord around his neck and takes the end with his teeth. Then it's the arms crossed Osiris-fashion over his chest with the cuffs opened to the last tooth and the Doctor is ready.

He holds his dream-catcher stretched taut in his hands. Finger-nails long and sharp. The dream-catcher is a little golden sack freshly made from the skin of the White Lotus seed-pod itself. Positioned right there in camera's field of vision.

He does a few warm-up exercises. Pulls on the cord to exert steady pressure under the Adam's apple and restrict the supply of blood to the brain. His cock balloons. He eases the pressure and backs off from orgasm. Air is sucked rapidly through the open windpipe into his lungs. Repeat sequence.

Time for the White Lotus ascent. The Doctor builds up a steady rhythm. Choke, hold, breathe. Choke, hold, breathe. He balances on the point of passing out.

The Doctor's head is a few inches above the lilies that grow in the pond near the bank. He cannot smell their heavy scent. He cannot hear the scarab beetles fertilising their flowers. Sweat collects on his forehead. Eyes roll into the back of his head.

He can no longer see the night constellations reflected in the water. He spits out the pollen that collects on his tongue. Touch the only sensory channel still open. His head very cool and discoloured now. His skin stretched tight over internal organs. His sex pulsing. There is a beetle crawling over white petals to the centre of a flower.

The Doctor transfers the ache in his testicles to the beetle. He dedicates this hurting channel to his spectre. Khepri, with the shaven head and the tattooed body, bound to him fast with the rings in her ears, the rings on her fingers and toes, the rings in her clit. Khepri, for fuck's sake.

The Doctor got that secret name for his spectre as a failsafe. Say the name and that spectre shut itself down come right back to him.

Big toe twitches and send button depressed on teleport camera. Timer kicks in with countdown from ten.

The Doctor breaks the boundaries of his skin. His spectre is tattooed with the beetle, tattooed with the flower of the lily. Their anagram of sexual co-dependence spelling out the name of the goddess Khepri.

Khepri can travel the Antarctic Leyline. This the astral highway between the Ukanian stay-behind cellnet on planet earth and the Crown operation in space. The Doctor's spectre riding it good. Tally-ho!

*Full Motion Video*
The Doctor hanging upside down from the cosmic tree over the zodiacal pond. Only the whites of his eyes show. He is squirming and wriggling inside his multiple restraints. "O baby, baby, baby." His face is going blue. "Errnnnggth!"

His cuffed hands fluttering like birds. A limp piece of fruit peel jerking between his fingers. His long nails skittering together.

A beetle flies up from the water-lilies below and settles on the Doctor's upper lip. Twitches its antennae and crawls into his nostril. The Doctor is choking. Another beetle lands on his eyelid. A flutter of the lashes. Soon there are dozens of beetles crawling over the Doctor's inert form.

Camera in tree reaches zero on its countdown and aperture opens for briefest of intervals. There is a flash of darkness. That seed-pod skin held between Doctor's fingers up and disappear.

*Screen Message*
WHITE LOTUS ASCENT MEDIA: ANTARCTIC LEYLINE

*Narrative Voiceover*
The Antarctic Leyline is the oldest axis connecting Crown geoworld and overworld

territories. It is a channel of communication between extremely high altitude airspace over the South Pole and the downworld island mud of London. Ascending and descending this channel routine for chaos magician Doctor Double Oh No. He entrust his divinely tattooed body Khepri only to the well-travelled leylines. No chance he fall into spirit trap.

Let's zoom in on the connecting points between Crown geoworld and overworld. The cosmic tree with the Doctor hung upside down over the zodiacal pond. And the top secret comm sat of the Crown orbital space ark. This an orbital geodesic sphere made of glass. It contain massive quantum teleport camera in zone known as Garbage Disposal.

The Sirian Leyline runs with fibre optic cables streaming out the quantum teleport cam of Garbage Disposal to connect light years away with partner cam in Sirius. They all been hauled there by autonomous drones manufactured on alien star and first contact now established. This the official version of events.

Hip hip hooray!

But the Doctor has his own back-channel. Eddie speaks to the Sirians direct when driven by the Doctor using sex magick techniques.

Never mind. Less said about Crossroads of Anubis the better.

*Screen Message*
WHITE LOTUS ASCENT: PROCEDURE

*Narrative Voiceover*
The White Lotus out-of-body travel procedure works according to a black psy op scrambles the good old Egyptian motifs of water-lily and scarab beetle. So let's look at the process. It's spring and a lotus seed sown at the bottom of the zodiacal pond germinates a bush of water-lilies out the mud. Zoom in on one of those long-stemmed lilies. Is pushes its head through the water, extends its stabilising leaves on the surface of the pond, sits there flat.

The flower of the lily opens one summer night, petals glowing white beneath the moon and stars. It's a female. Its strong scent attracts the scarab beetle, flying sex organ of the lily world. This promiscuous insect carries on his back a load of pollen from a male lily. Now what he's after antennae twitching is more of that finest pure nectar hidden in the deepest reaches of the female flower.

Beetle lands on the lily and folds up his wings beneath his carapace. Down he goes on the lily, clamping his jaws around the cup of nectar, drinking down that sticky juice. Well, the moon goes down, the sun comes up and the lily closes, wrapping the needy little beetle in its crisp embrace. Outside, the green sepals of the flower are tough and spiky. But inside there's a soft bed of petals.

O perfect day comes but once a year! The flower caresses the beetle, its long pink stigma sucking him hard, swallowing his rich load of pollen, taking it all the way down into the ovule. Fertilisation occurs and there are a bunch of lotus seeds. Only now can the lily afford to perform its female-to-male sex change. Its stamens fatten and stiffen, pollen spurts from the purple anthers, hitting the beetle, covering him good.

It's over. Night comes again and the lily opens its flower to release the beetle, newly loaded with fertile grains. The beetle prepares for flight, sleek forewings sliding horizontal out of carapace, and he's airborne looking for another fix. The lily's petals are pink now in acknowledgement of its sex change.

Time to dispose of those used mating assets. The big petals fall to the surface of the zodiacal pond. The sepals close over the head of the lily and it sinks underwater, leaves wilting.

So now it's autumn and the lotus seeds are packed tight inside a big round pod bristling with defensive spines. They are surrounded by the maternal tissue of the plant, a nourishing substance, the lily's own placenta.

The seed-pod ripens changing colour from green to gold and bobs to the surface of the zodiacal pond. Its rind breaks open and the healthy seeds pop out. They scatter to the four corners of the earth.

And so the cycle begins again.

*Player Status*
Now you get how to use this? Check that perfect summer's day again and crank up the scale. The leaves of the White Lotus now cover the surface of the earth, the petals now reach the stars in the sky. Become the beetle and you disappear from the world as the lotus petals fold in on themselves, the stars fade away, the sun makes its appearance. You are that ray of light streaming between geoworld and overworld. You are making the White Lotus ascent.

The root of the Pink Lotus bush hidden underwater.

*Screen Message*
WHITE LOTUS ASCENT
GAMEPLAY STARTING...

*Player Status*
Location: Crown orbital space ark@Parliament Hill zodiacal pond
    You hook yourself up to designated terrain peculiarities.

*Narrative Voiceover*

The Doctor's spectre takes off from Parliament Hill and hits the Crown orbital space ark over the South Pole. Connects with the water filtration plant at Garbage Disposal. Khepri travelling the Antarctic Leyline water-to-water.

Tally ho!

Water sacred for the Doctor's spectral body. That's why it taboo for his physical body. The Doctor is naturally hydrophobic.

The glass panels of Garbage Disposal's geodesic sphere underpinned by wrought iron struts and shielded by mobile sun reflectors. Suspended in a central chamber is the massive iron box of the teleport camera. It got a slit down one side. The camera rotates so that this aperture faces one by one the metal walkways radiating out to the edge of the sphere. The aperture opens and closes on each of the walkways in turn. Fibre optic cables sprout from the top and the bottom of the box to punch holes in the glass sphere and race away to Sirius.

Beneath the walkways is the water filtration plant. Sewage piped in from the distant palaces and apartments of the Crown orbital space ark and then filtered, processed and purified. Clean water dumped into reservoirs and recycled back into industrial system of Crown orbital space ark. Shit and garbage extract gets sent back as fertiliser.

Monorail station at the perimeter of Garbage Disposal connects with the Crown orbital space ark. Opens on to loading and unloading bay. This a platform with the curved glass panelled walls look back out on to the monorail track and the night sky beyond. Turn to face the yellow-and-black colour coded rim of entrance into the water filtration plant.

It's relatively safe here at loading bay. The floor is lined with black and white tiles in a chessboard pattern. There is a rusting metal stand-alone bath set in the floor. It is pitted and flaking. Got an old wooden board placed over the top.

Muddy footprints on tiles lead from monorail station to bath. Sound of pipes gurgling.

The starlight slants down from outside. The Doctor gets a fix on the psychotronic device implanted in his host. Settles into possession of a real live warm body hidden in the darkness.

Whoopee!

Khepri rides the body of Natasha Supanova.

*Full Motion Video*

The loading bay with the overflow bath. There is an image of an Egyptian deity painted on the wooden board covering the bath. The colours fading now. A woman with her ankles bound and her arms crossed Osiris-fashion across her chest. Her naked body tattooed with protective symbols and funerary motifs. A collar of intertwined pink flowers tattooed over her throat.

White lights seeps from the crack between the bath and its wooden lid. It crackles in the air.

The lid moves to one side. A hand emerges from inside the covered bath, fingers curling around the lid. They move it aside a bit more. A scarab beetle crawls out on to the rim of the bath and scuttles away. Rust flakes on to the tiles of the floor.

Bad Nat steps out of the bath. She is wearing a white coat with a one-piece bathing suit on underneath. Her head is covered with a swimming cap and her feet are enclosed in soggy white pumps. There are little blue goggles strapped over her eyes and a breathing apparatus over her mouth.

The front of her coat is open. The tools of her trade are strapped to the black leather belt that she wears round her waist. Surgical knives, scalpels, Nikon teleport camera, needles, reels of thread.

She carries in her hands a limp, sagging piece of fruit skin. It is the empty seed-pod of the white lotus.

*Player Status*

You have used your POV button to adopt the subject position of one of Doctor Double Oh No's alter egos. You are Natasha Supanova controlled from the inside by Doctor Double Oh No's spectre code name Khepri. You answer to the name of Bad Nat. You have no will of your own.

You do not know Professor Natasha Supanova an eminent gene splicer. You only know the trigger words of the Doctor's own spectre.

*Point of View: Bad Nat*

You don't do water. It gives you the creeps.

You are standing next to an old rusty bath in the loading bay at the end of the line. You walk towards the door edged with yellow and black threat colours. Your pumps leaving watery prints on the tiles. You know where you are going. There should be a fresh one inside the water filtration plant. That's where they get dumped. Offerings to the Sirian gods.

You should know. You drain them yourself of neuromelanin brand name Substance H during their short life cycle.

Now is the time for one of those posthumous operations. You got that empty seed-pod ready in your hand.

You enter the plant and soon you are moving along one of the iron grille walkways leads to the central chamber. The walkway is suspended over a tank of dirty water. You can see down through the little square holes in the iron grille. Steam rises from the bubbling sludge in the tank.

The walkway is lined with metal railings supporting flaking industrial pipes and long strip lights. The pipes drip urine and the lights buzz and flicker. There are gaps in the railings where vertical ladders connect the walkway with the sewage below.

The walkway has no ceiling. You can see far above the glass domed roof of Garbage Disposal.

The walkway twists and turns over the water. You are hot and sweaty inside your costume. You know this place. You have been here many times before. Far at the end of this snaking walkway is the central chamber with the huge telecam. You cannot see it. But you can feel it. Slowly, it rotates.

You are safe for the moment. But soon the telecam will focus on your walkway. You don't have much time.

You are searching. You have only one purpose. You turn the corners of the walkway, one after the other, your eyes hunting for a fresh one.

There is one floating in the water. But it too far away. Shame. A real fresh one with the puncture wounds over the body still leaking Substance H. You don't remember her. She got red hair and dark rings under the dead eyes.

You keep going. Maybe you should have picked another walkway. But you cannot predict where the victims get dumped. Out of your control.

You don't want to get too close to the central chamber. Longer to get back. More chance of getting snatched. You want to go back. Something urges you forward.

There is a wilted one on the neighbouring walkway. You can see it over the water. One you did last time. Decaying now. Arm dangling over the walkway. Belly burst open like over-ripe fruit, spilling faecal matter and blood and little white buds. You see the spores in the atmosphere.

The light on that neighbouring walkway goes out. You see the darkness rush down it like a wave. It spring out from the direction of the central chamber.

Strip lights on your own walkway go dim. There is the sound of a rushing wind. You are suddenly cold. You can feel that darkness over there on the walkway. It stops, collects itself, waits. Now it seeps back the way it has come towards that central chamber. It passes away.

Nothing there now on the walkway over across from you. That decaying one with the spilled insides is gone.

You move forward. How long before the darkness rush down your walkway? You don't know.

You turn the corner and there is a fresh one. She slumped against the railing with her chin resting on her collar bone. She got these rings under her eyes.

You feel the prompting from inside. Time to reach for the knife.

*Player Status*
You have just scored one unit of mana.

*Point of View: Bad Nat*
You exit the water filtration plant carrying that seed-pod packed full of good mana. You walk across the loading bay floor towards the bath. The black and white tiles squeak under the rubber soles of your shoes.

You set the golden seed-pod on the wooden board lies on top of the bath. That seed-pod stitched with black thread down one side. You unhook your little Nikon telecam from your belt and point it at the object. Set the exact focal length. Click the send button to take its ghost. The darkness leaps from the aperture to claim the seedpod. Black cut-out of the seedpod in space. Silhouette distorts sideways and jumps back through aperture into camera box.

Seed-pod no longer there. It gone far away.

You slide the wooden board across the top of the bath. Two inches of dirty water revealed beneath. You feel sick. You touch breathing apparatus hung round your neck. Blood jets from your nose.

You collapse.

*Narrative Voiceover*
Natasha Supanova suspends all thought as she lie there on the floor of the loading bay of Garbage Disposal connected to the Crown space ark in orbit above the South Pole. Doctor Double Oh No's spectre leaves her. Khepri tracks the passage of the seed-pod and disappears from her body taking a ride down the Antarctic Leyline back to the zodiacal pond on Parliament Hill.

*Full Motion Video*
The Doctor still hanging upside down from the cosmic tree. The beetles which cover him are active. Some of them are starting to fly back down to the lilies on the pond below. The Doctor's pink lips visible. He gasps the name of his spectre. He says: "Khepri!"

Now the beetles leave him in a cloud. Doctor twitches his toe. Hits switch on that telecam camera attached to a branch on the cosmic tree. Click as the receive button depressed. White light leaps from the aperture in the camera. Lands in the Doctor's hands cuffed at the wrists. Gives back the ghost of an object. There it is.

A distended seed-pod of the White Lotus stitched with black thread down one side.

The Doctor releases the cord round his neck. Spits a dead beetle out from between his teeth. Gulps air.

"Khepri!"

The Doctor shivers. He breathes deeply. His cock is shrinking. The little hairs on his skin are standing down. His spectre has returned to him.

It's okay.

The Doctor does his Houdini trick hitting the steel panic snap with his big toe to tumble in the air and land on his feet free at last on the bank.

The Doctor putting on his black coat: Nothing and nobody can make me come. There are no flies on me!

*Screen Message*
WHITE LOTUS ASCENT
COMPLETED

*Point of View: Doctor Double Oh No*
You get back to your bedroom cell in the hole under the hill.

You open a glass jar in the back of your closet and drop the unit of mana inside. It curls up deep inside the amniotic fluid. You screw the cap back on the jar and slide shut the door of the closet.

You sit cross-legged on your mattress. Pick up your long wooden Tally Stick. Carve a notch in the side.

*Screen Message*
TEZMA HOARD: 1

*Player Status*
Fold away navigational menu from North America screen and delete tactical level map of the Crown orbital space ark. Done.

You have just scored one unit of tezma.

*Screen Message*
PINK LOTUS DESCENT: PROCEDURE

*Player Status*
You need to score one thousand units of tezma before you are powerful enough to make the Pink Lotus descent. This terrible curse will effectively discreate the

world and launch you into your favourite parallel universe where Crown rules the world once again in a Secret Ukanian Combine.

Pink Lotus descent involves passage down axis connecting Crown geoworld and underworld territories. You must spend all your accumulated tezma in order to create your own personal black hole and use it to pass over into the parallel universe of your choice. The intervening passage across the narrow throat that connects universes is mediated by a singularity where infinite spacetimelines intersect each other. It is easy to become lost in this underworld, where every pathway looks the same as and yet also somehow different from its neighbour.

There are five leylines make the connection between Crown geoworld and underworld. Each marked by massive sacrificial event dedicated to Crown once every hundred years. These leylines make up the spinal column of the Old Ukanian Combine in spacetime. You can make the Pink Lotus descent down any of these leylines. You have to make a choice.

1997 Paris Leyline
1888 Whitechapel Leyline
1789 Manhattan Leyline
1695 Greenwich Leyline
1593 Deptford Leyline

Each of these dangerous spacetime crossroads is guarded by an avatar of Anu the Chameleon Kid. Be warned that she can adopt any shape and may appear to menace you in the most unexpected way. You must struggle to overcome her in order to successfully complete your passage.

The Pink Lotus descent is highly dangerous. Very few players succeed in making it. You must perform the White Lotus ascent one thousand times to even begin to attempt it.

*Screen Message*
WHITE LOTUS ASCENT
REPEATING...

*Player Status*
Location: Crown orbital space ark@Parliament Hill zodiacal pond

You are Doctor Double Oh No. You keep on making the White Lotus ascent. You are clocking up the tezma in your hoard under the hill.

*Screen Message*
TEZMA HOARD: 999


*Point of View: Doctor Double Oh No*
You are sitting cross-legged on your mattress in the hole under the hill. You carve another notch on your Tally Stick.

The wood of the stick is ridged with hundreds of notches. You remember when Eddie first got it for you the surface of the stick was shiny and smooth. The stick is made in the shape of two intertwined snakes. Eddie said he found it on the streets of London.

You blow the wood shavings from the Tally Stick.


*Screen Message*
WHITE LOTUS ASCENT
REPEATING…


*Player Status*
Location: Crown orbital space ark@Parliament Hill zodiacal pond

You hook yourself up to designated terrain peculiarities for the one thousandth time.


*Narrative Voiceover*
The Doctor's spectre takes off from Parliament Hill and hits the Crown orbital space ark over the South Pole. Connects with the water filtration plant at Garbage Disposal. Khepri cannot get a fix on his psychotronic device.

Uh oh! Looks like Natasha Supanova no longer hospitable.

Immediate return back to Parliament Hill.

The Doctor unhooks himself from the cosmic tree. Where is Bad Nat? He has to locate her.

Eddie! He gets his magic boy to tap into the Crown orbital space ark realtime CCTV conduct a full area search of the place where Natasha Supanova last publicly sighted. He scour the laboratories of the White Palace genetic pharm at the Home Sphere. Nothing. He expand the search to take in the peripheral sewers, rubbish dumps and basement corridors. Nothing again. He keep on expanding the parameters of the search area. Soon at Garbage Disposal.

The Doctor pull up the image. The rusty old bath empty of water. Its wooden covering knocked to the floor.

Take a closer look. Blood-stains inside.

Some kind of accident has occurred.

*Screen Message*
GAME SAVED

## Abortion

>>

Dead Girl sat on the edge of the lake on the Heath of London next to the old silver birch tree. She was wearing her white hospital gown and she had her fanny-pack on underneath. Her legs were made of blue light that shone over the water.

The water lilies were opening under the light of the moon. They opened right up. There were these beetles flying out of the flowers of the water lilies. The big white petals of the flowers turned pink and fell into the water. There was pollen in the night air.

Dead Girl clutched the Magic Wand. Its glass was cool under her hand. She had told Fairy Sugadaddy where Witch Doctor was hiding. She had sent him a message.

She tried to think of a wish to have come true.

<<

Dead Girl was this little ghost made of blue light. She was flickering at the edges like a naked candle flame. Only the middle bit of her was made out of flesh and blood. Only her torso was real.

Dead Girl was drifting through the Heath of London. She was in the woods with trees all around and branches covering the sky. She was looking for Witch Doctor. She was lost.

The ground was all parched and dry and cracked. There was no breeze. She was hot. The only thing she had on was her fanny-pack. Dead Girl had a sudden thought. She stopped and unzipped the pocket of her fanny-pack. It was empty. There was nothing inside.

Dead Girl panicked. She wanted to go back. She wanted her little black and white photo, the one with the torn edge. She wanted to touch it. She wanted to stroke the picture of the little baby. But she couldn't. It was gone.

Freak Boy must have taken the photo when she wasn't looking. It must have been when she used her Extra Special Powers on him. Dead Girl started to cry. Her tears were made of blue light.

She tried to remember what had happened. Freak Boy had reached her when she was lying on the strand of the Old River Thames. He had reached out for her fanny-pack. But she had used her Extra Special Powers on him. She had changed herself into what he secretly wanted. She became his Fish Girl and laughed at the desire in his eyes. Freak Boy had whimpered and gazed at her in fear. He had been transfixed.

That was when Dead Girl had found something at the back of his mind. It was deeper than his secret desire for Fish Girl. He didn't even know it was there. It was this radio connection. Dead Girl found the trace of an old signal. She decided to follow its trail back through the atmosphere. She wanted to see how far her Extra Special Powers would take her.

So while Freak Boy was distracted by her Fish Girl act she had pulled in the source of the signal. She had pulled it across the open skies of London Town until she could see it inside the mind's eye of Freak Boy. She was thrilled when she saw the vision of Witch Doctor. His white candyfloss hair floated above him like a vapour cloud and his eyes glowed a deep blue. It was a live image. She had to be careful. But she was so excited to find out where he lived.

Witch Doctor was crouching on the ground. He was in a damp place surrounded by patches of earth and swaying green leaves. He was wrapped in his big black coat but underneath he was naked. Dead Girl could see his loins beneath the tuft of hair on his belly. She could see the claws in his toes. He was moving around on his hands and knees. He was muttering something to himself.

Dead Girl could see that he had his Magic Wand. It was made of glass and spiralled round on itself like a snake. He took it and used the nozzle to draw some lines in the earth at his feet. He drew this circuit diagram and Dead Girl felt that it spelt out her name. She was frightened but kept on looking at the vision.

Witch Doctor put the Magic Wand on the ground and pulled a little black bag from his pocket. It was a drawstring bag made of black leather. Witch Doctor opened the bag and scattered its contents over the diagram at his feet. All these precious stones tumbled on to the earth. Dead Girl gasped. There were flashing green emeralds and deep red rubies and little white diamonds. She wanted them. There were eleven in total. She felt they belonged to her.

Witch Doctor began moving the precious stones around the circuit diagram. He moved them into a funny pattern, sat back to look at them and then leaned in to rearrange them once again. He was chanting now but Dead Girl didn't understand the words. She was hurting too much. Her stumps were enflamed. She was aching inside.

She began to pull back from the image of Witch Doctor. It was too painful to carry on looking. He was doing something to her. Somehow he was affecting her thoughts and feelings. She pushed the image away. Witch Doctor looked up and smiled. He smiled right at her. She was ashamed. She saw where he was hiding. It was in this little cave under a hill shaped like a big pregnant belly. The stars shone down on the hill. It was covered in grass. She identified the coordinates of the place in her mind. It was on the Heath of London.

Dead Girl had got rid of Freak Boy and come to the Heath of London. But he must have taken her photo out of her fanny-pack while she was inside his mind. So now she was lost in the woods with nothing to console her.

Dead Girl dried her eyes. She decided to go on. She wanted to check that the vision she'd had of Witch Doctor was true. She wanted to find out if he really lived under a hill. Then she could get back to Fairy Sugadaddy and tell him her wish.

>>

Dead Girl sat by a silver birch tree next to a lake on the Heath of London. She was wearing this white hospital gown. It was cold. The night was coming to an end.

Dead Girl kept unzipping the empty pocket of her fanny-pack. She tried to count the stars. She used the glass nozzle of the Magic Wand to scrape some bark from off the tree.

Fairy Sugadaddy had still not got back to her.

This breeze came up and dislodged some of the leaves of the birch. The chrome rings in the branches made a clinking sound. The green and golden leaves dropped on to the surface of the lake.

Dead Girl shivered and got into the water. Her legs glowed blue under the stars. It didn't matter. She couldn't think of a wish to have come true anyway.

<<

Dead Girl was fighting her way through all these brambles and sharp twigs on the Heath of London. She was battling through the undergrowth. The only thing she had on was her little fanny-pack.

It was dark. There were grey clouds sliding over the moon. Dead Girl was just this torso. The rest of her was made out of blue light.

She came to this clearing and saw the dark mass of a hill up ahead. It was in the shape of a woman's pregnant belly. The clouds parted. It was outlined against the moon.

Dead Girl saw there was a light shining at the bottom of the hill. It was a yellow light tinged at the edges with shades of green and red. She moved closer and saw an electric light shining out of an open window. The window was set into the side of the hill behind the leaves of this bush. Dead Girl crept up and moved the leaves aside. The window was oval-shaped and hinged into the earth at the sides. It was pushed half-open like a port hole. Dead Girl could see that the pane of glass was decorated. On the side facing her it was lined with a thick black paint. But on the side facing inwards it was beaded and lined with a trace-work of lead.

Dead Girl tugged at the window with both hands so that it swivelled open to its full extent. The yellow light spilled out from under the hill. Dead Girl poked her head through the gap. She saw an ornately decorated bedroom lined with arched doorways leading further back into the hill.

The room was empty. Suspended from the high vaulted earthen ceiling by a metal chain was a chandelier of shaded electric lights. Each bulb was screwed into a perforated silver clasp and ringed with a drop curtain of coloured glass beads. The shadows cast on the walls were tinged with yellow and green and red.

Dead Girl touched her fanny-pack. She didn't even think about how scared she was. Instead she climbed through the open window and shut it after her.

Dead Girl found herself crouched on the lid of a square-shaped box directly beneath the window. The wooden box was edged in brass and painted with geometric patterns of white and pink flowers. Next to it in the corner of the room was a brass four-poster bed. On top of its snow white quilt were these white pillows spattered with red dye at their tips.

The walls were made of dark earth and the floor was set with a mosaic of midnight blue tiles cut with swirling yellow star-shaped motifs.

One archway to the left of Dead Girl opposite the foot of the bed was set with a half-open slatted wooden door. Beyond was silence and darkness. The other archway in the far right-hand corner of the room opened into a shadowy corridor. Dead Girl thought it must be a walk-in closet or something.

The sunken chamber was warm and still. Dead Girl thought this must be the place where Witch Doctor lived. But how could she be sure? She remembered the precious stones she had seen in her vision. They had flashed with a hidden fire. They had seemed to wink at her. Where could they be kept?

Dead Girl looked under the bed but there was nothing there. She could feel her heart beating wildly. She felt under the mattress but there was nothing there either. Her breathing sounded very loud. Dead Girl pulled up the lid of the box and gasped when she saw Witch Doctor's Magic Wand inside. It was all made of glass and twisted around on itself just like she remembered it. It was lying at the bottom of the chest next to this black bag.

Dead Girl looked closely at the bag. It was made of leather and it had a brass clasp. It was much bigger than the little bag she had seen in her vision. She wanted to check what was inside the bag. But what if Witch Doctor came into the room? She thought about it and realised she didn't care. She released the clasp on the bag and opened it up. She was still half expecting to see all these sparkling gems inside just like in her vision. But instead she saw these hunks of dead meat.

Dead Girl felt sick. She nearly passed out. She recognised what was inside the bag. The grey flesh with the coarse black hairs? That was her skin. And all the red meat around the cut white bone? That was her flesh.

Dead Girl was very angry. She hauled the bag out of the chest and tipped its contents on to the bed. All these body parts spilled out on to the white quilt. Suddenly there was real blood on the pillows. Dead Girl saw her arms and her hands and her fingers. She saw her lips and her teeth. Her own sightless green eyes stared up at her.

Dead Girl picked up her head. It was cold and heavy and covered in all this long black hair. There was a hole in its forehead. She screwed the head back on. The blue light acted as a kind of solvent. It made sure that her head stayed stuck to her neck. She rolled her tongue over her teeth. She sniffed the damp air. She shook her hair all over the place. The head stayed firmly in place.

Dead Girl was ecstatic. She put her arms back on. The blue light showed up at the seams in the shoulder joints. She swung her arms and flicked her wrists. She clenched and unclenched her fists. Everything seemed to work fine.

Dead Girl had nearly put herself back together again. She had found all the parts of her that had gone missing except for her legs. The legs on her body were still made out of the blue light. They looked even more forlorn now she had got the rest of herself back. They were shivering and flickering like a bad television picture. Dead Girl climbed up on the bed and looked everywhere for her missing legs. She looked under the pillows and felt under the quilt. But she just couldn't find them.

That was when Witch Doctor appeared. He came out of the shadows at the back of the archway leading into the closet. His hair floated above his head in thin white cotton-candy wisps and his eyes glowed with a hypnotic blue light. He was wearing his long black coat and it was covered in these beautiful pink petals. Dead Girl thought he looked like a bride-groom. She was still kneeling on the bed in the corner of the room. She was transfixed by the sudden appearance of Witch Doctor. He was all naked and dirty under his coat. He smelt of dung. He had these long sharp nails on his fingers and toes.

He came up to the bed and he rolled up his sleeves. He was looking down at her. She shrank from him until she was lying on her back. What was he going to do? She wanted to disappear but she couldn't. She tried to get away from Witch Doctor but it was like she was pinned to the bed and couldn't move. There was only one thing to do. She would have to put him off with her Extra Special Powers.

She would have to do a number on him and hope that it worked.

Witch Doctor looked her up and down like she was a slab of meat or something. Dead girl shivered. She felt ashamed of the blue light which showed through at the seams all over her body. She wanted to cover her pathetic weakly glowing legs.

Witch Doctor's eyes were cold. Dead Girl had the sudden chilling conviction that he had expected to find her here. He had let her go and now he had brought her back. Wasn't that it? There was something inside her he wanted. Dead Girl thought that he knew all about her Extra Special Powers and that was what he had come for. He was expecting the blue sparks he had injected into her belly in the Beautiful Person Lounge to have grown into this Little Thing. That was what he was expecting. Dead Girl instantly became very calm. She knew what Witch Doctor wanted. That was enough. She was going to have to be very clever to trick him. But she was sure it could be done.

>>

Dead Girl was floating among the water lilies in the lake on the Heath of London. Her white hospital gown billowed out on the water. She held the Magic Wand over her chest. These dead leaves were blowing all around her.

She closed her eyes. She moved her legs against the coarse stems of the water lilies where they were underwater. Her legs were only made of blue light. She kicked and went under.

Fairy Sugadaddy didn't care about her.

Her head felt like it was bursting with emptiness. She breathed out and drifted down through the murk. Her fanny-pack felt loose. She let herself go all the way down towards the bottom of the lake.

<<

Dead Girl was lying on this beautiful white bed that was all covered with her own blood. Her joints ached. She was spilling all this blue light at the seams from where she had put herself back together. Her legs were still made of blue light and she had tucked them underneath her. She couldn't move.

Witch Doctor was standing over her in his long black coat. He was looking at her with his head tilted to one side. There was a grin on his white face. His long toe nails made a clicking sound on the floor tiles as he moved closer. He was panting. The nails on his fingers were long and hard and sharp.

Dead Girl was using her Extra Special Powers on him. She was concentrating hard. She was trying to pretend to be the one thing he loved so much he kept it hidden from all the world. He jumped back when Tattooed Lady suddenly pulsed out of her like a solid hologram. He gave a little yelp. But all she could do was laugh.

Witch Doctor stood there in shock. Something was happening to his mind but he refused to accept what it was. He could not speak the name of his secret desire like Crazy Lady had done.

Dead Girl lay on the bed doing her Tattooed Lady act. She was naked except for her fanny-pack, which was pushed up against her breasts. Her belly was all fat and lumpy. It was big and swollen. It felt really heavy and was pressing down on her. It was like there was something coiled inside. The strange thing was that her belly skin was all brown and hard. It was bristling with these soft spines which looked like big hairs. It was like she had this big hairy belly.

Witch Doctor was very agitated. Dead Girl kept pretending to be Tattooed Lady as he leaned in close to her grotesque belly. She could see there was this old wound in her belly. It was a cut. The two halves of the skin either side of the cut had been stitched back together with thick black thread. The stitches ran in a jagged line from the top to the bottom of her belly.

Witch Doctor leaned in close. His breath smelt of alcohol. The blue fire in his eyes was deep inside. He was a shadow now obscuring the light from the ceiling. He flexed his fingers and his glittering nails made a skittering sound. Then he sliced through all the stitches just like that. It was very quick. It was painless. Witch Doctor's finger nails were very sharp. All this water and seaweed and stuff gushed out of her. It soaked the bed. She stank of old fish. Witch Doctor didn't care. He was delving around inside her belly with both hands. He was hurting her. Dead Girl gritted her teeth. She could feel him pushing and pulling deep inside.

That's when Dead Girl really let him have it. She still had her little ghost legs tucked up beneath her. They were made of blue light. She concentrated on the light and pushed it up into her belly. Now she made the light into the thing that Witch Doctor wanted most of all.

Witch Doctor pulled this weird Little Thing out of her belly. It was made out of blue light but he didn't notice. He had found what he was looking for. He held it in both hands. The Little Thing was an old man the size of a baby with all this long white hair. It had wrinkled skin on its face and its eyes were half-closed. Its mouth was this bubble of wet flesh. It was squawking and giggling.

Witch Doctor looked very serious. He was taking deep breaths. It was like he was in shock.

Dead Girl sat up on the bed. She did this thing with her mind where she cut the cord of blue light that still connected her to the Little Thing in Witch Doctor's hands. It was easy. She didn't know why she had never done it before. She had made this spectre and now she was cutting it loose. She took down great lungfuls of air.

Witch Doctor was moving away from her back through the archway to his closet. He was carrying the Little Thing as if it were a prize. The lights in the ceiling were shaded with glass beads. They looked like veils. She thought the lights must be weeping. She slid off the bed and crawled after Witch Doctor. She wanted to know his secret.

Witch Doctor's closet was at the end of this snaking tunnel. The closet was a narrow space with a high ceiling made of stained glass. The glass was all in the shape of hundreds of flowers. They were of varying shapes and sizes and colours. Some had big blue ridged petals. Others had delicate little red petals. The glass flowers were lit from within. It looked like they were growing from the ceiling.

Dead Girl marvelled at how beautiful it all was. The last of the blue light which made up her legs looked very weak and feeble now. She felt faint and found it hard to breathe.

Dominating the closet was this open-framework four-storey tower made of wrought iron and laminated glass. It stretched from the floor to the ceiling. The core of the tower consisted of a four-sided column of open square-shaped shelves. Each of the shelves contained a rack of glass specimen jars. The jars were all filled with this thick red liquid and covered with a muslin cloth.

Witch Doctor had strapped himself into a leather harness and was rising up the outside of the tower. The noise was like one of those old lifts. There was this hydraulic pulley system next to all the glass flowers in the ceiling and it was pulling him up by these metal cables. He was still carrying the weird Little Thing and his black coat flapped in the air.

The noise of the pulley stopped when he got to the top storey. He swayed in the air as he reached out and selected a jar from one of the shelves. He pulled back the cloth lid and plopped the Little Thing inside. It dropped into the red liquid and Dead Girl saw its horrible grinning little face magnified by the glass. There was this brief smell of ammonia mixed with bananas. Witch Doctor covered the glass again and sealed the cloth tight round the rim with an elastic band. Then he began to write out a label.

Dead Girl looked at all the jars of red liquid stacked in the tower. They all seemed to have these little wizened creatures preserved inside. The creatures looked like the Little Thing she had projected except they were made out of real flesh and blood. It was like Witch Doctor was collecting them. There must be hundreds and hundreds of them. She squinted to read the label Witch Doctor had stuck on the jar. It said 'Horus 1000'.

Witch Doctor pressed a button on his harness and the hydraulics started up again. He started to come down. He was relaxed now. He was muttering to himself. Dead

Girl didn't move. She was still looking at the Little Thing trapped in the glass jar. It was made out of blue light but Witch Doctor hadn't noticed. He obviously thought it was something that was made out of nerves and skin and blood. Dead Girl saw the spectre open its mouth wide. It was shrieking from inside the red liquid but nobody could hear. It didn't matter. The Little Thing inside the jar popped like a soap bubble and was gone.

Witch Doctor had got caught up in the cables. The hydraulics had jammed. That was when he saw Dead Girl down below. She was no longer doing the Tattooed Lady routine. He shouted at her but she ignored him. He thought he had taken her Extra Special Powers away from her to add to his collection. But he hadn't. She had used her Extra Special Powers to trick him. He dangled helplessly above her. He didn't realise there was nothing inside that last jar.

Dead Girl ran back to the bedroom but now it was all different. It was just this dingy cave hacked out of the ground. There was a naked ten watt bulb hanging from this low ceiling by a twisted length of flex and in the corner was a stained yellow mattress and a screwed up plastic bag. The ground was sticky. It was covered in all these crushed brown seed-pods. They were in these layers. The ones on top were all bristly and springy and the ones underneath were all slimy and rotting. Dead Girl walked carefully over to the window. It was just this sheet of polythene tacked over a hole in the wall.

Everything was changed. She gave the room one last glance. Opposite the mattress was this open door leading into a dark passage-way. It smelt of damp. On the other side of the room where the walk-in closet had been there was just this pathetic wooden cupboard. The door had a full-length mirror on the front. It had swung wide open to reveal Witch Doctor's black coat hanging from a rail. Piled on the floor of the cupboard were all these old papers. There were Court circulars, kiddie porn magazines, death certificates and skull X-rays.

Dead Girl reached for her fanny-pack. It was underneath her white hospital gown. Suddenly she had got her old clothes back again. That was when Dead Girl realised she had done what Fairy Sugadaddy wanted. She had found where Witch Doctor was hiding. The polythene window fluttered in its earthen frame and this cool breeze wafted into the damp room. It was time to leave.

Underneath the window was this old cardboard box. The Magic Wand lay inside. It hadn't changed. It was still made of this twisted and braided glass. It looked like these two snakes made of crystal that were curled up around each other. It shone in the light.

Dead Girl hitched her hospital gown up around her hips. Her ghost legs were still giving off this soft blue glow. She climbed back out through the window on to the Heath of London. It was early morning. She had spent the whole night underneath the hill.

Dead Girl walked away from the hill. She ached on the inside. The sun was peeping through the green leaves overhead. She was carrying this twisted glass rod. It was hollow with a nozzle at one end. She knew it was really a Magic Wand.

>>

Dead Girl was falling down through the water in this lake on the Heath of London. It was a deep lake. She was wearing this white hospital gown over her fanny-pack. Her legs were made of this thin blue light. It was dark all around.

Dead Girl had this Magic Wand made of twisted glass. She was holding on to it ever so tight.

Every so often she would bump into the thick stems of all these water lilies. She would kick against them to make sure she kept on going down through the deep water.

Eventually she landed on this mud-shelf. This was where the water lilies were rooted. There were big fat seedpods all around. They were brown and bristly and ready to burst.

Over the edge of the mud-shelf the ground gave way to become a sheer drop. There was this chasm. Dead Girl peered into it. She had never seen anything so deep. Far away at the bottom of the watery chasm it was very dark. She could see this dark light.

Dead Girl wished she could go to the dark light. That was her wish. She wanted to disappear and start all over again.

That was when Fairy Sugadaddy came back. He spoke to her inside her head. His voice was like an amplified echo. It was much clearer than before.

Fairy Sugadaddy soothed her. He said that she had landed on the lip of a Silly Black Hole and that the dark light at the bottom of the chasm was what they call a Singularity. He said he would take her there. But first she had to go to a place called the Temple of Osiris.

## Contingency operation

*Screen Message*
GAMEPLAY STARTING...

*Real Audio Stream*
"Noone comes close to me. Not even Eddie."
—Doctor Double Oh No admiring himself in his closet mirror.

*Player Status*
You are Doctor Double Oh No, Crown agent, chaos magician and remote master of schizoid knife-wielding alter ego Bad Nat. She hunts mana for you on the Crown orbital space ark. You draw it down to your closet and convert it into tezma.

You have successfully made the White Lotus ascent nine hundred and ninety nine times. You have one less than one thousand units of tezma stashed in old jars at the back of your closet on Parliament Hill.

You are almost ready to make the Pink Lotus descent and win the game. You need only one more unit of tezma.

But you can no longer make the White Lotus ascent. Your designated mark Bad Nat no longer responsive to hypnotic trigger commands.

Time to revert to other method.

*Full Motion Video*
The Doctor handballing Eddie at his radio listening post on Parliament Hill. Eddie is strung up by one foot from the cosmic tree. His toes are free. He squirms in ecstasy as the Doctor supports the back of his neck with his left hand and drives him gently inside with his right fist.

Eddie's spectre floats above the zodiacal pond. He speaks in a low jerky voice from deep inside his belly: Fuck me! Fuck me harder! I'm in heaven. Ravish me! O Satis!

The Doctor fixes Eddie with his evil eye. Eddie giggles as the blood rushes to his face. He stiffens and maintains the Satis frequency. The Doctor's conference with the Sirian breed of space aliens begins...

*Narrative Voiceover*

So this is how the Doctor gets his secret intelligence from the Sirians direct. He uses Eddie as a medium. Writes up the results of the conferences in his little black book. Just to be safe, he records everything in the old Enochian cipher.

He always remembers to file his nails.

What's happening? There is a very narrow window of opportunity according to Satis. She is such a gossip. She tells Eddie everything.

Seems like Natasha Supanova crack up when it time to collect that one thousandth unit of mana. She decide to make her own intervention. Mutant holding that mana transformed into supermutant. Not an accident at all. Result of controlled exposure to gamma radiation. Origin of Anu the Chameleon Kid.

What a fucking drag!

Satis goes on say that Anu escape Crown orbital space ark and make an attempt fly the Antarctic Leyline to London. But she don't make it in one piece. Anu break up on entering earth's atmosphere. Her body parts rain down all over East London.

Anu's torso splash down in the Thames and drift with the tide. But she lose other pieces of herself in the courtyards and alleyways of Whitechapel. These are little knobbly bits of hair and gristle and bone. These are her extra lives.

The Doctor realise he no longer needs Natasha Supanova. Abandon that avatar. Get going instead with East London alter ego held in reserve.

*Full Motion Video*

The Doctor loitering outside the glass closet of his hermetic hole-in-the-hill. A Substance H roll-up between his yellowed fingers. He is on his mobile.

The Doctor speaking in his sternest fire-and-brimstone voice: Jack? Don't mind me giving you the trade name. It's time to get busy…

*Screen Message*
TEZMA HOARD: 999

*Player Status*

As Doctor Double Oh No you must vanquish the alien/human monster Anu the Chameleon Kid to have any chance of defeating the Caliphate of New New England and rebuilding a Secret Ukanian Combine. You must animate your familiar Jack the Mack with the power of your tezma and send him out to conduct a full area search of Whitechapel. Here Jack must capture the living remains of the alien/human monster and return them to you in your glass closet. This will give you the chance to reassemble Anu and extract her mana under controlled conditions. The tezma once added to your hoard should make you powerful enough to accomplish the Pink Lotus descent.

*Narrative Voiceover*

This is how it plays. The Doctor activates Jack's holy prophet routine. Tells him that Ashtoreth, traitorous angel of Allah, has given birth to twelve cunty demons. The fallen angel herself swims deep in the Thames. But her twelve little daughters have crawled up on the land and are even now defiling the sacred spots of East London with menstrual blood and used condoms.

The Doctor tells his man to leave the bitch muthah in her underwater lair. She much too tricky to catch. Just capture those twelve daughters using strict holy tech. Only two cautions specific to the area.

One. Avoid telecam gaze of mobile TV reporter Mark 23. This is strictly a black bag job.

Two. Watch out for those dyke warrior goddesses, the Karma Twins. They could be conjured by daughters for protection.

That's it. Simple enough for Jack. Once daughters have been bundled off the streets of East London, they must be brought up to the sacred hill on Hampstead Heath. Look forward to the end of the Great Work when there will be twelve demonic pieces in total ready to be sacrificed to Allah. Time when Jack, last prophet of Allah, is purged of the illusions of desire.

This is the cover-story the Doctor lays on Jack. He gives out information on a strict need-to-know basis.

Of course, what he don't say is that for Jack to name a demonic shaping he has to know the secret of his own desire. But then the Doctor always was an optimist.

He already working up his sympathetic magic routines. Once he got those twelve pieces of Anu in his bedroom cell it gonna be simple enough to attract her main body in from the Thames. Then he can get on with the real work.

*Full Motion Video*

The Doctor throwing the fag-end of his Substance H roll-up into the zodiacal pond. He is finishing up on his invisible mobile.

The Doctor: Very good, Jack. La ilaha et cetera. Let's just bring them up to the grove on the hill, okay? You know the tree.

*Screen Message*
WHITE LOTUS ASCENT CONTINGENCY OPERATION
CODENAME: PARLIAMENT HILL ASCENT

*Player Status*
You have used your POV button to adopt the subject position of one of Doctor Double Oh No's alter egos. You are Jack the Mack. Voice in your head says you are last prophet of Allah questing for the shape-shifting daughters of Ashtoreth. Your divine mission is to capture these killer demons armed only with a knife and a ziplock bag.

The demons are biding their time at various occult locations around the London double septagram. You must track them down and overcome them. It could be tricky. The demons are very seductive. They have the power to alter themselves. They can disguise themselves as whatever guilty thing is in the eye of the beholder. They can become dangerously provocative young dancing girls.

You must resist their temptations. Be warned that Ashtoreth's daughters have the power to suck the life out of you. They can take you to a place where you are no longer you.

Luckily, you have a shard of polished metal in your pocket. You can use this to catch the light from the moon and the stars and cast it at the demons. The daughters of Ashtoreth like shiny things from the night sky. Once they are distracted, you can move in for the close-up work.

You must name the shape thrown by each demon in time and place of your encounter.

Once called on their powers of enchantment in this way, the daughters of Ashtoreth will shrivel and collapse back into their original foul state. That is the time for you to scrape them up off the pavement and drop them in your black bag. The demons lose their power when deprived of a light source. So you better make sure your bag zips up nice and tight.

There are twelve daughters of Ashtoreth in total. Each one more powerful than the last.

Hunt the demons down one by one in East London to master twelve levels of magical ascent.

Once you have bagged the final demon you will have enough mana to ascend to Parliament Hill. Deposit the captured demons under the hill as a tribute to Allah.

You have one cheat mode at your disposal.

*Screen Message*
PARLIAMENT HILL ASCENT
GAMEPLAY STARTING…

*Point of View: Jack the Mack*
You are locked in your cubicle at the St George's Baths. "More hot here in Number 23." And the water comes pouring in. Magic!

You've got the TV on the reality channel. That wandering reporter Mark 23 is out there looking for you. You chuckle. It's an old show.

You get busy with the disinfectant and the Derbac soap. You must clean yourself for the Great Work ahead. You must get rid of everything stinking.

There's a barking from outside the cubicle. Guard dog knows the score. Your time is up.

You will step out into the Highway smelling like a new-born babe.

It's a penny extra for the towel. But you never have to pay.

*Full Motion Video*
Jack creeping through the streets of East London with his demon-laying kit. He's got his radar up. He knows where to go.

*Screen Message*
PARLIAMENT HILL ASCENT: LEVEL 1
GAMEPLAY RESUMING…

*Player Status*
Location: Water Street@North America screen

You are hit by the first daughter of Ashtoreth. That demon shape shift to become the image of your spectre in this time and place.

*Real Audio Stream*
It was here in a hotel room that you murdered me.

I have been called an Ascot snob. I can be a bit haughty and disdainful, it's true. I secretly think ordinary people are pods and scum and vermin. But that's okay because I am fantastic on an international scale.

I wear Paloma Picasso red lipstick. Just the one shade.

My favourite scent is Caron. It's very heavy and musky. You could say it's a slightly old-fashioned expensive perfume. I also wear Fracas by Robert Piguet. It's a vintage fragrance that's now been repackaged.

I wear La Perla underwear, if you must know.

My bags and accessories are all by Hermes. In fact, my dream commodity is a Hermes bag named specially after me, like the Kelly bag.

What is my name?

*Point of View: Jack the Mack*
You speak the name of the first demon. You say, "Carrie Shakespeare-Browne."

That demon shrink down and disappear. All that's left is a finger covered in nasal hair.

*Screen Message*
PARLIAMENT HILL ASCENT: LEVEL 1 COMPLETED

*Full Motion Video*
Jack hopping over the Atlantic pond. He does not deal with running water. He's got the first daughter of Ashtoreth stowed away in his black bag.

Jack: "What a man-eating vampire bitch she was!"

*Screen Message*
PARLIAMENT HILL ASCENT: LEVEL 2
GAMEPLAY RESUMING...

*Player Status*
Location: Old Swallow Gardens@North America screen

You are hit by the second daughter of Ashtoreth. That demon shape shift to become the image of your spectre in this time and place.

*Real Audio Stream*
It was here in the long crooked passage under a railway line that you murdered me.

I am like a solemn little child, really. I seem quite innocent. But I'm wise beyond my years.

I tend to appear at the moment of orgasm.

I wear very light, cheap perfume. Anais Anais by Cacharel. I use eau de toilette cos perfume is far too expensive for me.

I use Maybelline mascara on my eyelashes. I bought it from Superdrug by the H sign on Chapel Market.

The commodity I most desire is some face glitter.

What is my name?

*Point of View: Jack the Mack*
You speak the name of the second demon. You say, "Red Nell KFC."

That demon shrink down and disappear. All that's left is a foot with a puckered arsehole in the sole.

*Screen Message*
PARLIAMENT HILL ASCENT: LEVEL 2 COMPLETED

*Full Motion Video*
Jack dodging a night watchman. He waits for a train to pass overhead and uses its noise to cover the sound of his escape.

Jack: "Skanky fucking junky. What an old crone!"

*Screen Message*
PARLIAMENT HILL ASCENT: LEVEL 3
GAMEPLAY RESUMING…

*Player Status*
Location: Pinchin Street@North America screen

You are hit by the third daughter of Ashtoreth. That demon shape shift to become the image of your spectre in this time and place.

*Real Audio Stream*
It was here under a railway arch full of rubbish that you dumped what was left of me after you'd murdered me.

I can be a mischievous little sub, devious and cheeky, a real trouble-maker. I'm young but quite socially confident. I've been called a bit of a tart. But I'm really just saucy.

I have my hair in a perm or else scraped back in a ponytail. I like to wear lots of earrings in each ear. Gold hoops, mainly.

I wear lots of make-up, but it's always slightly off. I don't get it quite right.

The lipstick is applied too widely, it goes beyond the mouth. That's the one mistake young girls always make, isn't it? Lipstick at the sides of the mouth. That's because they apply lipstick all round the mouth while it's open in an O shape, rather than simply apply it to the top lip and the bottom lip.

My favourite lipstick is frosted pink made by Rimmel.

My blue eyeshadow is applied in a block to give me that 'panda' look. Like Agnetha in Abba.

My perfume is Charlie by Revlon. But I aspire to Dolce et Gabbana.

My dream commodity is a Dolce et Gabbana nylon bag.

What is my name?

*Point of View: Jack the Mack*

You speak the name of the third demon. You say, "Lady Lydia."

That demon shrink down and disappear. All that's left is a nose pitted with little tear ducts.

*Screen Message*

PARLIAMENT HILL ASCENT: LEVEL 3 COMPLETED

*Full Motion Video*

Jack pushing past the dossers drinking cans of Tennant's lager and pissing in the street. He is moving at a high speed.

Jack: "Call that a woman? I call it a piss poor imitation of a woman. Fucking dyke!"

*Screen Message*

PARLIAMENT HILL ASCENT: LEVEL 4

GAMEPLAY RESUMING...

*Player Status*

Location: Old Castle Street@North America screen

You are hit by the fourth daughter of Ashtoreth. That demon shape shift to become the image of your spectre in this time and place.

*Real Audio Stream*

You murdered me in this dimly lit alley, on the pavement.

I'm a rather queer bird. Some might say a scholar, even an intellectual. It's true I am patient, reserved and intense.

My signature scent is Jicky by Guerlain.

I get my nostrils plucked out once a month. It used to be at Simpsons of Piccadilly. But now it's at a gentleman's establishment in Jermyn Street.

I wear accessories by Daks and Aquascutum.

My dream commodity is a signet ring from Tiffany.

What is my name?

*Point of View: Jack the Mack*
You speak the name of the fourth demon. You say, "Crackpipe Ali."

That demon shrink down and disappear. All that's left is a hand with a pair of lips in the centre of its palm.

*Screen Message*
PARLIAMENT HILL ASCENT: LEVEL 4 COMPLETED

*Full Motion Video*
Jack fleeing the scene. He's scooting past the metal frames of the market stalls parked in the street.

Jack: "That chick had a beard! Grotesque, man!"

*Screen Message*
PARLIAMENT HILL ASCENT: LEVEL 5
GAMEPLAY RESUMING...

*Player Status*
Location: Gunthorpe Street@North America screen

You are hit by the fifth daughter of Ashtoreth. That demon shape shift to become the image of your spectre in this time and place.

*Real Audio Stream*
You murdered me here, next to the stairs, on the first floor landing of a block of flats.

I always have been a bit of a destructive saboteur. People say I have a baleful gaze.

My gender is a tricky one, that's for sure. I'm a trannie dominatrix, pre-op for sure. That's right, some really big bloke in thigh-high boots.

I wear stage make-up. The real pancake stuff that used to be made by Max Factor. I apply it almost as a block. It offers full coverage, giving me a mask with absolutely no definition. There's no natural skin tone showing through.

I have very red glossy lips. But the lipstick is slightly smudged. It's bleeding into the little cracks around my mouth, because it's not applied with a pencil.

After many hours under those hot video lights, my sweat causes the pancake to slide down and melt the lipstick. The pancake collects in thick streaks on top of my nostrils and upper lip. It has to be removed with stage make-up remover. I get it in a big blue tub from ScreenFace. It's like grease or fat. I dip my hand in, slap it on my face and rub the make-up so it dissolves. But I have to be careful, cos if I get any in my eyes then I'm seeing soft-focus for the rest of the day.

I have huge hands covered in hard silver rings. They are real thick silver bands which from a distance look like knuckle-dusters and they click when I move my fingers together.

I got cropped hair and wear a collection of wigs. They all smell of male sweat and cheap make-up and hair-spray.

My dream commodity is a facial which tattoos the make-up right on.

What is my name?

*Point of View: Jack the Mack*
You speak the name of the fifth demon. You say, "Big Mama Em."

That demon shrink down and disappear. All that's left is an eyeball covered in little grey hairs.

*Screen Message*
PARLIAMENT HILL ASCENT: LEVEL 5 COMPLETED

*Full Motion Video*
Jack nipping round the corner and out of sight. He's already collected five of the demons. His bag is getting heavy.

Jack: "Thankyou, Allah. Did you check it out? A stone-faced ball-buster. That was nasty!"

*Screen Message*
PARLIAMENT HILL ASCENT: LEVEL 6
GAMEPLAY RESUMING...

*Player Status*
Location: Henriques Street@North America screen

You are hit by the sixth daughter of Ashtoreth. That demon shape shift to become the image of your spectre in this time and place.

*Real Audio Stream*
You murdered me on this path in the back-yard of a club.

I'm a romantic little thing. I reckon I'm made of glitter and marshmallow. I'm a terrible sentimentalist. My heart is easily broken. What I'm really looking for is some kind of father figure.

My cosmetics are by Estee Lauder. L'Eau d'Hadrien by Annick Goutal is the fragrance I wear for the evening. My daytime scent is l'Eau d'Issey. It's a non-aggressive scent worn by feminists, very fashionable back in the day. A novelty perfume, blatantly non-natural smelling.

My clothes are by Ghost. They're very floaty.

I have a tiny beaded handbag, with room only for a mobile and a credit card. It's by Lulu Guinness.

I wear backless shoes—kitten heels by Jimmy Choo.

I attend private views at the Royal College and buy fashion garments there. I'm very London.

My role model is Anoushka Hempel and my dream commodity is a titled husband.

What is my name?

*Point of View: Jack the Mack*
You speak the name of the sixth demon. You say, "Lollipop Liz."

That demon shrink down and disappear. All that's left is a forearm with an ear growing out of it.

*Screen Message*
PARLIAMENT HILL ASCENT: LEVEL 6 COMPLETED

*Full Motion Video*
Jack blending into the background, one more passerby cutting past the deserted school.

Jack: "That one was exhausting. Talk about hysterical! Going on and on and on and on. Fuck me!"

*Screen Message*
PARLIAMENT HILL ASCENT: LEVEL 7
GAMEPLAY RESUMING...

*Player Status*
Location: Hanbury Street@North America screen

You are hit by the seventh daughter of Ashtoreth. That demon shape shift to become the image of your spectre in this time and place.

*Real Audio Stream*

You murdered me in the back-yard of this terraced house, near the outside toilet, next to the wooden fence.

I am a cyborg whore. I do the temple sex slave number.

I'm a tricksy little thing. But I'm nothing like Lady Lydia. I got too much social charm for that. More money, too.

Even so, I have to confess, I do think a D&B bag is the same thing as a Dolce et Gabbana bag. I guess I'm a victim of advertising.

I wear the latest cosmetics—Laura Mercier, Trish McEvoy.

I frequent tanning booths.

I have a handbag with a gold chain.

I like lots of different perfumes. D&G. Eternity by Calvin Klein. Or the new one by Calvin Klein, Contradiction. Or Tommy Hilfiger's bathroom range. What's it called? Tommy Girl?

I've been through my henna tattoo phase. My dream commodity is a diamond naval stud. I've got a piercing already.

My ideal type is Meg Matthews—common as muck but loaded.

What is my name?

*Point of View: Jack the Mack*

You speak the name of the seventh demon. You say, "Motown Anne."

That demon shrink down and disappear. All that's left is a severed tongue with a nipple at its tip.

*Screen Message*

PARLIAMENT HILL ASCENT: LEVEL 7 COMPLETED

*Full Motion Video*

Jack camouflaged by the throng of late-night revellers spilling out into the streets. He's got seven of the demons inside his black bag.

Jack: "White trash like her think they can just flounce around with their tits hanging out. Well, that should show the rest of them!"

*Screen Message*

PARLIAMENT HILL ASCENT: LEVEL 8
GAMEPLAY RESUMING...

*Player Status*

Location: Durward Street@North America screen

You are hit by the eighth daughter of Ashtoreth. That demon shape shift to become the image of your spectre in this time and place.

*Real Audio Stream*

You murdered me on the cobbles in this dim, narrow street, just outside the gates to a stable-yard.

I tend to spit and curse at random.

I am very overweight and clown around to compensate.

I am something of a tomboy. I wear very baggy unisex sports gear, like Gap combats in American sizes. I like them nice and big.

My underwear is mismatched. It doesn't matter, cos I'm never seen in it.

I poke fun at Motown Anne and Carrie Shakespeare-Browne while secretly admiring them.

I wear a Body Shop fragrance. It's oatmeal scrub.

I claim to be a vegetarian, but stuff myself with bacon sandwiches at night. It's true. I'm an Animal Liberation Front militant who secretly eats meat and craves a wardrobe full of leather goods.

I use feminism as a last-ditch resort cos I've failed as a glam woman. I've come to radical feminism cos I've no place else to go, rather than cos it's an informed choice.

I admit I'm young and confused. I'm still finding my way in the world.

I do have a tremendous sense of humour. I'm able to verbalise my anger safely.

I'm a popular person who feels unloved. I feel awkward, big, clumsy and unfeminine. But at least I'm valued for not being just a showroom dummy.

What is my name?

*Point of View: Jack the Mack*

You speak the name of the eighth demon. You say, "Pollyanna Goldenshower."

That demon shrink down and disappear. All that's left is a thumb with three joints.

*Screen Message*

PARLIAMENT HILL ASCENT: LEVEL 8 COMPLETED

*Full Motion Video*

Jack plodding along with the homegoing stream of Sainsbury's supermarket shoppers. Eight daughters of Ashtoreth trapped inside his black bag.

Jack: "A big fat troll I can handle. But a big fat *yid* troll? Fuck that shit!"

*Screen Message*
PARLIAMENT HILL ASCENT: LEVEL 9
GAMEPLAY RESUMING…

*Player Status*
Location: Mitre Square@North America screen

You are hit by the ninth daughter of Ashtoreth. That demon shape shift to become the image of your spectre in this time and place.

*Real Audio Stream*
You murdered me here in the darkest corner of this badly lit square, in the shadows of the silent warehouses, at the back of the empty houses, next to the railings of someone's back-yard.

I am cute and funny, kooky rather than sexy.

I wear very bright clothes, very loud floral prints.

I enjoy buying weird, cheap clothes from vintage thrift shops. I buy the cheapest I can find and then customise them myself with bits of fur, sequins, ear-rings and other jewellery.

My philosophy is that clothes should be worn to make people smile and brighten up the world, not to make the wearer desirable.

I often wear clothes inappropriate for the weather.

I can often be seen sporting a hat at a jaunty angle. A beret, for example.

The irony is that I actually have a really hot body, a well-proportioned body, which is hidden by all the clashing, mismatched clothes.

I have long hair. I am very ruddy-faced. My skin is scrubbed. I don't wear any make-up. Well, maybe a bit of lip-gloss if I'm going out in the evenings.

My eyebrows are unkempt.

I wear crazy nail-polish. I might have colours alternating on my nails. I like reds and blues, occasionally customised with bits of glitter.

I do not have a dream commodity.

I do not wear fragrance. Which means I smell of old clothes and Johnsons baby talc.

What is my name?

*Point of View: Jack the Mack*
You speak the name of the ninth demon. You say, "Kit-Kat Kate."

That demon shrink down and disappear. All that's left is a severed ear with a tooth growing out of the lobe.

*Screen Message*
PARLIAMENT HILL ASCENT: LEVEL 9 COMPLETED

*Full Motion Video*
Jack timing his exit to depart through a gap in the coverage of the surveillance cameras. He disappears into a warren of underground walkways.

Jack: "What a mess! Green and blue and red shit tattooed all over her belly, even on her, you know, her fucking thing. Vile!"

*Screen Message*
PARLIAMENT HILL ASCENT: LEVEL 10
GAMEPLAY RESUMING...

*Player Status*
Location: Old Dorset Street@North America screen

You are hit by the tenth daughter of Ashtoreth. That demon shape shift to become the image of your spectre in this time and place.

*Real Audio Stream*
You murdered me here in a ground-floor bedsit in one end of a paved courtyard, right by the bins of the terraced houses.

I am often like a very young child, an infant really.

I am easily mesmerised, by a ball of string being unwound, for example.

I experiment with lots of perfume all at once. I spray perfume dispensers in my face to see how they work. I have been known to spray myself with all the perfumes at a department store counter. But then I get migraines and other illnesses.

I always get the amounts of perfume wrong.

I buy perfume and throw it away after two days cos I'm bored of it.

I am actually wearing the first perfume that came to me. It's Calvin Klein's CK One, I think. Or is it Emporio Armani?

I always wear the same old clothes, old dungarees with old badges on the front. The badges have slogans. Animal Liberation Front. Spice Girls. Will Self Is Stupid.

At the front of my scalp, I have tiny bulldog hairclips, plastic sparkly ones.

My dream commodity is the full Spice Girls cosmetics range.
What is my name?

*Point of View: Jack the Mack*
You speak the name of the tenth demon. You say, "Mary J Kelly."

That demon shrink down and disappear. All that's left is a big toe with a urethral slit.

*Screen Message*
PARLIAMENT HILL ASCENT: LEVEL 10 COMPLETED

*Full Motion Video*
Jack nipping past the multi-storey car-park. He jumps the barrier and doesn't look back.

Jack: "Did you see that huge arse! Who the hell was she kidding, with her la-di-da bullshit? Stupid fat whore."

*Screen Message*
PARLIAMENT HILL ASCENT: LEVEL 11
GAMEPLAY RESUMING...

*Player Status*
Location: White's Row@North America screen

You are hit by the eleventh daughter of Ashtoreth. That demon shape shift to become the image of your spectre in this time and place.

*Real Audio Stream*
It was here near the vegetable market that you attacked me. A month later I collapsed in the workhouse and died.

I am a hard little worker, always stressed out. I'm often made into a scapegoat.

I'm one or two steps behind everyone else. I live with mental hand-me-downs.

My clothes are behind-the-times and slightly old fashioned in styling. I still wear leggings.

I never have the time or the energy to go to upmarket department stores. I rely on Chat magazine, instead.

I have lots of Yardley cosmetics. I like their heavy violet scented soap and their toilet water.

My usual perfumes are Tweed by Lentheric or Charlie worn in a non-ironic way. I've only just cottoned on to Calvin Klein perfume.

I buy supermarket copies of designer perfumes styled to fool you. So I get Opiate in Sainsbury's. It's the same colour and packaging as Yves Saint Laurent Opium. It also smells similar when first sprayed on.

My dream commodity? I am saving up for my first pair of designer jeans.

What is my name?

*Point of View: Jack the Mack*
You speak the name of the eleventh demon. You say, "Little Fanny Annie."

That demon shrink down and disappear. All that's left is a clitoris covered in eyelashes.

*Screen Message*
PARLIAMENT HILL ASCENT: LEVEL 11 COMPLETED

*Full Motion Video*
Jack appearing on the other side of the multi-storey car-park. He's bagged eleven daughters of Ashtoreth so far. Just one more left to find.

Jack: "Yeuch! She looked like a goddamned walking corpse. I did her a favour, really."

*Screen Message*
PARLIAMENT HILL ASCENT: LEVEL 12
GAMEPLAY RESUMING…

*Player Status*
Location: Maidman Street@North America screen
You are searching for the twelfth demon.

*Full Motion Video*
Jack lost in the maze of dark little streets behind Mile End tube station. He's going round in circles. Swivelling his head from side to side, tapping at the cracks in the ground.

Jack: "I don't know about this one. I just don't know. I can't be expected to remember all the places I've jumped on dumb cunts."

*Narrative Voiceover*
Jack is feeling disturbed. He senses a hidden influence at work. Something is

keeping him away from the twelfth daughter of Ashtoreth.

He remembers the stories of the Karma Twins. Flash suits, cheap grins, bodies buried beneath the paving stones.

This could get nasty. Very nasty.

*Player Status*
You give up searching for that twelfth demon. Time for a little cheating…

*Screen Message*
PARLIAMENT HILL ASCENT: CHEAT MODE
SKIPPING LEVEL 12…

*Point of View: Jack the Mack*
You no longer have to find that twelfth demon. It makes you feel guilty. You drift to the abode of Ashtoreth, mother of the twelve cunty demons.

*Full Motion Video*
Jack standing at Shadwell Dock Stairs. His wanderings have led him to the bank of the Thames. He is looking down into the water. His black bag is resting at his feet.

Jack: Ashtoreth! Come out, come out, wherever you are!

*Narrative Voiceover*
Jack is babbling nonsense. He's got too far into his cover story and is starting to lose it. Always a danger with someone as fucked up as Jack.

Doctor decides time to reel him back in.

*Full Motion Video*
The Doctor patrolling the bank of the zodiacal pond. He is careful not to get his feet wet. He is on his invisible mobile.

The Doctor: Forget Ashtoreth, Jack. We don't do water. Just bring me what you've got.

*Screen Message*
PARLIAMENT HILL ASCENT: RUNNING
SKIPPED LEVEL 12 STORED AS SECRET LEVEL

*Player Mode*
You are Doctor Double Oh No's alter ego Jack the Mack, clean-up boy and all-

purpose diversionary agent located in East London.

You have successfully resisted the advances of the daughters of Ashtoreth. You have accumulated enough mana to ascend to Parliament Hill.

*Narrative Voiceover*
So now Jack trudges up to Parliament Hill with his heavy black bag. Thinks he is on a pilgrimage to a hill sacred to Allah. He makes it into the hole in the hill and leaves his bag and its contents inside as an offering.

Then he's back to figure out the conundrum of Ashtoreth.

Silly old Jack.

*Screen Message*
WHITE LOTUS ASCENT CONTINGENCY OPERATION
COMPLETED

*Player Mode*
You have used your POV button to abandon the subject position of your alter ego Jack the Mack. You are Doctor Double Oh No.

Jack has done his work. He has deposited the scattered remains of the alien/human monster Anu the Chameleon Kid in your glass closet. Enough for you to attract the main bulk of Anu to your bedside through the operation of sympathetic magic. You need to reel in what is still drifting there in the Thames.

"This has been a message from hell, Jack." You are ending Jack's deep trance. "Yours truly, the Boss." Keywords which wipe out the Jack memory.

You return the hypnotic subject to himself with sensation only of missing time. Time to get busy.

Once Anu has been reassembled you will be able to extract her mana. Then it's you doing the Pink Lotus descent and showtime for the Secret Ukanian Combine.

*Screen Message*
TEZMA HOARD: 999

*Narrative Voiceover*
The Doctor is in closed conference with Eddie at the sacred tree. He going over plans for the Pink Lotus descent. He got the blindfold on.

Thanks a lot, Eddie Boy.

When the Doctor track back to the hermetic hole in the hill he find Anu waiting for him in his back bedroom. Damn, his sympathetic magic work fast! That supermutant already find the missing pieces of herself delivered by Jack.

She had put herself back together best she could while the Doctor was busy with Eddie.

Anu the Chameleon Kid got that one thousandth unit of tezma needed by Doctor Double Oh No for the Pink Lotus descent. Time to go get it.

No more Bad Nat. The Doctor got to do the dirty work himself.

*Point of View: Doctor Double Oh No*
You are gonna retrieve that mana from Anu the Chameleon Kid with your own two hands. You move deeper into your bedroom. Dumb creature lie there on the ground jerking and flapping. She hasn't got any legs. They taper away into a thin mist.

What the fuck.

You get busy with your nails. They are long and sharp.

Anu is kicking and giggling under your hands. She got the shaven head with the purple eye-shadow and the blue lipstick, she got two silver nose rings and a nose stud, she got the gold ring in her clit. Tattoos cover her body—bands of hieroglyphs on her arms, beads on her wrists, image of a beetle with spread legs over her lower belly. You dig in hard and get this acid or some shit spurt all over your face.

You got to be strong. Anu is using her mutant powers on you. She has got deep inside you and photocopied your spectre. Oh no! She has changed shape to become that guilty thing you keep deep inside. Anu is pretending to be Khepri, goddess of beetles. She is messing with your mind.

Your hands are shaking. You are digging into a creature that has your own eyes. It's as if you are hurting your own secret self.

You banish the thought.

You need that one thousandth unit of mana. You want to do the Pink Lotus descent.

*Full Motion Video*
The Doctor prepares Anu with his own hands. It's a simple operation. The belly cut open with a left-handed stroke. The cord severed. The trophy delivered in a rush of blood.

*Narrative Voiceover*
The Doctor reckons he has scored one unit of tezma. But he is deluded.

Anu the Chameleon Kid is running a number on him.

He stands there holding a mess of fish entrails in his hands. He sees what he wants to see. Places those worthless fish guts in a glass jar at the back of his closet.

The Doctor has turned his back on Anu. She ups and runs. She gets out of the hermetic hole in the hill.

*Screen Message*
TEZMA HOARD: 999

*Point of View: Doctor Double Oh No*
You reckon you got one thousand units of tezma in the back of your closet. Enough to perform the Pink Lotus descent.

You return from your closet to the place where you did Anu. There is only a blood-soaked mattress. The supermutant is gone.

Where is your Tally Stick? You want to carve that final notch into place. Confirm you got those one thousand units.

The Tally Stick is gone as well.

*Screen Message*
GAME SAVED

## Conspiratorial plots of the secret Osiris Club

Eddie is giving his captors what they want on audio and video. They've hauled in the latest equipment. He puts in a request for a make-up artist.

*A True and Faithful Relation of What Passed at Clarence House between Dr John Dee and the Devil.* Extract 5.1: They thought her untimely death was necessary. They would do what had to be done in the eternal interests of the Royal Firm.

She knew she had to go. There was due to be one heir too many. Kill herself she would not; so brought down she would have to be. They would have to give her an agonising push. The hell with it! Either it was necessary or it was not.

And that is how they broke with her. It was an eruptive necessity.

At the time, it was agreed that no glassy-eyed third party could be blamed for her weird death. It would be an inexplicable accident. They wanted no doubts about this untimely death; although doubts there would be—gnawing doubts, together with evasive whispers, unmentionable gossip, creaking rumours and terrible scandal.

But they cared not whether it was politic; they knew only that it was necessary.

Safety was there none in going through the malodorous French police. If they brought her down in the abysmal dark, they could probably get her out before anybody noticed what had occurred. The fiendish ambulance driver would be told to keep shut his gasping mouth. He would be instructed to say nothing absolute; as would anyone passing by when she was taken unto the desolate Pitie-Salpetriere.

For a blurred hour or two, they thought they could keep it quiet—delay the frantic publicity, the dangerous inquest. She would fit a chewed body bag.

They thought it was a marvellous way out of their stewing troubles.

And they farmed out the gruesome work unto a nebulous freelance. It was another job shunned inside the Palace walls. Brutal it was to employ a blemished freelance who did not qualify for that kind of damnable work. But they came to some putrid financial arrangement. It was necessary for them to open a numbered account for the Bulgarians. The Doctor always saved them filthy lucre.

Six paid out.

The unbelievable shock was not easy to bear. Faced with it, they ought to have had mercy illimitable upon her.

Her peculiar death had nought to do with the other prodigious evil. The Doctor was the one responsible for that. He said it was never pointless to reopen festering wounds.

EK Exegesis 5.1: I wasn't involved in the original decision, so I can't really comment, can I?

I do know that it was an outside job and the Bulgarians do come cheap. I mean, a Fiat Uno ain't exactly gonna break the bank, is it? But you get what you pay for in this life. And a little Fiat is hardly a match for a bloody great big Merc that's built like a tank. The real miracle is that they actually did manage to force it to crash. But they still bungled it, didn't they? Missed the target. I tell you, it was a botched job from start to finish.

Lucky the old man was there, that's all I can say.

*A True and Faithful Relation...* Extract 5.2: The straggling gendarmes explained what had happened. They herded the wild paparazzi together. They told them to stay put until the ghastly body was removed.

And the last person to see her alive was from the secret office. Noone else was about at that primal hour. The Doctor was working late into the unquiet night in the utterly locked ambulance.

At the time, he thought it strange that noone had asked him what he was doing. But he did not look out of place. He had the whitish coat, he had the black bag. There was nothing odd about it in hindsight.

A furtive check he gave her before she finally went all the way home. He looked inside her with the ethereal light on. Was there a Little Devil inside? Nothing did he say of it to the last.

No further mention of it has there ever been. The blasphemous coroner lied. He was instructed to lie plausibly and stay true to the lie.

EK Exegesis 5.2: It was an horrible business. No question about it.

So let's just be clear about one thing. The old man didn't kill her. He didn't do nothing to save her neither. But he didn't kill her. He just sort of let nature take its course, if you know what I mean. After all, blood *does* have a tendency to clot.

See, he was there on another job entirely. It dovetailed neatly with the job he'd been given, I grant you. But it was billable to a completely different account. *Teoqualo*, say no more.

Now, don't forget, he'd had lots of practice. Used to be the gynaecologist to Gloriana, doncha know? He was a man always prided himself on his intimate understanding of obstetrics. Thought of himself as a bit of an artist, if you wanna know the truth. In fact, he was always very hurt by all the stories in the penny dreadfuls about Leather Apron and all that.

"They are confusing my role with that of the abortion priest," he said. "When I take no responsibility for Jack's work. The slaughterman has always been by tradition an hired hand."

Course, later he claims memory loss about the whole event. Unlike the rest of the bleeding population!

*A True and Faithful Relation...* Extract 5.3: A hairless atavistic man was the Juggler, with luminous green eyes. Often his surly mouth refused to work; his astounding fingers spoke for him instead.

He sat with the depraved tarot pack clasped in his hidden lap. Trembling he was over the filthy cards. They were a meaningless confusion of occult symbols, until his elusive spirit guide took over and he was under supervision infernal. One by one, the hoary cards were intelligibly transposed on the table vast.

*The Lovers. The Chariot.*

Scared was the Sun Prince that the Juggler would slump over the haunted cards in an epileptic collapse. His brother the Moon Prince could not get his curious head around it. He thought it frightfully odd.

*The White Devil.*

The bloodless lips of the Juggler were apart. A long miasmal snake from his open mouth hideous emerged. Lined was it with gorgeous pink skin. The Princes were aware of its unimaginable appearance. Both were in a vivid state of shock. The serpent did coil in the air before their amazed eyes. It was crowned with ancient scales and displayed a slithering forked tongue.

The evil ghost was not to be laid until the end of its speech incoherent. It had a sibilant voice most low. Prohibited was all talk save its own. It droned on for several inauspicious hours. None else uttered a word.

Recorded was the hissing dictation; then was it played back. After an initial sinister silence, conspiratorial whispering could be heard by the Princes. They did listen to the reverberate sound of distant masculine voices as they became louder.

"The Doctor hath arrived...take away the infant's claim...stay there until it's all over...quick work no doubt...the job's yours if you want it...Dismissed!"

Twas not ended. The Juggler's scrabbling fingers had automatically found the next symbol obscene.

*The Tower.*

The taped spirit malign went on to give forbidden details of the secret membership list.

Terrific was the harm that was done to the Old King.

EK Exegesis 5.3: Course, as soon as Wills became heir apparent, it all started to unravel, didn't it? Never underestimate a boy's love for his mother, that's what I say.

He only got the Doctor to hold a seance. Right there in Clarence House under the nose of his bloody father, Charles.

How could the Doctor refuse? I carried his bags. I was just the medium, I swear.

Anyway, that was all the chance Set needed. He didn't get his bung like he was supposed to, did he? So naturally he was pissed off. He wasn't going to let this one ride. He was going to bring down the whole dirty lot of them. Even if that meant mucking things up for his brother Osiris.

The old devil names names. Which means that Prince William ends up with the full membership list of the Osiris Club.

*A True and Faithful Relation...* Extract 5.4: As precisely executed as a death warrant was the accursed book. This demonic record was anathema unto the Osiris Club. It reported they had a relish primordial for the sinister ritual of infanticide.

The nameless book was in the sudden possession of the Sun Prince.

Some took the deadly white powder; others had recourse to the automatic pistol; older more hysterical members, as a result of their previous repellent professional activities, the silent rope preferred. All thought death by one's own hand was not an unnatural end.

And it was good that all these nether souls belonged now to subterranean history. The Devil Osiris exacted had his own exquisite revenge.

EK Exegesis 5.4: It was quite a result, wasn't it? Wills with his little black book of evidence confronting the guilty members of the Osiris Club. Who could have predicted it? Suicides all round—except for that of the ringleader, of course. Well, Charles was still the boy's father, wasn't he? And he *was* still King.

Course, it helped that the Prince had Set on his side. It was that scaly bastard who dictated the book, wasn't it? Imagine if it had been published. Now that would have raised quite a stink...

*A True and Faithful Relation...* Extract 5.5: The nameless book was in production.

Awesome was the hype; as if its horrific disclosures could bring down the shadow government, discredit age-worn parliament and foreclose the tainted monarchy.

The book was withdrawn unseen. The Sun Prince let it go with no unwholesome struggle. It was obliterated so easily. He it was who broke the prehistoric family contract with the Devil Osiris

EK Exegesis 5.5: Well, he turned out to be quite the little politician, didn't he? Not just a dumb blonde, after all. Who'd have guessed it, eh?

I'm sure you know the rest. He uses the threat of full disclosure to force his old dad's abdication and suddenly he's on the throne. Only now it's a Sunni Muslim prayer mat and he's a full-fledged Sheikh. It was all too much for his father wasn't it? He never really coped with the trip into exile.

So now it's old King Charles up there and young Sheikh William down here and never a kind word between them.

The old man didn't come out of it too well. He got the blame, didn't he?

But let's just look at the facts, now. It was Set who talked. Well, that's his privilege, you might say. But who was it benefits? Who was it renounces the Great Satan and goes all monotheistic? Who is the young master now?

## Dream girl circuit

'JAMES BOND' EPISODE

MARK 23: *(Voiceover)*   Assalamu alaikum, godly people. Here's your host Mark 23, crazy old vigilante and reality TV signifier, marching down the streets of East London with a hidden TV camera. I was still obsessed with the same old riddle—who was Jack the Mack? But now I felt the answer could be found only by solving another riddle first—just who was the enigmatic creature known only as A.?

*Cue titles and music*

VISIT TO AN OLD BATTLEFIELD
*Fade up on the daytime exterior of Mudchute in the Isle of Dogs in East London. A mound of earth reclaimed from the bank of the Thames has been landscaped to form a putting green. There are bunkers of sand and leafy trees at the edge of the green. Canary Wharf tower is visible in the background.*

   *MARK 23 enters the green in his motorised wheelchair. He wears a beige Mao jacket on top of baggy blue jeans and Adidas Gazelles. His hair is shaped into an unruly moptop and flops over his collar. His stickered aluminium flight case rests in the basket at the front of his vehicle. It is covered in a motley display of record company stickers.*

   *Trotting along behind is his sleek black dog SHAITAN. Riding beneath its soft hide are powerful muscles. Its eyes are red slits. It stops to sniff the grass every few seconds and growls.*

   *Track MARK 23 and SHAITAN as they move across the grass to the red triangular pennant fluttering from a pole in the hole in the green. SHAITAN cocks his leg at the flagpole and a stream of thick urine splatters against it.*

MARK 23: *(Voiceover)*    I needed somewhere safe to conduct my psychic research.

FLASHBACK TO A TRANCE INDUCTION
*Interior daytime shot of a bunker deep underground. Whitewashed brick walls dug out of the earth, a concrete floor marked with tape, metal lights suspended from*

*the ceiling in a row. This is the Crossroads of Anubis.*

*Move in on a workbench littered with micro-electric circuitry, soldering irons and bottles of barbiturates. A FACTOR sits at the bench beneath the glare of an anglepoise lamp. He is dressed in a white lab coat. He holds up a radio microchip for inspection, nods and passes it to his boss, the MOBSTER.*

*Track the MOBSTER in his long black coat as he moves over to the SUBJECT spread-eagled on a white dais. The SUBJECT's arms and legs are bound with rope. His face is a video blur. He wears baggy blue jeans and a Shoom T-shirt.*

*Close in on the radio microchip on the tip of the MOBSTER'S finger.*

MARK 23: *(Voiceover)* They said a bunker was built under Mudchute during the bombing raids of the Second World War.

## SAXE-COBURG-GOTHA AS A SYSTEM OF SIGNS

*Exterior daytime shot of the putting green at Mudchute. Canary Wharf tower glittering in the background.*

*MARK 23 sits next to the hole in the green. He holds a little black box in his hands. It has a long narrow slot at one end and a rectangular blue screen at the other. This is a Psychic Image Reader.*

*MARK 23 removes a torn black and white photo from his jacket pocket. Close up on the image. A little baby asleep in a shoe-box. MARK 23 inserts the photo into the slot of the Psychic Image Reader. The interior mechanism grips it and takes it all the way inside.*

*SHAITAN places his front paws on MARK 23's lap. He stretches his body and yawns. His teeth are very sharp.*

*Move in on the blue screen of the Psychic Image Reader. A stream of messily spliced imagery begins to signify...*

MARK 23: *(Voiceover)* The little machine would take a psychic reading from A.'s photograph. From this I was to learn how the Silver Birches had trafficked children up to the Royal Spaceship, where they had been abused and transformed into shape-shifting mutants. It was horrible...

## THE DREAM GIRL FACTORY

*Interior shot of an ancient hospital ward whose floor is lined with mattresses. Paunchy middle-aged Caucasian men wrapped in white Terylene robes lie on the makeshift beds with their heads supported by pillows. Their bodily needs are ministered to by teams of professional courtesans who move from bed to bed equipped with lit candles and boxes of Kleenex. One of the courtesans is opening the long shutters which bar the windows around the ward.*

*Close-up on the courtesan. A gaunt young girl with black hair plaited at the back and garlanded at the side with a white lotus. She is dressed in a white blouse, navy blue skirt, long white socks and black patent leather shoes. Diamante jewellery glints at her neck. She has sparkling green eyes.*

MARK 23: *(Voiceover)*    A. was destined to become a leading role model for all the girls. But for now she honed her research skills.

### THE MATERNAL SECRETARY AND THE DISFIGURED HENCHMAN

*Exterior shot of a hospital quadrangle surrounded by grey stone barrack-style buildings. Two rows of courtesans sit cross-legged facing each other in the covered walkways on either side. They are dressed in navy blue knickers and grimy white gym-slips. An elderly mistress wearing heavy dark robes and a gold-leaf veil settles into a chair at the far side of the quadrangle. She is accompanied by a male factor who eases in behind her and occasionally leans down to whisper in her ear or slip her a paper wrap.*

*Close up on the factor. A mixed race man of indistinct features whose ears are clipped at the tips. He is dressed in a beige safari suit and a Panama hat. The fraying edges of white cuffs peep out from his sleeves.*

*A gong is beaten. Two of the courtesans rise from either side. They approach each other, turn to bow to their mistress and her guest, then face each other again. They exchange a ritual kiss and then begin a very fast competitive exhibition of their seduction skills. After a few minutes of highly controlled physical exertion, they retire slightly hurt to their original places.*

*The gong is beaten at regular intervals as the process repeats and all the courtesans take turns to show off their skills. The factor leans in close and nods at one or another of them now and again. The mistress writes in a notepad on her lap.*

MARK 23: *(Voiceover)*    A. was always disappointed not to be chosen. She promised herself that she would get away somehow.

### THE RIVER GETAWAY

*Exterior shot of a riverside quay lined with gaudy suburban mansions designed to resemble Ancient Greek temples, Chinese pagodas and English Tudor country-houses. The portico of an old hospital visible in the far distance above them. At the edge of the quay an emerald green lawn abuts a flight of stone stairs leading down to a motor launch. The factor is helping a single file of courtesans to descend the stairs and settle into the back of the launch.*

*Close in on the courtesans. Six anorexic girls of varying racial designations.*

*They are dressed in bikinis overlaid with diaphanous wraps and sport chunky sunglasses on their heads. One of them has a white lotus in her hair.*

*Cut to the factor unmooring the launch, pull-starting the engine and breaking surf on the flat expanse of the grey river.*

*Aerial shots of the journey downriver to the estuary. The courtesans eyeing each other superciliously and trying to catch the attention of the factor.*

MARK 23: *(Voiceover)*   A. knew her designer labels. She was confident this gave her the edge in life.


THE UNDERWATER DIORAMA

*Exterior underwater shot of a biomorphically contoured submersible. Its headlights cut through the deep gloom. Pan across the snub-nosed transparent plastic-covered cab, the round portholes in the side of the craft, the slowly rotating propeller blades at the rear. Bubbles of exhaust gas stream upwards.*

*Cut to interior shot of the submersible. The factor sits alone in the cab checking the instrumentation panel and adjusting the controls. He is costumed in a neopreen diving suit with patched elbows. The courtesans are tightly strapped into bucket seats behind him. Their faces are masked with cosmetic creams and paints. They stare blankly ahead. One of them has a white lotus in her hair and glittering green eyes.*

*Cut to exterior shot of the submersible disappearing into the gloom. Shoals of fish swim over coral reefs. Rays stir in the sand. A baby shark swims into view.*

MARK 23: *(Voiceover)*   A. was enchanted by the marine creatures. But only if they were smaller than she was.


CARIBBEAN ISLAND HIDEOUT

*Exterior shot of a motor cruiser idling in clear blue waters with the factor at the wheel. The deck of the cruiser supports a red winch whose iron cable is still attached to the dripping submersible. The round hatches have been opened on its surface. The courtesans are climbing out and dropping down to the deck. They congregate at the prow of the cruiser and lean over its rail to gaze out at an approaching tropical island. One of them throws a white lotus into the water.*

*Close in on the island. Lush green foliage covers its entire surface. Nested in the hills high above a cove are the brilliant white lattices and verandas of a leisure complex. Its low-rise sprawl is dominated by a church bell-tower.*

MARK 23: *(Voiceover)*   A. had always dreamed of being taken to a place like Monte Carlo.

## THE WHITEFACE VOODOO RAVE

*Exterior night-time shot of a garden party in the grounds of a converted church. The nightclub advertises its name over the gate of the old churchyard in electric blue neon sans serif script: CATHEDRON-A-GO-GO. Outside the gate is a posse of big native islanders in tight black flying jackets gripping clipboards and Heckler & Koch machine-guns. They are checking off the names of arriving guests.*

*Dolly through the gate to frame the clipped hedges, raked flower beds and candy striped awnings of the garden party. The distinguished guests are wearing lycra evening sportswear, Hermes bum bags and highly engineered training shoes. The factor presides over the decks in the DJ booth adjoining the converted church bell-tower. He sports a smudged white dinner jacket and black bow-tie and is crowned with a Sennheiser head-set. His fingers rise and dip over the rotating discs and spin the crowd into a voodoo trance with Old English garage rhythms.*

*Move in on the crowd. Haughty male-to-female transsexuals in top hats, tails and stockings elegantly weave through the press of bodies bearing trays of Substance H. Writhing in ecstasy above them all are the courtesans on the high podiums.*

*Close in on one of the courtesans. She is dressed in a long white ermine-trimmed gown slit to the thigh. Her green eyes roll back in her head as her name is called by the factor. There is applause from the crowd as the transsexual waiters swing up on to the podium to catch her as she swoons. They bear her aloft through the chanting crowd to the open door of the converted bell-tower where the titles of old ancestors are bestowed.*

*Close in on the door of the converted bell-tower. The chill-out room announces itself with a gothic sign over the lintel hand-painted in goldleaf: BEAUTIFUL PERSON LOUNGE. The courtesan moans and cries as she is taken inside.*
MARK 23: *(Voiceover)*   A. was determined to be made into one of her betters.

## THE UNDERGROUND LAUNCH BAY

*Interior shot of an underground cavern which seems to have been carved out of the rock. Echoing voices issue from the public address system. Statues of ancient Afro-Atlantean ancestor gods line a wide industrial corridor. Men and women in bright yellow flak-jackets direct the movement of two-lane traffic.*

*Move in on the traffic. Electric carts piloted by men in hard hats pull trolleys stacked with cargo. The advancing vehicles cut the gloom with their headlights before turning into a launch bay. They are loaded with courtesans in short white tunics sitting demurely back to back. The receding vehicles trundle along to the exit ramp. They are freighted with aluminium canisters.*

*Close in on the canisters. Each is stencilled with a name: ROYAL COMPANY*

*OF SUBSTANCE MANUFACTURERS. Beneath that is stamped the logo of a bare-breasted mermaid wielding a net and trident.*

*Cut to the launch bay. Suspended behind an iron gantry is a space shuttle whose nose is directed to the metal ceiling above. A winged orbiter is attached by its undercarriage to a huge white fuel tank and two long column-like rocket boosters. A metal walkway connects the gantry to the hatch of the orbiter's crew cabin. Elevators move up and down the supporting walls of the gantry distributing cargo between the orbiter and the bay.*

*Cut to the interior of the orbiter. The factor lies in the pilot's seat wearing a sheepskin jacket over his oily blue jumpsuit. His head sports a brown leather aviator's helmet and microphone chinset. Cut to scores of courtesans strapped into couches in the payload bay behind him. Suspended from the roof by breathing cords are the oxygen masks which cover the lower halves of their faces. One of the courtesans is distinguished by her fiery green eyes.*

*Cut to the launch bay. The gantry is retracting into one of the supporting walls. The ceiling slides back to reveal a patch of blue sky fringed by palm trees. A countdown proceeds from the public address system. Fire blooms from the rocket engine exhausts to propel the shuttle upwards into the lower atmosphere.*

MARK 23: *(Voiceover)*   A. thought the other girls were scum.


THE GLAMOROUS SPACE STATION

*Exterior shot of a massive space station composed of geodesic struts and spheres and spaces which interlock to form the overall shape of a pentagonally-inflected globe. It hangs against the blackness of space above the white rim of the upper atmosphere shielding the watery blue planet below. Its double-glazed polycarbonate panels reflect light from a distant sun. Tiny orbiters are arriving and departing from the brightly lit nodal spheres which gird its outer support structure.*

*Close in on one of the perimeter spheres. It is honeycombed with brightly lit port hangars some of which contain powered down orbiters. Track along the jointed strut connecting this terminal to the distant sphere at the centre of the open meshwork of the space station.*

*Close in on the strut to reveal its dimensions as a connecting corridor whose skin is intermittently punctuated by windows. Move up to a window to discern the monorail traffic flashing past within. The courtesans are stacked three deep in transparent plastic sleeper cars which speed along the rails. Their eyes are upturned in their sockets. Only one of them is awake. She has green eyes.*

MARK 23: *(Voiceover)*    A. stared into space. She knew how to hum and rock.

## THE DELUXE MODEL CAGES

*Interior shot of a sunken bath set into a tiled floor. A courtesan wearing a lotus-print shower cap dabs her upper arms with a sponge. Soap bubbles cover the surface of the water shielding her lower body from view.*

*Pull back to discover a wall-mirror, a low shelf stacked with white fluffy towels and a cabinet filled with bottles of cosmetics and perfumes. A trail of silk under-garments litters the floor tiles. Next to a lacy brassiere sits an open tray of Belgian milk chocolates and a white porcelain chamber pot.*

*Quick fade through a wire mesh screen to reveal the bathroom now housed within a padlocked cage. Pull back to discover a long row of cages. Pan round to disclose four rows of cages within a pitched-roof shed.*

*Pull back on the shed interior. The factor is leading a team of men with clip-boards round its straw-covered passageways on an inspection tour. He is dressed in a flat cap, white lab coat and muddy green Wellingtons. An electric stun gun rests in the palm of his hand.*

*Cut to exterior shot of the shed. A boom-supported observation deck is parked outside. Its cab occupied by a driver smoking a Substance H roll-up.*

*Cut to aerial shot of multiple rows of sheds laid out within the chain-link guard fence of a factory farm. A monorail station sits at one end. At the other is a covered mall.*

MARK 23: *(Voiceover)*    A. always took great pains to prepare herself for the arrival of her keeper.

## THE SECRET LAB

*Interior night-time shot of an empty glass-walled laboratory constructed within the atrium of a covered mall. A stationary conveyor belt leads from sliding elevator doors to an operating table with huge overhead light and suspended hand-drills and circular saws. The belt curves past the table and exits the lab through a flap in the opposite wall. Next to the flap is an aluminium door.*

*Close in on the aluminium door. It opens to dimly reveal a yellow-and-black biohazard warning sign on the other side. The factor enters the lab. He is dressed in a paper mask, stained white lab coat and surgical gloves.*

*Cut to the factor as he unlocks a massive steel refrigerator next to the table. Electric light floods the room from its interior as he pulls open the doors. Close in on a miniature carousel of metal-capped crystal test-tubes on a shelf. The factor lightly spins the carousel and selects a test-tube. He holds it up to the light and inspects the golden smudge of Substance H contained within.*

MARK 23: *(Voiceover)*    A. would always fear the consequences of yet another operation.

## THE PACKING PLANT

*Interior shot of a big shed. A moving conveyor belt snakes across the industrial floor. It leads from a flap in the wall at one end of the shed to a gated pneumatic tube at the other. Six foot long wooden crates rumble slowly along the belt.*

*Close in on the crates. Each is stamped with the logo of a bare-breasted mermaid wielding a net and trident. One of them has a lid coming loose.*

*Cut to an exterior close-up shot of one of the double-glazed polycarbonate panels of the space station. Its skin unpuckers around a slit as with a burst of compressed air a wooden crate is squeezed out into the starry blackness of space.*

*Pull back to discover a trail of wooden crates falling away from the space station towards an articulated geodesic sphere that surfs the lip of a nearby black hole. Move in on the black hole.*

*Cut to the brightest star in the firmament.*

MARK 23: *(Voiceover)*    A. was forever beguiled by the moon and the stars.

## SOFT PORN FANTASIA

*Computer animated fantasy sequence of a host of naked courtesans silhouetted against the watery blue haze of the night sky. They tumble through the air performing jack-knifes and scissors-kicks and other obscenely tinged gymnastic manoeuvres. Their synchronised movements together form the shape of a water lily whose long petals open and close in repeat bloom. Faintly superimposed over vibrating female sex organs are the hooded eyes of the factor.*

*Roll credits listing the names of the dead.*

MARK 23: *(Voiceover)*    A. rather preferred to dance alone with herself.

## THE ENCHANTED BASE

*Exterior night-time shot of a rock-pool in a cavern which is partially exposed to the elements. A waterfall gushes at the back of the cavern. A shaft of starlight enters from high above. A crystal radio apparatus, aerial and set of head-phones cluster at the ferny edge of the pool.*

*Move in on the pool. Suspended upside down from a crane above its boiling and foaming waters is the bound and gagged mobster. He is a shaven-headed transvestite clothed in a pair of black fishnet stockings. The albino skin of his exposed chest is imprinted with a black image of the skeleton beneath. His merciless face is tattooed with two diagonally aligned checks.*

*Close in on the blood seeping from the freshly reopened wounds of his tattoos. Its dripping maddens the ferocious marine creatures whose existence is indicated beneath him.*

*Cut to an underwater shot of gills venting a cloud of swirling bubbles from snaky golden flesh. Pull back to discover a massive tail which flips over to reveal an open maw set with sharply pointed teeth. The jaws snap closed to betray for a brief moment the insanely contorted features of a human face.*

MARK 23: *(Voiceover)*    A. was used to the sight of blood in the water.

THE HOME FOREIGN OFFICE

*Exterior night-time shot of a stepped pyramid in the starlit glade of a forest. An open passage cut into its base.*

*Cut to interior shot of a dark wood-panelled office filled with studded green leather armchairs and shaded lamps on side-tables. Gilt-framed spin paintings and shelves of leather-bound pornographic volumes line the walls. At one end is a desk whose surface is populated by a red cradle-set telephone, a syringe rack, a wooden in-tray containing sheets of paper and a bare white human skull. At the other end is a padded red leather door with a round brass handle.*

*Move in on the door. It opens inwards to reveal a dark upward-inclining passage. The factor steps into the office and stands facing the desk. He is wearing a beige leisure suit and a fatly knotted striped kipper tie. The tips of his ears are bleeding.*

*Reverse cut to where the mobster now sits at the desk. He is wearing a long black coat and crotchless panties. His face is wet.*

*Cut to a shot of the mobster and the factor in conference. The mobster puts his bare feet up on the desk and injects himself in the fleshy inner thigh with Substance H. The factor loosens his tie and smirks.*

*Close in on the factor as he moves smoothly behind the desk and leans in to snog the mobster. Pan along to discover the factor flipping up the cap of the hinged skull and pressing the red button beneath without looking.*

*Cut away to the swirling multi-coloured canvasses retracting into their frames to reveal the screens behind. Visible through these windows are the shady depths of a rock-pool. One thousand disturbed faces press up against the glass. The closest has a third eye in the middle of her forehead. She mouths a name.*

MARK 23: *(Voiceover)*    Allegra. That was it. That was A.'s hidden name.

BACK TO REALITY

*Pull back from the blue screen of the Psychic Image Reader in MARK 23's lap. Fade up on the daytime exterior of Mudchute. MARK 23 is asleep in his motorised wheelchair. Dried blood is on his upper lip.*

*Cut to SHAITAN racing round and round the putting green. He is panting heavily. His eyes are aflame.*

*Cut back to the Psychic Image Reader. There is a whirring noise and a torn photo is ejected from the slot at its base. Close in on the image. It is blank.*

MARK 23: *(Voiceover)* Now that I knew the name of the mutant creature I had found on the bank of the Thames, I was confident I would be able to make her speak. But first I had to locate her once again.

TO BE CONTINUED...
*Roll credits*

## Tracking the water serpent Ashtoreth

Old Castle Street
O U INFIDELS OF THE EAST END OF LONDON STILL WORSHIPPING
THE FALSE IDOLS OF CAPITALISM IN THE SAME RHYTHM FACTORIES
AFTER ALL THESE YEARS OF GRIEVOUS BODILY HARM MAKING JAM
MATCHES CLOTHING NOW MUSIC & FASHION KNOW THAT I JACK AM
BACK HERE I AM THE VOICE THE EYES THE EARS OF THE CALIPHATE
OF NEW NEW ENGLAND AMONG THE IMPORTERS AND EXPORTERS
OF DAMAGE THE PROPHET APPOINTED BY THE ULTIMATE POWER
WHO NEVER SEE NO EVIL NEVER HEAR NO EVIL NEVER SPEAK
NO EVIL ASHTORETH AND HER SPAWN ARE CONSPIRING AMONG U
INTERNATIONAL DRUG DISTRIBUTORS DANGER OF DEATH BUT I WILL
TRACK THE WHITE TRASH WHORE DOWN THE NASTY SEXY ASS SCENT
OF THAT PUSSY IS FLOODING YOUR MARKETS IN INTERNATIONAL
BABELICIOUS CALL RATES BY THE FENCE OF THE EAST END
COMMUNITY SCHOOL U WANT SUPPLEMENTARY EDUCATION IN
THE MOTHER TONGUE? IT IS AGAINST ALLAH OOOO BABY FUCK ME
FUCK ME WOLFMAN I HEAR U MOANING I CAN SMELL YOUR HOT
JUICY WASTEFUL DEEP HONEY SHIT HOLE O DID U HURT YOURSELF
WHEN THE ALMIGHTY ALLAH HURLED U HEADLONG FLAMING
FROM HEAVEN WITH HIDEOUS RUIN AND COMBUSTION COME TO ME
ILE TAKE CARE OF U ILE HAVE YOU ALWAYS AND 4EVER HERE AT
THE EMERGENCY RECRUITMENT POINT OUTSIDE THE GUILDHALL
UNIVERSITY WHERE THE SOLDIERS OF ALLAH FREE THEMSELVES IN
FASTING AND UNITY

Gunthorpe Street
THIS TOWN IS POLLUTED A DEAD DOG MOUNTAIN HERE AMONG
THE BROKEN GLASS AND THE CUM STAINS OF RAPE AT KNIFEPOINT
YOUTH OUTREACH RECYCLE YOUR MINDS O SLAVES OF EAST
LONDON UNITE AGAINST CAPITAL PEOPLE NOT PROFITS ORGANISE
NOW FOR A CALIPHATE OF THE WORLD GET RID OF THE DEMON
SCUM ROYALS BABY ALIEN KILLERS STOP THE TORTURE ON THE

ARK OF OLD ENGLAND WHAT ARE U STARING AT? ALIEN LIBERATION
FRONT YES I AM LAUGHING I AM FEELING PRETTY GRIM OVER THE
MURDERS IN CROWN CUSTODY ALL ARE WELCOME ALLAH'S ARMY
DONT U KNOW ME FROM SOMEWHERE WHO IS JACK THE MACK?
PLEASE FUCK ME BABY I DONT CARE I WANT TO SUCK U NOW DYKE
HONEY I AM VERY SAD WE CANT BE 2GETHER IN YOUR PALPABLE
OBSCURE NAUGHTY ASS CRACK O ASHTORETH INTO THE NIGHT I
CALL OUT YOUR NAME

Henriques Street
BE AWARE O INFIDELS OF EAST LONDON U R AN ACCIDENT WAITING
TO HAPPEN U HAVE BEEN CAUGHT ON VIDEO AND THE IMAGES HAVE
BEEN SENT TO THE ANGELS OF ALLAH DO U EVEN KNOW WHAT THAT
MEANS? THE POLICE VIBE THAT HOLDS A NATION UNDER ITS SPELL
NO 2 CORRUPT REPRIVATISATION YES 2 ISLAMIC NATIONALISATION
SPEARHEADED BY THE MOSQUE WITH TWO MINARETS JESUS WAS
NOT CHRISTIAN ADAM WAS NOT CHRISTIAN AND HERE JOY RIDING
OUTSIDE THE PRIMARY SCHOOL MINISTERING TO THE KIDDIE
GANGS I AM NOT CHRISTIAN TOO HA HA BE UPSTAIRS READY MY
ASHTORETH I LIKE YOU IM THE ONE 4 YOU SUCK MY BIG FILTHY
BLACK DICK DEEPER AND DEEPER INTO YOUR NASTY SEXY VAST
ABRUPT MOUTH WHEREVER YOURE GOING IM GOING BABY NOTICE
I AM THE DEATH PENALTY OF THE POWER THAT ABIDES

Pinchin Street
THIS IS A FORMAL MESSAGE TO THE INHABITANTS OF THE RAILWAY
ARCHES WORKING ON HIT AND RUN VEHICLE REPAIR COMPUTERISED
EMBROIDERY DRUG DISTRIBUTION YEH YEH SURE WHATEVER CROWN
DAMAGE COME 2GETHER RIGHT NOW AND INFORM ME WHERE
ASHTORETH IS OR HEAP ON YOURSELF DAMNATION IM GOING TO DO
IT GOOD AND NASTY AND SEXY TO YOUR VOID PROFOUND HONEY
SHIT CHUTE HEY HEY BABY WANT 2 GET LUCKY? OPEN YOUR WET
STICKY WHITE NAKED ASS CHEEKS AND TAKE A RIDE WITH ME

Old Swallow Gardens
ITS TIME TO LEAVE THE ARK OF OLD ENGLAND IN A MOVEMENT
AGAINST THE MONARCHY EPIDEMIC CHARLES AND HIS CREW WHAT
A LOAD OF OLD SHIT A FLU BUG TRAVELLING AT 120 MPH RISING

EAST LONDON DEATH RATE ALONG THE OLD CHOLERA TRACKWAYS SCIENTIFIC WILD GUESS U MAKE ME SICK AN ALIEN IS FOR LIFE NOT JUST FOR EID JOIN THE MUSLIM POSTHUMAN DEFENCE LEAGUE CAUTION HIGH VOLTAGE OR GO PLAY IN TRAFFIC UNDERNEATH THE RAILWAY BRICK AND WIRE MESH TUNNEL WITH ELECTRIC LIGHTS IN METAL GRILLES O BEWARE INFIDELS ALLAH'S PROPHET WAS HERE A GUARD DOG PATROL SNIFFING OUT THE GRANTS VODKA BOTTLES DRUG DEBRIS ENAMEL TOILETS THROWN IN THE YARD SYCOPHANTIC PROPERTY WASH VALET SERVICES YES SIR NO SIR ART FOR YOUR EYES ONLY SIR ALL I HAVE TO DO IS DREAM OF LOOKING DOWN AT U SEXY THING ASHTORETH LAYING HERE WRITHING AND BUCKING AND MOANING FOR ME BY THE UNESSENTIAL NIGHT WASTE COMPACTOR CLOSE DOOR ENGAGE CATCH PRESS START BUTTON I BELIEVE IN MIRACLES DO U?

Mitre Square
TWO VIEWS ONE PRICE WEST THE CITY OF EMPTY TOMBS POLICE PATROLS & STREET CLEANERS IN OPERATION EAST THE LARGE SCREEN SATELLITE PAGAN LANDS HERE THE SECCAM DOG'S HEAD SIGN OF THE HOLE IN THE WALL I AM DRUNK WITH LAUGHTER WAITING 4 THE VEILED WHORE CIGARETTE STUBS ON THE GROUND OUTSIDE THE PRIMARY SCHOOL EMERGENCY ACCESS FUCK U ASHTORETH FUCK U REMEMBER U R MINE IN DARKNESS VISIBLE JACK THE MACK WAS HERE BYE BYE LOVE U WHITE DOVE O BABY ITS U

Water Street
404 FILE NOT FOUND

White's Row
I AM RABID CURSING I CANT STOP THINKING ABOUT DRUGS N GUNS PULLING YOUR SKIMPY TOP OFF YOUR PLUMP SEXY TITS I NEED U 2NIGHT U R THE DEVIL IN DISGUISE KING CHARLES DROP DEAD IF U KNOW WHAT I MEAN & I THINK U DO MAKE THE ARK OF OLD ENGLAND A ROYAL FREE ZONE REVOLT INTO ISLAM KILLS ALL KNOWN SPECIALISTS IN CAPITALIST DOMINATION HERE AMONG THE BROKEN PAVEMENTS PADLOCKED VACANCIES & BRAINDEAD BOOZERS IM ON TENTERHOOKS THINKING OF U AND THE THINGS U

DO TO ME LET ME TELL U BOUT THE ABORTIVE GULF OF ALLAH THE CREATOR ABOVE

Old Dorset Street
DO U BELIEVE THERE ARE DELIVERIES TO BE MADE VIA THE REAR DIRECT UP YOUR NASTY SHORT TIGHT NO PARKING NO ALIENS NO SMOKING NO FOOD OR DRINK NO EUROS BRING BACK THE POUND REAL SOON NOW NO ALLAH JUICY SHIT ASS CRACK PRIVATE COUNTER-REVOLUTIONARY FEELGOOD MONARCHIST FITNESS CLUB? FIGHT AGAINST THE NUMBER ONE RENEGADE BLOOD SPORT OF THE ROYAL SUBSTANCE LAB A CIRCUS OF HORRORS WANTS TO FORCE FEED US PROPAGANDA FOR PROFITS AVOID ALIEN CRUELTY NEAR DEAD ON ARRIVAL THE FIX IS IN AT THE NIGHT REFUGE SEEKING ASYLUM ON THE COASTS OF DARK DESTRUCTION I AM LICKING MY LIPS BURN BABY BURN IN ENDLESS PAIN EAT YOUR HEART OUT ASHTORETH U SUB FEMALE FIEND JACK THE MACK GUIDED WALKS DOWN HERE SEE U IN MY DREAMS

Hanbury Street
CANT WAIT 2 HOLD U ASHTORETH & FUCK U BETWEEN YOUR BIG NASTY LAP-DANCER SEXY VOID IMMENSE THIGHS OH BLIMEY! U DONT KNOW THE MEANING OF THE WORD FEAR THANKING YOU PLEASE I HAVE NO PENIS 4 THE TOY BOY TRAMPS BUT I WILL SEEK U IN THE SMASHED WINDOW DRUG DEN HELL U SAY GHETTO GOLD THEMEPARK WITH CASH & CARRY BAGS OF H WHEN THE MAGIC DAY COMES TO GO DEMENTED IN A MILLENNIUM WEDDING VIDEO IN THE NAME OF ALLAH FEEL THE NEED IN ME ADVERTISING THE INVISIBLE JIHAD FOR THE HOMEGROWN CALIPHATE THE ONLY SOLUTION TO THE CRIMES & ATROCITIES COMMITTED BY THE CROWN MASSIVE ANTI-FASCIST ACTION IN THIS AREA EXPECT NO MERCY GUERRILLA GARDENING BY THE HOLY MISSION AGAINST CAPITALISM A PUBLIC OBLIGATION UPON EVERY MUSLIM TO SUPPORT THE LAST FILM EVER MADE ROLLING ON THE GROUND WITH TEARS IN MY EYES BOO HOO YOULL BE SORRY THOUGH U R FAR AWAY YET I AM HERE TO STAY THE SAGA CONTINUES

Durward Street
WISH U WERE HERE TASTY & TENDER BY THE FENCED OFF VACANT

LOTS WITH HOLES IN THE WIRE TRUANCY GROUNDS 4 PUSSY BOYZ
& DIRTY BITCHES BEHIND THE SCHOOL I USED 2 LOVE U BUT NOW
ITS ALL OVER RUBBISH 4 THE RATS HARD DRUGS SAFE NEEDLES
WINTER WARMTH WARNING U SLAGS CONTROL ROOM MANNED 24
HRS I AM YOUR DESTINY ROAMING THE AREA NO NUCLEAR TEST
MORATORIUM FOR A BETTER WORLD ALLAH LOVES YOU & HE RULES
U NOT PROFITS DO NOT DIE IN IGNORANCE STOP MULTINATIONALS
SPOUTING PROPAGANDA AND SUPPRESSING CRITICISM & FREE
LEGAL ADVICE NO WIN NO FEE COMPENSATION ILLEGAL EVICTION
IMMIGRATION BLOCKED DRAINS I WILL NOT SUCK OUT YOUR SAUCY
JUICY PUSSY HOLE SLASH PUNANI MASSIVE I WILL MAKE SURE
U R SMILING EAR 2 EAR FLYING VIRGIN RED DEVIL DOCTOR RUIN
UPON RUIN YEH I GOT THE POISON I GOT THE MEDICINE YOUR NAME
ASHTORETH UPWARD TITS AND DOWNWARD FISH TA TA 4 NOW BE
BACK LATER HA HA I REMAIN 4EVER ALLAH'S OBEDIENT SERVANT
JACK NO REPLY NECESSARY

## Infant sacrifice planned on Hampstead Heath

Eddie is directing the cameras from behind his chair. Asks for the lights to be softened. Offers suggestions for questions.

*A True and Faithful Relation of What Passed at Clarence House between Dr John Dee and the Devil.* Extract 6.1: The tiny shrieking result of the premature delivery in Paris was a hybrid firstborn. But the Little Devil was never permitted to become an unmanageable trophy dangled betwixt the Old King and the coronation ultimate of the Sun Prince.

The only one of the Whore's unbalanced brood next to the Sun Prince who would have had the remotest chance to the right of succession was indeed the Little Devil. The fevered wound-bedecked prophesying brigade would have had a convulsive place taking it up.

The extravagant funeral of the Whore in London suspended chaotic disorder.

EK Exegesis 6.1: Personally, I've always had a soft spot for Sunni Muslims, know what I mean? Well, of course you do.

Now imagine if you lot had found out there was an actual Muslim child—even a girl child—with an half-plausible claim on the throne? Like as not, you'd have dumped the boy wonder when it came to it and taken up her cause instead.

And who could blame you? Certainly not the Osiris Club. Which is why they called in the old man to sort things out.

I tell you, he thought it was gonna be his finest hour. Here was his big chance to kill two birds with one stone. He thought he could keep the Osiris Club happy and at the same time make a real proper sacrifice to Osiris for the first time since the good old days.

See, he thought the *teoqualo* ritual had got all pussified down the centuries. I mean, it is meant to be the Royal Firstborn, right? Royal cos it's the Royal Firm who ultimately benefits. And Firstborn cos the gods always get offered the first fruits of the litter. Not some piss-poor fourth-rate substitute. Except the last time it happened, there the old man was capering around in Whitechapel with some smackhead royal fuckwit temporarily possessed by Osiris, trying to get him to squirt a load in some no-good whore just so he could open her up nine months later and his man Jack could finish off the job. I mean, it's just insulting for Osiris, ain't it?

No wonder this time round the Doctor decides to go straight for the mother of the heir to the throne. His only mistake was to nick-name the sprog once he'd delivered it. He must have come over all mumsy when he was bringing it back home from Paris.

That could have messed things up for Jack. Horus is the proper name for the infant sacrifice in the *teoqualo* ritual. Horus and Horus alone!

*A True and Faithful Relation...* Extract 6.2: An occult order was issued by the Doctor unto the Clown Jack. It said that the White Devil was to be secreted in the bubbling throat of the Black Dog. The White Devil was astrally projected.

No little time did the Clown take to remove the gouged cable of flesh from his shapeless pants and place it inside his familiar uncanny. The Black Dog had been designated by the Juggler.

Doubt was there none that it was a demonic possession transfer. The Doctor did send the White Devil unto the Clown. His evil spirit was the seed malevolent deposited inside the Black Dog.

EK Exegesis 6.2: It's true I had me eye on Jack's dog. I thought better a dog than a person, know what I mean? They're easier to control and if something goes wrong, you're in less trouble with the law.

Set had to go somewhere once the old man had invited him to stay. He was worried about his brother, wasn't he? I mean, this secret understanding he had with the old man was a betrayal of Osiris's confidence.

The old man wasn't bothered. He just didn't care.

*A True and Faithful Relation...* Extract 6.3: The Clown did make his creeping way down the twisting entrance tunnel to the cave unplaceable under the perilous hill. His vacant name he spake aloud in the darkness unreal. There was hot stifling air a-blowing. He turned and did gasp in wonder when he saw the apocalyptic burst of light from the single high stained glass window ever unwashed.

And his skeletal host to meet him did appear. He cradled the Little Devil in a ripped shoe-box as like it were an unexploded bomb.

Obvious it was that the Clown was expected. The Doctor was anxious for him to demonstrate his anomalous status.

"Have you the tools of your ghastly office?"

"Of course."

Never before had the Clown been asked for his infanticidal credentials.

The clawing trophy of the Doctor was soft-boned with dark ill-starred skin. She was swaddled with crushed tissue paper. Allegra was her lonely name.

The Doctor had learned to recognise and outwit the stratagems chaotic of the female stellar gods. The Weird Sisters were here today and gone tomorrow. They told him they desired a variety most wide of atrocious experience before settling on a contract no longer indefinite. They were less than direct.

The Doctor preferred dealing with his own hateful sex. The Devil Osiris offered no freedom from mortal contracts. His cosmic bargain was always a lock-in. On the one side, there was rising quickly to a blighted fame and fortune; and on the other, there was the tending and reporting of the graveyards fathomless. It was difficult to ascertain where the one did begin and the other did end.

What was the Little Devil? A useless gratuity that required silent handling.

And the Clown was led by the strange figure of the Doctor into his sucking bed-sitting room. An evil spirit rushed out to meet them with a noxious stench that mixed the repellent smell of human vomit with a scent elusive and distant. The unknown physical closeness of the White Devil brushed against the Clown's own morbidly heightened senses. The miasmal air smelt of bodies acrid and dank.

Filled was the small brittle room with infinite shelves all tightly stuffed with crumbling bundles of papers. There was material unaccountable in the nameless graveyard files. The Doctor knew how long unmanageable files should be kept and when they should be destroyed.

There was a splintered wooden floor, a rotten table, a dusty closet, an unmade bed. Closer the Doctor and the Clown did move towards the insidious bed. Here was a charred letter addressed in disjointed green handwriting to the gruesome abortion priest who was Jack.

*If the slaughterman intends to kill a child most innocent, he should do so outside his own clammy home...noone looking...a nasty cut at the neck...the violated child shuddering violently at death...shut the wriggling mouth; close the yawning eyes...no freakish coffin...the icy river the clutching undertakers...Grab and squeeze the gleaming heart!*

The Little Devil was a sacrifice, a tip; something cherished for the White Devil. It was he who dictated the letter abhorrent. The Doctor wrote everything down.

*Use Jack...he is too familiar with death to be sensitive.*

The Clown received the detestable message. He was to kill again for the Doctor. This unholy man terrified him. Sorrow fell upon him in a sudden tide of melted feeling, released either by an eruptive precognition of shock or the torrential release of repressed memory. He fought for control intermittent. There was something frightening and too familiar about this uncanny death-cell.

The apprehensive figure of the Doctor moved back into the wasting shadows of his closet diseased. It contained an ominous collection of extraordinary objects: tiny scraps of baffling metal; feeble strips of silk and lace; shrivelled fruit; dry flowers; a baleful stick wrapped round with the shapes of multitudinous snakes; an unkempt long black coat.

The Little Devil was left on the viscous bed. She was watching the Clown with restless eyes from inside her dismal paper-lined cell. She was enchanting. A convulsive madness seized the Clown. Possessed he was by a frenzied urge to cradle the Little Devil in his arms and dance with her unto the unhallowed lip of the glistening Thames. His straining need for violent release was a morbid animal delight mixed with the impossible envy of youth.

What became of the Little Devil? The Clown did not waste his mocking pity. He knew it was an unnameable sacrifice. They were alone and there was a desperate need for innocent blood. She did not blink a kaleidoscopic eye.

The purple little torso sank beneath the ensanguined river. Discovered was it not until it began to stink.

Alone lived the Clown. He preferred stark nothingness to consciousness of his loathsome existence. And he did continue with the tainted drugs and the drink.

Bloody sacrifice is not a crime. He did it with his own savage hand.

EK Exegesis 6.3: The old man had his little hidey hole set up centuries before there was a real need for it. Said the hill on Hampstead Heath was one of the most powerful spirit traps in London. But what would he know? It was me actually called up Osiris back in 1587.

That was the start of it, wasn't it? Soon Osiris and the Doctor have an understanding. Well, it was only the oldest deal in creation. The Old Ukanian Combine got all the luck it needed when it came to conquering half the world. And in return, the mana of its victims got dedicated direct to the Lord of the Dead.

Very cosy. Except Osiris—being the old devil that he is—wants a little bit extra. So every hundred years, the Old Ukanian Combine has to give him a bung. A back-hander collected by his kid brother, Set.

It was the Doctor set up the *teoqualo* account. Though obviously he never actually soiled his own hands. That was down to the abortion priest at the end of every century. That was dirty work for Jack.

It's a simple enough ritual. The infant sacrifice is dedicated to the baby Horus on the altar. The abortion priest takes on the aspect of Set. He nips off the head, quick as you like. He plucks off the limbs, he extracts the internal organs. The heart is always a good bit. All this juicy stuff goes to make up the communion feast and is dedicated to Osiris.

The torso is offered to Isis and flushed down the ditch to the Thames. Least, that's what's supposed to happen. But quite often Jack would leave little human remains lying all over the place. Shocking!

Set gets to keep one thing, as a little souvenir. And that's the nub of flesh between the legs. Call it a penis, call it a clitoris. It's all the same to him. It's a token of his prestige, see.

The whole thing went quite well the first time round. Well, it was Greenwich in the 1590s. They was very wild days. An abortion meant nothing to Gloriana. And the Apollo Club was prepared to eat it raw.

The old man loved it! He never could get used to modern methods. The idea that the internal organs are ground into a paste and mixed with flour to make nice little cakes. Well, he thought it was too Christian by half.

That's why he was so excited by the Paris business. Gave him a chance to get back to basics.

But Jack was a bit of a poor specimen this time round. I never really trusted him. He wasn't a patch on the honest psychos the Doctor used to employ.

He comes up to the hill in an hypnotic trance and takes the little thing off in its cage. Says he was going to kill it at Shadwell Dock Stairs. That was the last we saw of it.

I can't say exactly what happened next. The old man said that Osiris got it too late and was all pissed off as a result. I dunno.

I *do* know that Jack had access to clinical waste products from the London Hospital in Whitechapel. I *do* know that abortions are performed there regular. I *do* know that it don't take much to swap a dead baby for a live one.

Have I really got to spell it out for you?

I blame Jack.

## Secret level

*Screen Message*
GAMEPLAY RESUMING...

*Player Status*
You are Doctor Double Oh No, Crown secret agent and radio controller of the Ukanian Stay-Behind cellnet. You are sitting cross-legged on a carpet of lily seed-pod rinds in the hole under the hill.

You do not know for sure how many units of tezma you have accumulated. You lost your Tally Stick.

*Screen Message*
TEZMA HOARD: 999

*Real Audio Stream*
"Jack? I know how much you love your work. It's time to start again."
—Doctor Double Oh No on his invisible mobile issuing kill orders from behind radio-opaque tinted glass.

*Point of View: Doctor Double Oh No*
You turned your back on Anu the Chameleon Kid for only a minute and she made off with your Tally Stick. You got the Old South Eastern Leyline up. Jack is easy to locate.

Fuck sake! If only you weren't so neurotic. Seems you already got the last unit of tezma there from Anu the Chameleon Kid. You reckon you got the full one thousand units. Time to get going with the Pink Lotus descent finally put the kibosh on those fucking towelheads in Westminster, show them who's boss. But, no! You gotta carve that last notch on the Tally Stick. You gotta check the numbers with your very own eyes.

Of course, you could always count the glass jars in the back of your closet. But you don't trust yourself. Too much chance of getting lost and making a mistake. Sitting there forever counting jars.

Let Jack track down Anu the Chameleon Kid and come back with the Tally

Stick. You can afford to wait.

"Uproot the Devil's Claw, you hear me?"

Jack is a sucker for romance. The cover story you lay on him this time is a doozy.

*Screen Message*
PINK LOTUS DESCENT CONTINGENCY OPERATION
CODENAME: PARLIAMENT HILL DESCENT

*Player Status*
You have used your POV button to adopt the subject position of one of Doctor Double Oh No's alter egos. You are Jack the Mack. Voice in your head says you are the holy prophet of Allah on a mission to purge the East End of London of Ashtoreth, muthah of all killer bitch demons.

Word is that Ashtoreth been roused from her slumbers in the Thames and walks the streets of East London looking for her missing daughters. She wailing and lamenting and swishing her tail from side to side. She stinking up the place.

You got your orders direct from Allah. Slay Ashtoreth and recover the Devil's Claw. Seems that demon muthah got a knobbly wooden branch growing between her legs she use to fertilize herself. Ashtoreth steals from Allah the power to divide male from female and collapse them into her own monstrous form.

Time to revisit Whitechapel. You got the blade to do Ashtoreth? Check, one steel hunting knife with worn ivory handle. You got a bag for the Devil's Claw? Check once again.

No more excuses.

Word is that old Ashtoreth more dangerous than all her daughters put together. She will suck the life-force out of you. She will shape-shift into the one guilty thing you desire in that time and place where you meet. You gotta name your guilt right there wherever it is. Then that muthah demon will collapse back down into its original form. This is your chance to intercept it.

Get it? Distract Ashtoreth with the light shining from your blade and then move in to chop her to pieces. Keep on working that knife until nothing but the Devil's Claw is left.

Allah ready to receive you himself when you take that monstrous root up to Parliament Hill. It will be a time for rejoicing.

One thing, though.

Ashtoreth got a twelfth daughter still at large. You failed to take her out last time. Now she lives on a secret level can be sprung on you at any time. This level is not a shortcut. It is an extra hazard. That last daughter of Ashtoreth extremely fucking dangerous.

Capture no longer an option for Ashtoreth and her last daughter. Kill them both instead.

Better be careful. You got no cheat mode now.

*Screen Message*
PARLIAMENT HILL DESCENT
GAMEPLAY STARTING...

*Point of View: Jack the Mack*
You switch off TV and get out the water. That roving reporter Mark 23 got nothing on you. Just new theories and old crimes. Repeat showings. Forget it.

You appear out the St George's Baths shaking yourself dry. That devil dog left behind to guard your cubicle.

You hit the streets of East London. That evil bitch whore Ashtoreth just round the corner. You sniff out her trail. You seek the part between her legs offensive to Allah so brazenly displayed. That briny smell of rotting fish sprayed all over Whitechapel. You track through the back-streets and court-yards you know so well. Your old haunts. You make a connection with Allah report back on the defilement created by Ashtoreth. Busy there punching out the text messages on your holy tablet. It make you so angry.

Where the fuck are you? You are back where you were before. Lost in the maze of alleyways behind Mile End tube station. Going round in circles. Panic spot. Ground sacred to the Karma Twins. Don't think of them. Forget it. Concentrate on the job in hand.

Ashtoreth is close. You got the taste of her almost in your mouth. You hit the telephone exchange box at Eric Street and slide under the manhole cover there. Easy does it. You drop into a concrete inspection chamber filled with old cables duct taped to the walls. There's a shaft in the floor one hundred feet deep. You swing your legs over and climb down the ladder. It's dark. Your feet hit the ground. You move across an abandoned platform and leap into a disused tube tunnel.

You keep on tracking Ashtoreth through the bowels of East London. You move through sunken corridors and covered streets. Everything is empty. Just old electric lights shuddering and sparking in the walls. You come to the secret entrance to the Osiris Club on Maidman Street.

There is a red door with an ivy wreath and a torn Save the Children sticker. You don't bother to knock. The door is ajar.

*Screen Message*
PARLIAMENT HILL DESCENT: LEVEL 0
GAMEPLAY CONTINUING...

*Player Status*
Location: Maidman Street@North America screen
   The demon muthah Ashtoreth is waiting for you inside.

*Point of View: Jack the Mack*
Deep breaths now. You got your blade? Check. You got your bag? Check!
   Who are you? You are Jack the Mack.
   You adopt the defensive position. Hunting knife held out before you in both
hands a good old-fashioned demon repellant. You move into the Osiris Club.
   You are gonna do in that Ashtoreth and chop out that Devil's Claw hot
between her legs. And if her last daughter spring up you are gonna mess her up
too. Fucksake! You know what you gotta do. Your orders are clear.
   You find yourself in a long empty hall filled with shadows. Looks like an old
cinema theatre decked out with Ancient Egyptian stylings, sarcophagi built into
the walls, friezes of hieroglyphs, lots of flaking gilt pillars carved with the heads
of jackals and falcons. The floor is covered in an old red carpet marked with damp
and strewn with wet brown leaves.
   There are two massive granite coffins on the floor. They each got a table on
the top covered in the green baize. The cloth is smooth and worn. There are string
sacks suspended from under the tables with the billiard balls inside. Wooden cues
lie abandoned on the floor.
   Okay.
   Check out that sobbing comes from the other end of the hall. You squint into
the darkness. Tiny creature standing in the corner with her back to you, one pale
leg twisted up behind the other. She wearing this white hospital gown ties up at the
back. Scratch marks on skin. A stained bandage wrapped round damp black curls
on her head. She rocking from side to side. Bones sliding under the skin of her
back. Those little legs transparent, ghostly, not really there.
   Ashtoreth? But she just a little girl. You move closer. See the rubbish heaped
up against the back wall there. Wooden chests spilling mouldy old curtains and
smashed earthenware pots. Empty wine bottles and tin cans.
   You put your knife away and stretch out your hand. The wild little girl so
miserable. Shaking and trembling. She supporting herself with this ridged wooden
stick. The stench is horrible. She begin to turn her head round towards you. Your

hand begin to shake. What the fuck? The pock-marked cheeks. The huddled, yellow teeth. The pitiless glint in the eyes.

"Ashtoreth?"

It's a trick! That wild little girl change shape on you to become this real weird creature. She looming over you in this inflated white body suit. She standing there big and wide and threatening. Head covered in rubber with the seams running down the front, mouth sucking on a metal pipe so she can breathe. Them legs big and wide but still fading away. Something not right with the legs. Like a ghost only solidly materialised from the waist on up.

"Ashtoreth!"

Your knife is back in your hand. It is a heavy dull thing. There is so little light for it to catch in the hall. The weird creature moves towards you, her hood bobbing in the gloom. She got these diagonal eye-slots zipped up tight. She cannot be blinded by any light you throw at her. She moving by instinct alone.

You reckon she is going to kill you.

She got this metal harness strapped round her waist. There's this ridged wooden stick screwed into the mount. It gotta be the Devil's Claw.

*Player Status*

You are hit by the demon muthah Ashtoreth. She has shape-shifted to become the image of your spectre in this time and place.

*Real Audio Stream*

It was here in the front-door passage of a two-room flat that you stabbed me twice in the throat. You put me in the hospital for thirty days. But I SURVIVED.

I am very angry. I use up my energy in short, sharp bursts of ranting.

I am older than Pollyanna Goldenshower.

I'm single and not particularly well-off. I feel like I've been left on the shelf, to be honest.

I always have used and will continue to use the same skincare and cosmetics. And that's Lancome. I've been buying it for twenty years now and will carry on buying it for the next twenty years.

I wear perfume a couple of times a year on a big night out. It's usually Christian Dior's Poison or Elizabeth Taylor's White Diamonds.

My most precious commodity is an inflatable white rubber body suit from DeMask. I've had it for years and am always cleaning the metal pipe in the hood.

What is my name?

*Point of View: Jack the Mack*

You are jabbering. You move forwards a step. You call out the name of Ashtoreth again and again. You call out the names of those eleven daughters of Ashtoreth you done the last time. But it no good.

What the fuck is going on?

This demon answer to no name you remember. But somehow she familiar. You move another step through the curtains and bottles and rubbish silted up on the floor against the wall. Fucksake! You can't be expected to put a name to every dumb cunt gets ripped up.

Ivory handle of the knife wet in your palm. Still no light for your blade to catch. Only shadows. The creature a pale swollen baggage in the corner. Floating on these two wisps of light. White rubber skin puffed up all round the body. That head closed up tight. Her breath coming and going through that metal pipe in her face like wind in a tunnel.

You make a slashing motion with the edge of your blade. Slice open the rubber at the throat, draw blood. Second time you use the tip. It goes in deep. Something gives. Creature fall back, clutching throat with gloved fingers. Blood sprays out in fine mist.

You jump backwards.

It's like the demon is deflating. It wobbles and shivers in the air. There are countless little drops of blood all over the front of its white rubber suit. The creature all messy now.

"You fucking whore!"

The blade of your knife is streaky with blood. You are getting it on your hands. You have to wipe it clean somewhere. You back away from the injured creature. Your feet get tangled up in those curtains. You are unbalanced. There is something under the curtains. Logs or pipes or something. They roll under your feet and you fall over. You land in the middle of the junk. Stuffed head of an ox mounted on a wooden plaque facing you. It's got these long curved horns.

You could have impaled yourself. Where is that knife? You dropped it. The creature with the blood on her white rubber suit is hanging there in the corner like a sodden plastic bag. She got the hand clapped to side of her neck there. She speak out. What? You cover your ears. She is saying something. You can hardly see her. It's so dark. There is blood on your sleeve.

What were those lumpy things tripped you up? You twitch the edge of the curtain on the floor beside you and see these two bulbous human feet, tight shiny skin, dirt under the toenails. What is this? You pull back whole curtain to see there are two legs dumped there on the floor. They been hacked off somebody like joints of meat badly cut at the thigh. Not you.

That demon, Ashtoreth or whatever her name is, the one you cut. She got her free hand round that wooden stick grow out of her dildo harness. She is frigging the Devil's Claw. Moving her fat rubber fingers up and down notches in its side in obscene gesture.

She is saying something over and over again. Forcing the words from the blow-pipe in her secret mouth. She says it in a sing-song voice and it comes out sounding like a malign chant.

She wish for something. She wish for protection.

This white stuff oozes out the nozzle in the tip of the Devil's Claw. It jets all over the legs on the ground. It covers them good.

*Screen Message*
PARLIAMENT HILL DESCENT: SECRET LEVEL
GAMEPLAY STARTING...

*Player Status*
Location: Eric Street@North America screen
You are hit by the twelfth daughter of Ashtoreth. That demon shape shift to become the image of her mama's spectre in this time and place. Nothing to do with you any more.

*Point of View: Jack the Mack*
You are sprawled on the floor in the Osiris Club when those amputated legs jump up and start dancing to the tune of the demon muthah's song. They melt into silvery liquid blobs and hang and twirl there in the air. The blobs push outwards at the edges until they become pale shimmering ghosts. Two creatures made of light and mist. They pulse and glow. The outlines of two human figures beginning to appear from out of the mist. They are coming as if from very far away.

Slowly they manifest themselves. Two creatures in electric blue suits and shiny alligator-skin shoes. You cannot drag your gaze away.

The two stone coffins in the junk-filled corner of the Osiris Club begin to creak and shake. Then the green baize lids fly off and shatter in the air.

You push your nose to the ground. You seek refuge with Allah.

The two of them have arrived. They are tough-looking women. One is huge and brawny and the other is slim and delicate. But they have similar physiques with well-developed chests and tiny feet.

That big one got a mean face full of these lumps of scar tissue, looking down at you like you a piece of shit. She opening and closing her hands like she spoiling for a fight. The small one all lean and wiry, with pouting lips and drooping eyelids. She got a pen and a notebook, like she gonna take down your personal details.

Twin bitches from hell! What do they want? This don't look good.

Now that demon muthah Ashtoreth or whatever slide in between them and point you out. The blood not yet dry on the front of her white inflatable rubber suit.

The little bitch writes something in her book and nods. The big one unscrews the Devil's Claw from the harness worn by Ashtoreth or whatever. She slap it in the open palm of her hand.

Those two stone-faced dykes look at each other and laugh. Like they gonna enjoy what happens next.

You want to say it's not your fault. But it's too late for that and it's not even true. So fuck that shit.

What happens next is you're not here. Got it? You are gone.

Forget those demons. Grab your knife. Get the fuck out of the Osiris Club.

Track back through those underground corridors. Grab daylight and move through the streets of East London. Retreat to your cubicle at St George's Baths. Your devil dog to greet you.

Get going. Disappear now!

*Screen Message*
PARLIAMENT HILL DESCENT: ALL LEVELS
GAMEPLAY TERMINATING…

*Point of View: Jack the Mack*
You are panting when you get back to your cubicle. You have a real bad migraine. Satan your guard dog is barking like crazy. Big and black and slavering at the mouth. Straining at his rope leash. You cut him loose while you clean your hunting knife with a wet cloth. The sweat is cold on your face. You unlock your case and put away that knife with the scalpels and the iron hooks and the bayonets and the adze and the bronze rod. All your bits and pieces lined up just the way you like them. You just about to shut the case when you notice Satan stopped barking.

Just the sound of water lapping at the edge of the big pool. What happened to that crazy devil dog? You creep out your cubicle and sneak a peek. Those two stone cold dykes are there at the side of the pool. The big one stands there checking out the waves of light reflected on the walls and ceiling. She got the Devil's Claw in her hand. The little one is kneeling down beside that stupid dog lies at her feet. Her head is buried in the long tufts of hair between Satan's legs. She is doing something to that dog. His hind legs twitch. She is making slurping noises.

This is intolerable. "You sick fucks. Stop it!" So this is you coming up to them. You ain't even got your knife. How dumb is that? Your headache is really bad now.

The two of them look up and act all surprised. That Satan turns his head and he looks up as well. Call that a devil dog? That big pussy is meant to be protecting you! Instead he's letting himself get nasty sexual kicks from a bunch of dangerous intruders here in your own hidey-hole. For some reason that burns you up more than anything else. Like you can't even give a good blow job to a miserable fucking dog.

That headache comes down hard now. It beats at your temples like something knocking to get out of the side of your head. You got the blurred vision. The pool spins around you. What happens next you see only in flashes.

You are on your back on the floor. It's wet. That little bitch in the suit is leaning over you. She is in your face. What the fuck? You thrash your head from side to side. But it's no good. That big bitch in the suit cup your head in her hands and squeeze so your jaw nearly pop. You are pinned down. Fuck.

Now that weird sister appears in between the two bitches. She got the white rubber suit with the blood spots all over it. She got this thin bronze rod between rubber-tipped fingers. She found your box of instruments.

The little bitch take the bronze rod and shove it up inside your left nostril. She begin to pull and rip the flesh with the jagged part of the rod. She smash the bone in your nose. You go into this spasm. That big bitch press down on your chest with her forearm. You piss yourself.

The three of them look at each other all ecstatic. That stupid dog is licking your ear. The little bitch withdraw the rod from your smashed nose. It got this little square thing on the tip. A silicon wafer. Looks like a radio chip.

The reason your headache stops is you can't feel it any more. Everything goes black. Last thing you see is these little points of light swimming in the darkness like bright motes of dust.

*Screen Message*
PINK LOTUS DESCENT CONTINGENCY OPERATION
SUSPENDED

*Player Status*
You have used your POV button to abandon the subject position of your alter ego Jack the Mack. This an action forced upon you. You got no other choice. You

expelled from Jack by means of exorcism. You are Doctor Double Oh No.

No time to say the keywords wipe out Jack's memory of occupation. No time even for the auto-destruct.

The hypnotic mark returned to himself with total memory of missing time.

*Screen Message*
PARLIAMENT HILL DESCENT: ALL LEVELS
TERMINATED

*Full Motion Video*
Jack slumped against the tiled wall one side of the pool in St George's Baths. He got this bandage over his nose. It's edged with plasters and stained with blood.

Jack belches and opens his eyes. He coughs and starts to puke.

Jack: Who the hell am I? What is my name?

*Narrative Voiceover*
Everything come together in St George's Baths. Doctor Double Oh No's spectre has left the building. What more is there to say?

Jack in his awakened state watching the light bounce off the pool. He wearing this ragged old T-shirt say SHOOM on the front. He looking at this blood-stained silicon chip in the palm of his hand. Jack got to understand his criminal career as a radio-controlled mark, operating under Doctor Double Oh No's spell. How did that happen? Track back to Eddie at the Battle of Mudchute…

What is happening with Satan? He no longer behaving like a dog possessed. He is all calm and serene and sniffing at some puke on the floor. He got this swelling in his belly. Something new there looks like.

Check out that damaged creature over in the corner of the baths. She completely covered in inflatable white rubber. Breathing with a hoarse rattle through a metal pipe in the hood. She not all there. She lying on her back with her hips in the air. She got these stumps where her legs oughta be. There is blood all over the front of her suit. Her rubber-gloved hands slide over herself like they a pair of flippers.

She never did have her name shout out by Jack. No surprises. She Anu the Chameleon Kid.

As for them two killer bitch demons in the midnight blue suits. They lounging together in bucket seats at the side of the pool. That little one slip her pen and notebook inside her jacket pull out a packet of Dunhills. That big one accept a gold-tipped cigarette and light up. Pass the flame back to her sister in a cupped hand so she can light up her own.

"Regina Karma!" Anu calls to the little one from the corner of the baths. She speak the name of the demon. That little one drop her fag into the pool.

That big one stand up now. She got this ridged wooden stick at her feet. Doctor Double Oh No got his Tally Stick from Eddie who found it in the street.

"Rhona Karma!" Second demon get her name called by Anu, who is still lying on the floor. Anu choking with laughter.

The Karma Twins open their mouths to scream. First the little one, then her big sister. They open up wide but no sound comes out. They already fading away. Those bitches going back to where they came from, into the mist. They are just these two silvery liquid entities shimmering in the air. They merge into a single blob and pulsate.

Anu clap her hands. That silvery thing glide through the air toward her. She tilt up her head all covered in rubber show it the open end of the pipe. Down it goes.

Anu is coughing and shaking. She arches her back on the floor. Her stumps begin to elongate. She sprouts these legs like a breathless fish come up from the sea to evolve. She flips over on to all fours. That white body suit cover her now entire. She stands up.

Anu the Chameleon Kid made whole again. She saunters over to the edge of the pool picks up the Kingsize Dildo.

*Screen Message*
TEZMA HOARD: 999

*Point of View: Doctor Double Oh No*
You reckon you've got the full one thousand units of tezma. There is no room for any more self-doubt.

Forget the Tally Stick. Forget Anu the Chameleon Kid.

Yes, mummy! Dump those alter egos, they are falling apart. Bad Nat always was flaky. She's gone back to original Commie programming, liable to cut you up real good. Jack has gone AWOL. No longer responsive to hypnotic trigger-commands, he is free to track back in to you.

Thank Set for Eddie and his conjuring powers. Eddie Boy Krishna will get you out of this fix.

*Screen Message*
GAME SAVED

## Exorcising the inner demon Jack

Eric Street to Maidman Street
FUCK U ASHTORETH I CAN SMELL U WIDESPREAD BELOW THE BITCH
IS BACK TRYING TO DRAG ME DOWN WITH LIES PRAISE BE 2 ALLAH
KNOWS INFIDELS DONT COUNT THEY DESERVE SPECIAL TREATMENT
ALL WOMEN R WHORES ONLY LITTLE GIRLS R CLEAN VICTIMS BRING
IT ON THEMSELVES POOR PEOPLE NEED TO BE TOLD WHAT 2 THINK
U BETTER BELIEVE IT R U READY TO BE HEARTBROKEN ME ME ME
THATS ALL U EVER THINK ABOUT I NEVER FUCKED A DEVIL WOMAN
DRIPPING JUICY SHIT ASHTORETH I WANT TO DO IT 2 U NASTY AND
GOOD DEATH THROES 4 A SLIPPERY PREDATOR LAST SEEN IN THE
THAMES RIVER OF OBLIVION ROLLING HER WATERY LABYRINTH
WHEREOF WHO DRINKS 4GIVES THE HARDEST WORD I THINK YOULL
FIND IM RIGHT ENTERING THE NO-GO ZONE OF THE UNDERGROUND
CLUB TRUE NAME TEMPLE OF OSIRIS I DONT KNOW IM SO ANGRY I
AM CRYING IN SWEET REMEMBRANCE OF ALL PAIN AND WOE IVE
MADE UP MY MIND ABOUT U AND YOUR DAUGHTER BOTH A PAIN IN
THE NECK IM SURPRISED U CANT GUESS HOW I FEEL BRIGHT LIGHTS
ON AT THE END OF A LONG DARK TUNNEL DOOR OPEN JACK IN

Ratcliffe Highway/Cannon Street Road
WAIT FOR ME BENEATH ST GEORGE'S BATHS ASHTORETH I AM
MAD FOR U KNOW WHAT U CAN DO 2 ME ALL OR NOTHING ALLAH
COULDNT CARE LESS IVE GOT A TICKET TO HELL JUST WHO THE
FUCK IS THAT DAUGHTER EXCLUSIVELY YOURS ON THE WILD SIDE
DANGER TWO MYSTERY MARKSWOMEN OPEN FIRE ON THE ENEMY
AS I CROSS INTO THE CHURCH OF SET I DO KNOW SAFETY QUEERS
R NOT REAL MEN HANGING HEAD IN SHAME PLEASE DONT SHOOT
OOH IM SCARED PAEDOPHILE JACK SHOT DOWN BY ASHTORETHS
HIRED DAUGHTER HITWOMEN RHONA & REGINA KARMA GUN THUGS
SAYING HELLO FOR THE FIRST TIME TO FRESHLY MADE GOD CHILD
HORUS KNOWS WHAT THAT MEANS A LAST-CHANCE BLOOD WEDDING
THE BIGGER THE BETTER GET ONE FREE AUTOCATALYST A WOODEN

SELF-LOADING PHALLUS FOUND OPPOSITE THE SILVER BIRCHES CHILDRENS HOME IN EAST LONDON KEEP CLEAR FOREVER IN THE THOUGHTS OF SATIS & NEPHTHYS PULL MY SHIT STAINED BLACK SILK KNICKERS OFF PLEASE KISS MY NASTY VIRGIN ASS CRACK ILE TAKE ANYTHING U WANT TO GIVE MY RADIO CONTROLLED HEAD BACK TO ME EMPTY SOMEBODY IS CALLING MUTHAFUCKAH 23 THATS ME TO INCUBATE SOMETHING A DIVINE GIFT DEEP INSIDE MY BLACK DOG BOWELS NOW A FLESH CAR DRIVEN BY A YIN & YANG CROSSROADS GOD ITS THAT SIMPLE MY OWN SATAN CONCEIVES A GROWING BURDEN 2 FUCK WOMENS RIGHTS IM VERY VERY SHOCKED HUGS & KISSES SALAM BYE BYE JACK WAS NOT HERE YRS TRULY THE BOSS NAME UNKNOWN

## Offworld power games

'COLONIAL PUPPET SHOW' EPISODE

MARK 23: *(Voiceover)*    Assalamu alaikum, godly people. Here's your host Mark 23, good old bad old shaman and reality TV signifier, wandering the streets of East London with a hidden camera. I was about to ask the mutant Allegra about the identity of the creature who had assaulted her. I was sure it was Jack the Mack. But before any of that could take place, I had a minor identity crisis to deal with. Just who the hell was I?

*Cue titles and music*

THE RE-ENCOUNTER

*Fade up on the daytime interior of St George's Baths in Shadwell. An underwater grotto made from coral and driftwood. There are precious stones scattered on the sand floor and polished jewels set in the walls. At the back of the grotto is the statue of an Afro-Atlantean fish god made from burnished metal. He is named Set.*

*Propped on a chair fashioned from a huge clam shell is a broken doll. It is the upper half of a BLUE MYSTERIOSO with aquamarine scales, genital fronds and two ragged holes at the base of its hips. The doll has bug eyes and spiked teeth and its square head is crowned with fins.*

*Resting beside the BLUE MYSTERIOSO is a wand of black driftwood. It is made in the shape of two intertwining snakes which rear up from a common silver tip to form a handle out of their crossed heads.*

*MARK 23 enters the grotto on his motorised wheelchair. In the front basket is his aluminium flight case covered in a mass of fading stickers. He wears an open black zip-up military tunic over a Shoom T-shirt, blue baggy jeans and Adidas Gazelles. He sports a buzz cut and there are two white plasters over his smashed nose.*

*MARK 23's little black dog SOTAN races ahead over the sand. He skids to a halt beside a pile of twigs and noses out some cut-up pieces of GalPal Kylie smeared with ketchup. They are two legs each with a rough plastic socket at the end. SOTAN's Real Glowing Eyes burn with an electric red light.*

*Move in on MARK 23. He carries a radio microchip in the palm of his hand.*

*It is covered in blood and snot. He holds it up to the BLUE MYSTERIOSO and*
*laughs. She begins to scream.*

MARK 23: *(Voiceover)*     Allegra was at my place. I now knew her name and this
gave me power over her. But what power did she have
over me? Did she know who had implanted me with a
radio microchip? I had to find out.

### FLASHBACK TO AN ACT OF BESTIALITY

*Interior night-time shot of St George's Baths in Shadwell. An underwater grotto*
*of glitter and papier-mache. Lying on the sand floor are various antique items of*
*branded merchandise.*

*Move in on mugs decorated with transfers, lapel badges, a Waddington's*
*board game, boxes of Dinky cars and Barratts Sweet Cigarettes picture cards and*
*clear plastic-fronted boxes of Pedigree action figures.*

*Close in on the boxes. Two have been ripped open and are empty. One describes*
*MARK 23, the other his faithful dog SOTAN.*

*Cut to the black moulded plastic body of SOTAN. He has Real Shaggy Hair.*
*His head is buried in the denuded crotch of his master. MARK 23 has no clothes*
*on. The eyes have been half-rubbed out on his head and he has a blue chin.*

*Close in on SOTAN. He has yoghurt on his lips. His Real Glowing Eyes start*
*to work for the very first time.*

MARK 23: *(Voiceover)*     It only happened the one time. But after that my dog
was no longer tame.

### AUTO-INTERROGATION

*Fade up on the daytime interior of St George's Baths in Shadwell. An underwater*
*grotto made from coral and driftwood.*

*MARK 23 sits in his motorised wheelchair with his flight case on his lap. His*
*dog SOTAN is at his side. SOTAN's eyes flash red.*

*Seated opposite them on the clam shell is a completely nude GALPAL KYLIE*
*with Real Bendable Knees. She is perched with one leg crossed over the other. Her*
*vinyl skin has a dark tint and her hair is fashioned in a bubble cut.*

*GALPAL KYLIE picks up the wand in her lap and points it accusingly at*
*MARK 23. He cringes. SOTAN takes fright and slinks off into the shadows.*

*Move in on the square aluminium flight case on MARK 23's lap. He peels the*
*record company promotional stickers from its lid one by one. Revealed beneath is*
*the embossed logo of a bare-breasted mermaid with net and trident.*

*Cut to MARK 23's shocked face. Close in on his eyes. They are filled with tears.*

MARK 23: *(Voiceover)*   Allegra knew me better than I did. I had intermittently been a radio-controlled agent of the Saxe-Coburg-Gotha mob without even knowing it. Repressed memories came flooding back of life on the Royal Spaceship far away in the sky…

## A DRUG SOURCE

*Interior shot of an operating theatre with red plastic swing doors and a mock-marble floor. The white nylon blinds are pulled down and the ceiling lights reflect off the glossy walls. GalPal Kylie lies on the silver quilted surface of an operating table. She is nude.*

*Move in on GalPal Kylie. Her synthetic blonde hair has been pulled out of her scalp to leave tufts and a rotary pattern of round stitch marks. Strips of white gauze are wrapped round her body. They are stained with blobs of ketchup. GalPal Kylie's eyebrows are arched for dramatic effect.*

*NightNurse Natasha stands over her. She sports a white cotton uniform and buttoned blouse topped with a navy cape. Her kohl-lined eyes are framed with bat-wing specs and her nails are painted red. She is hooking up a drill together with its flexible extension cord to a ceiling carousel of power tools suspended low over the operating table. She unhooks various rubber suction tubes and feeds them under GalPal Kylie's bandages into her open flesh wounds.*

*Cut to BoyChick Jason seated at a work bench in a white lab coat, shirt and tie. He inserts the other end of the tube into a plastic flask and waits for it to fill up with pure liquid Substance H. He has a blank expression.*

MARK 23: *(Voiceover)*   It was always cold in the Royal Substance Lab.

## A SATANIC PARTY

*Interior shot of a lounge environment with sliding glass doors, a swimming pool and port-holes set in the walls. The decor includes gravel and shells, ornamental brass fishes and plastic tables and chairs. There are chunky glass ash-trays, books of matches and little shot glasses on the tables. The place is filled with a collection of Jasons in various costumes and different poses.*

*Flash cut to MoneyLaunderer Jason in black & white hounds-tooth check-shirt and skinny red tie. He is reclining on a lounger with his cowboy boots up on one of the tables.*

*Flash cut to DrugTrafficker Jason in maroon dressing-gown and velvet black collar. He is standing with his hands round the shoulders of two BoyChick Jasons in bathing costumes.*

*Flash cut to ArmsDealer Jason in an orange paisley shirt and blue rimless shades. He is seated in a rattan chair smoking a big fat cigar.*

*Cut to QuikTrick Eddie moving among his guests with a tray of plastic soda siphons containing Substance H. His face is obscured by big square-shaped blue plastic spectacles. He is wearing a beige lounge-suit over a white polo neck jumper with a pair of mocassins. He offers drugs to everyone in the room. The Jasons help themselves.*

*Move in on the pool. NightNurse Natasha stands in the shallow end wearing black bra and panties. She is dunking underwater the head of a nude GalPal Kylie whose vinyl body is punctured with cigarette burns.*

MARK 23: *(Voiceover)*     The pool water in the Home Sphere always tasted of urine.


SEX ORGY INVOLVING A CHILD

*Interior shot of an industrial corridor whose ceiling is lined with metal pipes, electrical cabling and extractor fans and whose concrete floor is lined with a runnel leading to a drain. The bare walls are pitted, stained with yoghurt and ketchup and set with manacles at regular intervals.*

*Move in on a GalPal Kylie chained to the wall by her hands and feet. She is dressed in gold metal hoop ear-rings and white plastic high heels. The hole in her forehead is filled with ketchup. Surrounding her is a horde of partially costumed Jasons in various poses.*

*DrugTrafficker Jason wears a gas mask over his mouth and is smearing GalPal Kylie's Real Kissing Lips with melted chocolate. ArmsDealer Jason is sporting a scarlet cummerbund and poking a plastic kitchen fork between her Disco Dancing Legs. MoneyLaunderer Jason is wearing black zip-up Chelsea boots and flogging her dented Push-Up Breasts with barbed wire.*

*Move in on the drain. It is clogged with chocolate, yoghurt, ketchup and strands of synthetic blonde hair.*

MARK 23: *(Voiceover)*     The Home Sphere basement always smelt of stewed cabbage.


A SECRET SERVICE SEX TRAP

*Exterior shot of a two-storey ranch-style house made of glass and concrete set in a rocky outcrop. It is protected by shrubs, palm trees and white picket fencing and connects via an open-air staircase to a circular landing pad covered in sand. Beyond is a lawn swing and the rolling green fields of a landscaped golf-course.*

*Move in on the landing pad. It is occupied by an outside broadcasting unit run by three SexCop Jasons dressed in peaked caps, blue nylon jump-suits with epaulettes and knee-length zip-up boots. SexCop Jason 1 has a camera with a zoom lens and flash attachment slung round his neck by a leather strap. SexCop Jason 2 holds a microphone and is turning the dials of a reel-to-reel tape recorder. SexCop Jason 3 is directing surveillance of the house and its occupants with the aid of a pair of binoculars.*

*Standing back from his troops is TransFag Jonny, dressed in chrome studded armour-plated smoking jacket with quilted tartan sleeves. His head is a smooth vinyl dome and his lidless blue eyes are wild and staring. Close in on TransFag Jonny as he presses a stud on his jacket.*

*The landing pad moves downward on hydraulic machinery leaving a gaping hole in the landscape.*

*Cut to the lawn swing and move in close. Lying on its cushioned seat is a GraceKelly Kylie in pink satin evening gown and white fur stole. Her arms and legs are tied behind her with rope to reveal white tricot elbow gloves and silver glitter pumps. Her jewellery includes drop ear-rings and simulated pearl necklace while black tape covers her mouth and eyes.*

*Cut back to the landing pad to reveal an empty field of raked sand.*

MARK 23: *(Voiceover)*  The White Palace was always very quiet.

A BLACKMAIL OPERATION
*Interior shot of an industrial corridor whose ceiling is lined with metal pipes, electrical cabling and extractor fans and whose concrete floor is occupied by a plastic table and chairs. The bare walls are pitted, running with soapy water and set with cameras and microphones at regular intervals.*

*Move in on the table. Resting on its surface is an open black plastic briefcase with silver-effect aluminium trim. QuikTrik Eddie is sliding black & white prints across the table to DrugTrafficker Jason, ArmsDealer Jason and MoneyLaunderer Jason. Eddie is sitting with his legs crossed and his blue-stripe trainers unlaced. The Jasons are all standing in sober two-piece suits and ties.*

*Pull back to reveal a film studio with a gantry running high above the corridor and a collection of powerful klieg lights pointed at the set. Move in on the gantry. TransFag Jonny and his SexCop surveillance crew slide into place on a platform of sand. They are checking their equipment.*

*Cut to GalPal Kylie in an unzipped semi-transparent white plastic body-bag lying on the ground. Her lips are painted blue.*

MARK 23: *(Voiceover)*  The Home Sphere basement was always full of noise.

## THE SPIN MACHINE

*Interior shot of a circular monitoring room whose curving wall is lined with screens and speakers. Sloping out from the wall is a desk of buttons, dials and faders. Stationed in front of the desk on the mock-marble floor is a black plastic recliner chair on wheels.*

*Move in on the chair. Cradled inside is QuikTrik Eddie in white T-shirt, boxer shorts and deck-shoes. His spectacles are propped up on his head and his Real Gripping Hands are busy at the dials. Standing behind him massaging his neck is TransFag Jonny dressed in sheer nylon stockings, high heels and a floor-length black coat.*

*Close in on the screens. They are leaking images of tabloid scandals, stock market prices and porno sex scenes. Flash cut to tabloid item on a drugs raid. Mix in GalPal Kylie's arms and legs. Cut to the rising share price in electricals. Fade up on GalPal Kylie's torso.*

*Flash cut to images of military jets over the desert. Move in on GalPal Kylie's head, the face streaked with oil, the open eyes obscured by strands of synthetic blonde hair.*

*Cut back to QuikTrik Eddie's deck-shoes. Move in to reveal their corrugated rubber soles lined with ketchup.*

MARK 23: *(Voiceover)*   The White Palace was always cleaned twice a day.

## THE CLINICAL WASTE DUMP

*Interior shot of a lounge environment with sliding glass doors, a drained swimming pool with the cover rolled back and port-holes set in the walls. The decor includes disturbed gravel and crushed shells, toppled brass fishes and overturned plastic tables and chairs. A dry wind blows from nowhere. The place is vacant.*

*Move in on the pool. NightNurse Natasha stands on the edge of the deep-end. She is wearing a white lab-coat smeared with ketchup. She holds a red-tipped cigarette in her hand.*

*Close in on the pool. It is filled with red plastic uteruses removed from HumanAnatomy Kylie. They have been tossed one on top of the other.*

*Cut back to NightNurse Natasha. She is melting. Close in on the flames and the acrid black smoke.*

MARK 23: *(Voiceover)*   It was never clear what lay beyond Garbage Disposal.

## A VITAL UNDERSTANDING

*Pull back from MARK 23's watery eyes. Fade up on the daytime interior of St George's Baths. MARK 23 thumbs open the locks on his aluminium flight case. There is a click.*

*Cut to SOTAN approaching from the shadows of the underwater grotto. He moves with his old calmness. His Real Glowing Eyes are broken. He sees clearly now.*

*Pull back to discover GALPAL KYLIE seated on the clam shell. She is clothed in a white bridal dress. A rayon wedding gown under billowing layers of flowered nylon tulle is complemented by a formal train and mock pearl tiara holding a tiered bridal veil. Short white nylon gloves and white slippers complete the look.*

MARK 23: *(Voiceover)*    Allegra had only ever wished to be whole again. Now I could ask her the question I had wanted to put to her all along. Who was Jack the Mack?

SECRET IDENTITY REVEALED

*Daytime interior shot of St George's Baths. GALPAL KYLIE throws her wand to the bronze statue of Set at the back of the underwater grotto. SOTAN races to fetch it.*

*MARK 23 opens the lid of his aluminium flight case. Revealed inside is an array of scalpels, medical scissors and forceps. They gleam in the watery light. MARK 23's face is bloodless.*

*SOTAN trots back to GALPAL KYLIE with the wand gripped firmly between his teeth. He drops it her feet.*

MARK 23: *(Voiceover)*    How could I not have guessed the truth? Knifeman Jack the Mack was none other than myself. My quest was over. But Allegra had a new mission for me. She knew where the Saxe-Coburg-Gotha mob had quartered its secret base in London. There was a way for me to have my revenge.

TO BE CONTINUED…

*Roll credits*

## Pollution of the divine source in Shadwell

Eddie flipping through the file led to his arrest. He congratulates his captors on their professionalism. A smile creeps across his face…

*A True and Faithful Relation of What Passed at Clarence House between Dr John Dee and the Devil.* Extract 7.1: On a bounding leyline stood the Osiris Club and the Church of the White Devil. Now a cryptic memory only was there of these two ill-fated stone circles north of the black corrugated waters of the Thames.

   Either side of the straggling leyline had the Wells of the Three Weird Sisters been dug. From the Well of the Third Weird Sister grew the half-glimpsed root of the Devil's Hoof.

   Satis was able to undo the cancerous signature of the Devil Osiris. She had started to remove his polypous name from the Devil's Hoof when the Juggler did appear. Her own fungous identity oozed strongly enough to be loaded into the Devil's Hoof instead.

EK Exegesis 7.1: Well, well, well! So you know about what happened in Shadwell. What can I say?

   You've gotta laugh, really. No wonder Set was pissed off. I mean, he only gets the altar boy job in the first place cos he's willing to have his bollocks lopped off. That way Osiris knows for sure that the only one getting his three wives up the duff is him and him alone. Well, there has to be some compensation for poor old Set, right? That's why he's given charge of the Jizzum Stick, which is basically an artificial version of what he's given up, thank you very much, except with Osiris's germ-plasm loaded inside. So Set can have all of the fun with none of the responsibility, if you know what I mean.

   Well, that all got bolloxed up by Satis, didn't it? She thought she'd got everyone fooled. But I caught her red-handed. When I hopped down to her toilet cell at St Mary's, she'd already made the pick-up at Set's bunker on the Highway. She was already very busy tampering with the Jizzum Stick. Emptying it of Osiris's germ-plasm and substituting her own. I tumbled at once.

   I didn't blame her. I told her, I says, good for you girl. She looks at me. She was a right slut. She says, why should it always be the male gods who get all the glory? Why shouldn't it be one of the wimmin instead? I says, too bloody right.

I never said anything to the old man. It would have added one wrinkle too many to the complexion of things, know what I mean? That new deal he managed to put together with Osiris for the New Ukanian Combine was complicated enough. It was much tougher than the old deal as well. Suddenly, the Lord of the Dead ups his tax rate. Used to be he wanted a bung once every hundred years. Now he wants a little something on top of each and every victim. Luckily, he leases us the Jizzum Stick so we don't have to find some demented aristo to spunk up a load. But we do have to industrialise the whole process. See, it was only ever meant to be Osiris's progeny that the old man was making with the girls he nabbed from the likes of the Glamis Road kiddie stash. Osiris wanted to use the New Ukanian Combine to replenish his stock, didn't he? Only he got fucked by the Doctor who made a secret deal with Set. And everyone got fucked by Satis.

*A True and Faithful Relation...* Extract 7.2: One multiform night the Second and the Third of the Three Weird Sisters lay together in the sepulchral magnitude and silence of the Church of the White Devil. It was a jubilant tryst. They were sick with tense excitement.

The two combined more than their crackling minds. Nephthys did support the demoniac propagation of Satis. Ashen-faced were they at the crazy thought of being visited by the White Devil. It was all inevitably overwhelming.

The Little Devil had its moment stewing inside the belly of the Black Dog. The growling host was prodded by the Second Weird Sister and found to be over-nourished enough.

The Black Dog was implanted with the Little Devil having had no prior knowledge of its devilish conception.

No longer was maternity an exclusive female burden in Shad.

EK Exegesis 7.2: So Satis and Nephthys descend to East London and reincarnate as a couple of local deities. They're living it up in the Osiris Club when whaddya know? The Jizzum Stick appears. Almost as if it had a life of its own.

Well, that girl Satis buggered up the Jizzum Stick in the first place, didn't she? Now she can finally have a go with it herself. I mean, she's got leeway. She's out on a spree and there's no interference from Osiris, her Lord and Master.

So what does she do? She scrams over to the Church of Set just to be on the safe side and makes a test-tube Horus with Nephthys. That's right. She takes the Jizzum Stick and transplants her germ-plasm into an egg extracted from her sister's ovary. Bingo! They've got a result. It's Horus in embryo. Only thing is that this time round he's kin to Satis and not Osiris.

All the pair need now is an host for the Horus. Luckily, Jack's guard dog is on hand and he's got an highly over-developed gut. Poor old doggie. The goddesses implant the Horus into his bowel tissue while he's out for the count and that's him fucked for the duration. He can't do his job anymore, he's no good for anything.

Now whaddya think of that?

A *True and Faithful Relation...* Extract 7.3: The glamour and dread of the Church of the White Devil laid its fateful spell on the unlit Well of the Third Weird Sister early through vanished association.

The screaming innocents had been removed unto the cannibal altar of the Church of the White Devil.

It was by a law unwritten that the unfortunate offerings rejected for some unseen blemish bore witness to the bestial delicacy of the crossroads Oracle. Transported were these imperfect victims over the road untrodden to the nethermost sanctuary of the Third Weird Sister.

So it is found by prophecy and shall be ever more

EK Exegesis 7.3: See, what you got to remember is that back in them days it was no crime to be a sacrifice, was it? In fact, it was a privilege and people had to queue. You should have seen the lines of mums and babies outside Set's altar! Course, not every kiddie was up to scratch, was it?

This is the bit missed out by Wallis Budge, ain't it? What does he know about the part played in the Horus ritual by that tricky jackal god, Anubis? Nothing. When I know from my own researches that he had the run of the place in the sacred fields of Shadwell. Cos if he cocked his leg over a little innocent on the altar, then that was it, the kid was spared. Quite an oracle, that Anubis.

Now, this is where the goddess Satis comes in. She was the last of Osiris's women. Quite the motherly one, you might say. It was her got to look after all the no-good little bastards that weren't fit to be consecrated. She tended the litter from which were drawn the priests of Set.

And that, my friends, is that. Good enough for you?

## Secret Deal

ANUBIS: Osiris, I have a message.

SATIS: No need to bother Osiris.

NEPHTHYS: Whyncha let *us* handle it?

ANUBIS: Prior permission required. My message is for de Lord of the Dead.

SATIS: Dont look-look me so. I hear Osiris with Isis, you know?

NEPHTHYS: She is *occupied* with her husband.

SATIS: Who da message from deh?

NEPHTHYS: Come here, little doggie. Want me to keep company with you? Hmmm?

SATIS: *Nephthys!* Do not pass your hand so! Let Anubis give up da shout.

ANUBIS: O you royal bitches! Da message is from the fair-maid Allegra One Zero Zero Zero.

SATIS: And Allegra say what deh?

NEPHTHYS: I got needle-stitches in my neck-back. Brrr!

OSIRIS: Ladies, ladies! Hello, sweet ladies! Are you losing time with Anubis?

SATIS & NEPHTHYS: (*Together*) Roger, Osiris! We are in the advisory area!

ISIS: Hello, my sisters. Break. Hello, sweet pup.

SATIS: Hmmph! Like we dont know what she been doing with Osiris.

NEPTHYS: She is so *pretensive*!

ANUBIS: Osiris, I have a blind transmission from Allegra One Zero Zero Zero.

OSIRIS: I read you, Anubis.You are cleared to pass the message.

ANUBIS: Allegra say she has found Doctor Dee hiding in a radar-screened scotch under Parliament Hill.

OSIRIS: Well, well, well. Who would have guessed it?

ISIS: And those Horuses missing from the New Ukanian Account?

ANUBIS: Allegra counts nine hundred and ninety nine live ones stashed under Parliament Hill.

ISIS: Doctor Dee has *certainement* been busy with your Jizzum Stick, my lord.

NEPTHYS: That big-eye kaba-kaba! He has made nine hundred and ninety nine baby Horuses on da Lord of da Dead's account.

ANUBIS: He *thinks* he has one thousand. Allegra say Doctor Dee took one from her but give it cut-eye when she stewed it.

SATIS: Doctor Dee is an asseboo!

OSIRIS: I will take them all. Every last manjack of them.

ISIS: Calm yourself, my lord. We must settle our debt with Allegra before she loss away. Anubis?

ANUBIS: My lady?

ISIS: Does Allegra have a first wish for Osiris to grant?

ANUBIS: She want to be whole again so I send her to da Temple of Osiris on

Maidman Street to collect her missing legs.

OSIRIS: You did well.

ISIS: And does she have a second wish?

ANUBIS: She wish for protection against Doctor Dee's rangatang duppy-agent Jack. She want the Karma Twins deh.

OSIRIS: Who?

ANUBIS: They are local deities, my lord.

ISIS: No more than hurry-come-up media avatars.

SATIS: Rhona Karma is cool!

NEPHTHYS: Regina Karma is irie!

ANUBIS: But Jack is a moko.

OSIRIS: *Who?*

SATIS & NEPHTHYS: (*Together*) Let us do the Karma Twins!

ISIS: You are willing to descend?

ANUBIS: They can mount Allegra's missing legs.

OSIRIS: Go then. Airdash fast.

SATIS: Anubis, get us a true bearing for da Temple of Osiris.

ANUBIS: Wilco. Break. Allegra? Prepare to receive the Karma Twins.

NEPHTHYS: We descend.

ISIS: *Au revoir*, sweet sisters.

ANUBIS: Now we must wait.

OSIRIS: I am eager to mash up dat kabba-kabba, Doctor Dee.

ISIS: Patience, my lord!

ANUBIS: Nephthys and Satis ascending!

ISIS: Already?

SATIS & NEPHTHYS: (*Together*) We return!

ISIS: Whappen?

SATIS: We made a Horus with the Jizzum Stick.

NEPTHYS: Satis impregnated my egg with jizzum. It was *so* wicked.

OSIRIS: I dont understand…

ISIS: Artificial insemination, darling! So where is dat embryo now, huh?

SATIS: We put it in da belly of dat fenky-fenky dog follow Jack round de place.

NEPHTHYS: Jack didnt care nutten! He too busy getting and talking to Allegra about Doctor Dee.

SATIS: He *such* a poor-me-one.

NEPHTHYS: He was really overdoing da long-tongue business.

OSIRIS: Whatever! Thankyou, ladies.

ANUBIS: Allegra's second wish is fulfilled.

SATIS: Theres just one tiny *lickle* other thing?

OSIRIS: Yes?

NEPHTHYS: About this chupid dog…

SATIS: We needed to keep its tail quiet?

NEPHTHYS: Before we buss its belly…

SATIS: So Nephthys give him sweet-eye? She suck doggy cock.

ISIS: No!

NEPHTHYS: And it turn out that dog had really got the spirit!

ANUBIS: Deity ascending. Expected approach time two point five seconds.

SATIS: Set was hiding in that dog!

NEPHTHS: He been there the whole time!

SET: Hey, hey, hey. What is all this old talk?

ISIS: My lord. Its been a long time.

OSIRIS: Welcome, brother.

ANUBIS: Osiris is devoted to his younger brother, Set. Who in those early days could tell the voices of Sam and Dave apart?

ISIS: Osiris has discovered the missing Horuses from the New Ukanian Account in Doctor Dee's off-radar scotch.

NEPHTHYS: Watch Set play fobler!

SATIS: He will admit nothing!

SET: I confess I had a Secret Deal with that powerful-foolish Doctor Dee.

SATIS: So brazen!

NEPTHYS: Set is *proud* of his anancyism.

SET: I promise him the secret of the Pink Lotus in exchange for one thousand baby Horuses.

OSIRIS: This pains me, my brother.

SET: One thousand is enough for me to start my own line! I am no bamsie man. I deserve my own ting!

OSIRIS: I have always looked out for you.

SET: You have always been my *boops*! I wanted something for me on my own!

SATIS: Set is too sensitive.

NEPTHYS: Pshaw! He is dont-care-a-damn!

ANUBIS: One thing stays true...

ISIS: Whats that, little dog?

ANUBIS: Doctor Dee prepares to receive the secret of da Pink Lotus at Hampstead Pond. He thinks he has da full one thousand Horuses to give in exchange; but he only got nine hundred and ninety nine.

OSIRIS: Its time for me to collect!

ISIS: Wait, my lord.

ANUBIS: Allegra One Zero Zero Zero has made her third and last wish deh at Shadwell Dock Stairs.

SET: What?

ANUBIS: She wish for justice to be served.

OSIRIS: I shall stick in Doctor Dee's skin. Make way!

ISIS: *My lord*! Please…

OSIRIS: I attend you, my lady.

ISIS: I have a plan. If Anubis directs Allegra to route to Hampstead Pond with dat rass-clate dog in tow behind Jack then we have a lanyap Horus in place to honour Set's deal.

SATIS: My embryo!

ISIS: Uh huh! Allegra must sacrifice dat embryo at Hampstead Pond.

NEPHTHYS: Why so?

SET: The secret of de Pink Lotus concerns safe passage through the black hole deh at da bottom of Hampstead Pond.

ISIS: If my plan works we can hag Doctor Dee into that black hole and still collect the one thousand Horuses. Catch my length?

SATIS: A harsh form of justice!

NEPTHYS: Allegra will not complain.

ISIS: My lord Osiris. Now is the time for you to mount Doctor Dee and collect the Horuses he has to give. Only pretend that you are Set.

NEPHTHYS: Such gorgeous trickery!

SATIS: Hmph! Dey hardly favour each other no more. Osiris has gotten all hum-grumshious.

SET: I am lost in amazement.

OSIRIS: Very well, my lady. I shall do as you say. Anubis?

ANUBIS: Roger, my lord…

OSIRIS: Get me a true bearing for Hampstead Pond. I descend.

SATIS & NEPHTHYS: (*Together*) *Au revoir*, Osiris.

ISIS: Farewell, my lord.

NEPTHYS: Eeeogh! *Farewell my lord.* What a ballahoo!

SATIS: Isis always did know how to pick a fare.

## Alpine dance sequence

ANOTHER 'BOLLYWOOD' EPSIODE

MARK 23: *(Voiceover)*    Assalamu alaikum, godly people. Here's your host Mark 23, archaic vibe controller and reality TV signifier, dancing through the wild woods of London with his hidden TV camera. Now I had a new mission—to find the secret base of the Saxe-Coburg-Gotha mob and wreak my revenge. My cohort Allegra had given me detailed instructions, which she assured me were divinely inspired.

*Cue titles and music*

RETURN TO THE SOURCE OF THE CRIME

*Fade up on the daytime exterior of a wooden shack leaning against a rocky outcrop at the bottom of a hill on Hampstead Heath. Cut to interior shot. Standing at the back of the shack on top of some piled stones is a carved wooden statue of LORD KRISHNA with a cap pulled down over his ears. The little mannequin has a mouth organ pressed to his lips between the palms of his hands. His skin is painted blue and he has the merry look of a Peter Pan.*

*Dominating the centre of the shack is a cylindrical glass carousel stacked with square-shaped glass phials. There are little burning candles placed in saucers all around the base of the carousel.*

*Entering the shack through a narrow wooden door opposite the carousel is MARK 23. He is riding his motorised wheelchair. Stowed in the front is an aluminium flight case, embossed with the logo of a bare-breasted mermaid. MARK 23 has a bright saffron robe draped over his shoulders and he sports blue Adidas Gazelles. He has the narrow fin of hair over his bald scalp. There are the remains of white paint on his brow.*

*MARK 23's djin SHETAN trots round the carousel. His head-dress of horns bobs in the candle-light. SHETAN's eyes smoulder with a deep red light.*

*Track MARK 23 as he motors between the candles up to the carousel. He reaches up to one of the phials and removes it from the shelf. Revealed through the glass is a golden foetus preserved in alcohol. MARK 23's fingers tremble as he gazes at the tail-like legs, the curled shrimp-like body, the vein-work in the bulbous black-eyed head.*

MARK 23: *(Voiceover)*     I counted exactly nine hundred and ninety nine of the preserved embryos in total. Allegra would be pleased.

## FLASHBACK TO AN EARLIER PICK-UP

*Exterior night-time shot of a wooden shack built over sloping rocks at the bottom of a hill on Hampstead Heath. Cut to interior. Dominating the centre of the shack is a wooden statue of LORD KRISHNA. Clouds of dry ice drift across its booted little feet.*

*Close in on MARK 23 as he moves towards the statue. From the dry ice at the back of the shack emerges a villainous MOBSTER in his long black coat. He is carrying a wrought iron bird cage with a little white shoe box inside.*

*Cut to the box through the bars of the cage. Lying on a bed of bubble-wrap inside the box is a black-haired infant. Her green eyes have a furious energy.*

*Cut back to MARK 23 as he accepts the package. His djin waits for him at the narrow wooden entrance to the shack.*

MARK 23: *(Voiceover)*     I no longer dreamt of Jack the Mack. Instead I called up the repressed memories of my past.

## A SACRIFICIAL BURNING

*Exterior daytime shot of a wooden shack piled up against the rocky base of a hill on Hampstead Heath. Cut to interior. A statue of LORD KRISHNA stands at the back. In the middle of the floor surrounded by candles is a carousel of glass phials.*

*Close on the phial in MARK 23's trembling hand. The pickled embryo inside the glass has a tube attached to its belly.*

*Cut to the statue of LORD KRISHNA. His eyes seem to twinkle above the mouth organ he presses to his lips.*

*Cut back to the glass phial as it slides to the ground from MARK 23's nerveless fingers. Close in on the phial shattering against a saucer of candles and the alcohol igniting.*

*MARK 23's djin SHETAN barks at the flames as the whole carousel erupts. Black smoke billows from the melting glass.*

MARK 23: *(Voiceover)*     I had no need of the matches given me by Allegra. Fate had taken a hand.

## THE WILD HUNT

*Exterior daytime shot of Hampstead Heath in the deepest part of the wild woods.*

*Built into the rocky base of a hill is a two-storey hide-out obscured by trees and foliage. It is built of wood with a sloping corrugated iron roof and a little dry stone doorway.*

*Flames lick the wooden supports of the shack. MARK 23 exits the doorway coughing and spluttering. He is followed by his djin SHETAN. A column of black smoke rises from a popped seam in the roof.*

*Cut to the MOBSTER in his long black coat as he runs away from the shack. He is barely visible through the enclosing brambles and trees.*

*MARK 23 shouts after the MOBSTER and gives chase. SHETAN races ahead through the undergrowth.*

MARK 23: *(Voiceover)*   I recognised the guilty man. It was he who had made me an unwitting agent of the Saxe-Coburg-Gotha mob. Allegra assured me he would pay for his crime.

## A FATAL SEDUCTION

*Exterior daytime shot of Hampstead Heath restyled as an Alpine setting. Stock footage of a lake at the foot of a waterfall with a snow-covered mountain in the background. The lake is surrounded by pine trees and there are rolling green fields covered in masses of yellow edelweiss in the foreground.*

*A COURTESAN dances towards the trees pursued by the MOBSTER. The COURTESAN is dressed in a white ankle-length bridal gown with long sleeves and a high neck. There are henna tattoos on the sides of her hands and feet. Her moon face is partially hidden by a white veil. Her white bridal train blooms behind her across the fields. The MOBSTER keeps trying unsuccessfully to snatch it. He is dressed in a long high-collared black coat. His head is shaved and he has a tattoo of a six-legged beetle on his forehead.*

*Move in on the chase as it enters the trees. The COURTESAN skips ahead, stops with one hand on her hip and turns her head to flash her teeth at the MOBSTER. He swaggers blindly towards her and she darts round a tree to tap him on the shoulder. He turns and tries to encircle her waist with his arms. She places her finger on his lips and shakes her head. She dances on, leading him towards the edge of the lake.*

*Cut back to the fields. MARK 23 is visible far away as a figure in a bright saffron robe. He is piloting his wheelchair over the grass. The aluminium flight case stowed in the front glitters in the sun. MARK 23's djin SHETAN races ahead. The pair are far behind the dancing couple.*

*In the far distance, a column of smoke begins to rise from the base of the mountain. It is as if the backdrop were catching fire.*

MARK 23: *(Voiceover)*     Allegra was quite capable of leading the Saxe-Coburg-Gotha mob boss a merry dance.

## REMNANTS OF AN ALCHEMICAL WEDDING

*Exterior night-time shot of a neem tree whose branches extend over the surface of a moonlit lake. Golden leaves on the tips of the branches. A snow-capped mountain dimly visible in the background.*

*The mobster's black woollen coat hangs over the water from one of the branches of the neem tree. It billows in the wind. Lying coiled on the surface of the water is the courtesan bride's white silk veil. It reflects back the cold brilliance of the moon.*

*SHETAN launches himself into the shallow water. His jaws close on the white bridal veil. He shakes it from side to side. He jumps up and bats the flying coat with his front paws. He is playing.*

*MARK 23 is in his wheelchair at the side of the lake. He is shouting at his djin. There are black smudges on his broad Sikkimese features. Fire rages behind him in the trees.*

*Move in on SHETAN. The white veil spread out on the surface of the water, the black coat twisting in the breeze. Move out to discover bobbing in the water the big round seed-pods of the water-lily. They are ripe. Some have burst. SHETAN laps at the little black seeds that float in the water.*

*The green leaves of the water-lilies are turned-up at the rims. They float on the lake like vegetable pontoons.*

MARK 23: *(Voiceover)*    The lake was dragged but no bodies were ever found.

## SACRIFICE TO A DEITY

*Exterior night-time shot of a neem tree at the side of the lake. A carpet of golden leaves on the ground. Fire all around.*

*SHETAN lies on his side at the base of the tree. His belly is grossly distended. His chest cavity rises and falls with effort. The horns on his head are askew. He is whimpering.*

*MARK 23 has climbed out of his wheelchair. He is on his knees before his aluminium flight case. He pulls the saffron robe tight around his shoulders and looks up at the moon. His pink eyes are fanatical and his smashed nose is covered in plasters. The old horizontal markings on his brow are vivid as red welts.*

*Close in on the flight case as MARK 23 flips the locks and opens the lid. His fingers trip along the gleaming tools displayed inside and come to rest over a scalpel with a bone handle and a serrated edge.*

MARK 23: *(Voiceover)*     Never before had I said a prayer to Lord Osiris. But Allegra had been clear in her instructions.

## THE VISIT OF THE HIJRAS
*Exterior night-time scene of Hampstead Heath restyled as the Alpine setting for a musical production number. An army of beautiful young male-to-female transsexuals pour out of a hole in the bottom of a snow-capped mountain. They are dressed in glittering red and gold saris and sport head-dresses of ostrich feathers. Each trannie models a jewelled nose-ring and a red bindi dot in the middle of her forehead.*

*The transsexuals stamp out the fire on the ground with their bare feet. They are singing and dancing as they go.*

*Track the dancers as they head over the rolling hills towards a forest of pine trees surrounding a lake. Move in on their flashing anklets and glittering bangles as they approach the lakeside neem tree where MARK 23 kneels over his djin SHETAN. Close in on the tip of MARK 23's scalpel as it moves towards the distended belly of SHETAN.*

*Cut to the giant green leaves of the water-lily bobbing gently on the surface of the lake. There is an inhuman shrieking sound.*

*Cut back to the transsexuals as they dance around the tree and sound their finger cymbals in coded gestures of praise scored to the beat of a dholak. The knee is bent and the heel is flexed, the hip is swayed and the bosom is lifted, the arm is extended and the palm is raised. Blessings are showered upon the small CREATURE delivered by MARK 23 from the belly of SHETAN. The figure is a special effect.*

MARK 23: *(Voiceover)*     Lord Osiris was reborn as Baby Horus every one hundred years. The ceremony was conducted by a specially chosen priest. So said Allegra.

## A NECESSARY JOKE
*Exterior night-time shot of Hampstead Heath restyled as an Alpine setting. The moon is covered by clouds. The corpse of a black dog lies under a neem tree beside a lake.*

*Move in on the dead animal. It lies on its side, exposing the long slit in its belly. Blood and guts spill out. Flies are gathering.*

*Follow the wide trail of blood across the ground from the dead dog's innards to the edge of the lake. A long wide track of gore. Keep moving across the surface of the water towards the floating leaf of a water-lily.*

*Move in on the wide flat expanse of the leaf in darkness under the covered sky.*

*A time of waiting and stillness. Something stirs…*

*Cut to the clouds parting from the face of the moon. They move aside as if gently pushed.*

*Cut back to the wide expanse of the leaf on the surface of the lake. Something naked is visible at its centre. A CREATURE the size of a small child. It is seated cross-legged in an attitude of* padmasana, *as if posing for a photograph. The figure is a special effect.*

MARK 23: *(Voiceover)*     Never before had Horus been reborn as a girl. Allegra had no need to tell me that.

TO BE CONTINUED…
*Roll credits*

## **Crash**

\>\>

Dead Girl had been through the Singularity at the bottom of the lake on the Heath of London and was trying to get out of this Silly Black Hole. She was being carried along by this torrent of boiling water. She couldn't get a grip. Everything was soft and slippery.

Her hospital gown was in tatters. She had lost the Magic Wand. Even her fanny-pack was gone.

The water surged over Dead Girl's head. She was tumbling through all this loose mud. There was a silence in her head where Fairy Sugadaddy used to be. He was gone now and he wasn't coming back. She knew that much. The skin had grown over the hole in her head.

Dead Girl wanted to slow down. She wanted to get back to her life.

\<\<

Dead Girl was falling down through the dark water in this lake on the Heath of London. She was wearing her hospital gown with her fanny-pack on underneath and she was holding this Magic Wand made of glass.

Fairy Sugadaddy was guiding her. He was whispering soft words at the back of her head.

Dead Girl landed on this mud-shelf with these big fat seed-pods all around. The jolt went through her legs. Fairy Sugadaddy said this was the opening into a Black Hole. She massaged the pain in her knees as she looked down over the mud-shelf into this watery chasm. That was when she realised she had got her legs back. They were thick and strong and hairy.

She tried to remember how she had got her legs back. She couldn't think. The memory was dim. Fairy Sugadaddy had taken her to this place called the Temple of Osiris. It was like a big cave full of rubbish. Her legs were lying on the ground.

She crept towards the edge of the mud-shelf and peered over it. Far away at the bottom of the chasm was this dark light. Fairy Sugadaddy said it was called a Singularity. It was where she wanted to go. But there was just one problem. Witch Doctor wanted to go there as well.

Fairy Sugadaddy said she would have to leave part of herself in the water at the mud-shelf to guard against Witch Doctor. She would have to split up. So that's what she did. She used her Extra Special Powers and pretended to be Tattooed Lady again because she knew that would confuse Witch Doctor the most. She made Tattooed Lady out of the blue light she still had deep inside and cut her loose just like she had with the Little Thing.

Tattooed Lady crouched down on the mud-shelf with her eyes wide open. Dead Girl gave her the Magic Wand to hold. She thought she might need it to frighten Witch Doctor and ward him off. Tattooed Lady grinned through the water.

Fairy Sugadaddy said it was time for Dead Girl to go. So she jumped off the mud-shelf into the Silly Black Hole. The muddy water slid past her. She was going very fast. She was aiming for the dark light there at the bottom of the lake. She could see that it was very far away.

>>

Dead Girl was caught in a Silly Black Hole at the bottom of this lake on the Heath of London. She was trying to find a way out but the muddy water was battering her from all sides. She no longer knew which way was up or down. Her white hospital gown was in shreds.

She closed her eyes. She tried to remember what Fairy Sugadaddy had said. He had taken her to the Temple of Osiris and something had happened. She had lost nearly all of her Extra Special Powers. The blue light had started fading away inside of her from that moment on. Now she could only use it to make the spectres she remembered from the past. She couldn't pretend to be new people anymore. That's what Fairy Sugadaddy had said.

Dead Girl's ears were bleeding. She was grinding the enamel from her teeth. There were these painful little rashes flaring up all over her skin.

What else had happened at the Temple of Osiris? She couldn't remember. Someone else had been there. Hadn't he been dangerous or something? She had reached for the blue light one last time. She had used her Extra Special Powers to frighten him off. She had laughed at him. Wasn't that it? She had pretended to be one last person. She had become this big person clad head to toe in rubber. Who exactly was that?

Something tough and hard brushed against Dead Girl's fingers. It was this gnarly root growing out of the mud.

Some last part of Dead Girl hidden deep inside took over and made her grab the root. The big person she had become in the Temple of Osiris was in charge now. Dead Girl sighed with relief and let go. Her Extra Special Powers faded away to nothing. She was all that was left of the blue light now.

She thought she must be a Dreaming Girl.

<<

Dead Girl was sliding towards this Singularity at the bottom of a Silly Black Hole. She was moving very fast. She was sat in the back-seat of this big car in just her white hospital gown and her fanny-pack. The car was painted black. It had smoked glass windows and lots of armour. It was what they call a Merc and it was out of control.

Dead Girl couldn't see who was driving. It was very shadowy inside the car and all she could see out the window was this long thread of water flashing past. Fairy Sugadaddy said it was the Old River Seine in the City of Paris. He was guiding her now.

Then everything went dark as the Merc shot into the mouth of this tunnel. Time slowed down as the car got faster. Dead Girl gripped the edge of her seat and pressed her feet against the floor. She was bracing herself for a crash when this brilliant white light went off in front of the car from the end of the tunnel. It flooded the windscreen so she couldn't see what was going on. She closed her eyes and felt the wheels of the car go into this skid.

Fairy Sugadaddy was whispering in the back of her head. He said that the Singularity was not far away and she had to get through it. She felt exhausted. Her metabolism had seized up. She was very sluggish. The light faded away and she opened her eyes to see this pillar in the central reservation of the roadway coming to meet the car. Her bowels refused to work. She was full of shit. She felt very very heavy. She felt like she was gaining weight. She couldn't move.

The pillar hit the Merc between the front headlights and the car buckled. Dead Girl was thrown forward into the seat in front as the windscreen shattered and all these little pieces of glass showered over her like confetti. The force of the impact went into her chest. Then she was thrown back as the car rebounded from the pillar and sailed through the air. It was like she was in this funfair waltzer as the car span round and she felt sick. Then there was this jolt which came up through her spine as the Merc landed back on the roadway facing the way it had come.

She shat herself. It was all warm and sticky inside the hospital gown she was wearing. She was in a state of shock. The Merc was a wreck. Its horn was blaring too late and there was all this steam coming out of its busted radiator. But all she could think was that it was a good job she still had her fanny-pack on.

She looked out of the crumpled door to see this surveillance camera mounted on the roof of the tunnel. It had these tiny gripping feet and it was moving round to track her. She squinted up at the lens of the camera. It was round and dark. She thought the Old King must be watching her on closed circuit television somewhere to check she really was dead. She imagined him sitting at a leather desk in his dressing gown with the Royal Crest or whatever stitched on his pocket. He was looking very furtive. There was the ghost of a smile on his lips.

Dead Girl thought about using her Extra Special Powers. She found some more of the blue light from somewhere inside herself and she pretended to be the Lost Princess. That would show the Old King. That would teach him not to grin at her. That's what she thought. She rested her eyes. She imagined how shocked the Old King would be to see his Lost Princess lying in the tunnel. She saw him crying and whining. She laughed as she coughed up some blood…

*What is your name again? Someone wants to know. It's important. What is your name? You don't know your name. You don't have a name. You are dreaming you are no longer alive. You are this Dreaming Girl who thought she was a Dead Girl. That's how it is.*

*You are bleeding. There is the taste of blood in your throat…*

>>

Dreaming Girl was coming out of this Silly Black Hole at the bottom of a lake on the Heath of London. She was using this tough old root to climb up through all this loose mud. She pulled herself up hand over hand and kept helping herself along with big powerful kicks of her legs. She was tired.

Dreaming Girl was rising through the thick muddy water. She was covered in this protective gear from head to toe. It was a white rubber body suit with a hood a bit like a deep-sea diver's outfit. The suit was partially inflated with air and it was cinched in at the waist by this green leather strap thing. The strap thing was buckled up really tight. It was what they call a dildo harness.

Dreaming Girl had this little metal pipe coming out of the hood at the mouth. It was like so she could breathe. She unzipped her eye-slots. There was sun-light coming down through the water from above. Below her was this dark light at the bottom of a chasm.

Dreaming Girl saw that the root she was holding on to was connected to all these other roots. There was this network of stems in the mud and water. Climbing was easier now. She found foot-holds and hand-holds. Soon she poked her head through a crack in this sloping mud-shelf. There were all these rotting seed-pods in the water and brown leaves and dead water lilies all around the place.

Dreaming Girl hauled herself out on to the mud-shelf where the water lilies were growing. There was no sign of Tattooed Lady or the Magic Wand. She looked back down through the crack in the ground. The roots of the water lilies went down through the mud and the water. Far away down below caught in some of the stems was this Dead Girl. She was wearing a ragged white hospital gown that billowed in the water. Her skin was glowing with this shimmering blue light.

Dreaming Girl stopped looking. She didn't want to think about the Dead Girl. She didn't want to think about what had happened at the Temple of Osiris. She remembered that Freak Boy had come back. Only this time he had been wielding a knife. Dead Girl had been in danger. That was why Dreaming Girl had been called up. She had frightened Freak Boy off Dead Girl. It was Dreaming Girl who had been this spectre made out of blue light.

But now Dead Girl was made out of the blue light and Dreaming Girl was real. Wasn't that it?

Dreaming Girl closed her eyes and swam back up to the surface of the lake.

<<

Dead Girl was lying in the middle of this Singularity at the bottom of a Silly Black Hole. She was alone in the back of this stupid Merc which was all smashed up. All she had on was her fanny-pack and her white hospital gown. There was a deep pain in her chest and she could hardly breathe.

Dead Girl did this thing where she separated from Lost Princess and got out of the car. She looked down at Lost Princess. She was just this hologram made out of blue light. Dead Girl felt lighter. Fairy Sugadaddy was still saying things to her in the back of her head. His voice was very calm. He said she had to get into the Antigravity Universe which was behind the crash scene at the Singularity. So she left Lost Princess flickering on the back seat of the wrecked Merc and drifted across the empty roadway towards the central reservation. There were these orange sodium lamps set in the walls of the tunnel. They were flashing and buzzing. She was looking for the pillar which the car had crashed into. She used her sense of touch to find it. It was like she didn't trust her eyesight or something.

There was this vehicle coming towards her from the mouth of the tunnel. It was like it was following her. She could see the twin pools of its headlights and hear its engine. It was a big white vehicle and it was moving very fast.

Her hands closed on this door handle that was set in the pillar. She worked it and the door in the pillar opened. She stepped through into the space beyond and the door sprang shut behind her.

Dead Girl found herself on this old stairwell like something out of a multi-storey car park except it stretched to infinity up and down in both directions. Fairy Sugadaddy said it was the Antigravity Universe. The square walls were made of red brick and the stairs were made of concrete. There were cigarette butts and old plastic bags on the landing.

She moved up to the next landing and opened the door a crack. It looked out of the central reservation pillar on to the crashed Merc with the Lost Princess lying in the back with her legs like a broken doll made of blue light. There was all this glass rubble on the road but this time it was quiet. The car horn was not making any kind of a sound. Fairy Sugadaddy said she was looking out on to a parallel universe which was only a bit different from the one she had just left. She let the door close and moved on.

Dead Girl checked the view from lots of different doors as she raced up and down the stairwell. One thing at the Singularity always stayed the same. The Lost Princess was always lying in the back of the crashed Merc. But little things would change. Sometimes she was on the left seat rather than the right seat. Other times the Merc was facing in the direction it was originally going in rather than back the way it had come. One time the Merc was on fire and there was all this thick black smoke in the tunnel.

Another thing that also stayed the same was the other vehicle racing up to the scene. Dead Girl could see after a few times that is was an ambulance. It had a red cross painted on its white side and its windows were all blacked out. It usually turned up at the crash scene and stopped next to the Merc with its engine running. For a while nothing happened. There was just this electric light leaking from the gaps in its blacked-out windows.

Fairy Sugadaddy told Dead Girl that Witch Doctor was in the back of the ambulance with Tattooed Lady and she was stopping him from getting past the Singularity. She was giving him what he deserved with his own Magic Wand. It was the same in every parallel universe Dead Girl looked at. Witch Doctor could not follow Dead Girl into the Antigravity Universe. He was trapped.

Dead Girl was unbelievably happy. She thought she would faint with euphoria. She sat down on one of the concrete steps in the Antigravity Universe and took these deep breaths. Fairy Sugadaddy said she could go back to any parallel universe she wanted now. He had granted her wish and taken her this far. The rest was up to her. He started to croon an old song deep inside her head. It was like a lullaby. But she couldn't catch the words. It was like there was all this static on the line. Fairy Sugadaddy was fading out.

Dead Girl lifted her fingers to her forehead to feel the hole in her head. But there was just this knotted lump there now. The skin must have knitted back together.

It was time to go. Dead Girl lifted up her white hospital gown and undid her fanny-pack. She ran the belt through her fingers until she got to the little purse. She unzipped it one last time. It was still empty. It was made out of mock crocodile skin. Dead Girl left it on the step. She didn't need it anymore. She got up and opened the nearest door.

Dreaming Girl walked out of the pillar in the central reservation. The emergency lights from the ambulance cast red and blue shadows against the roof and the sides of the tunnel. Lost Princess was lying in the back of the crashed Merc. Her skin was glowing with this blue light. There was blood coming out of her ear and she was shivering. She had these cuts and bruises on her face.

Sitting next to the wreck was the ambulance with the blacked-out windows. Its engine was still running. It was emitting this low throbbing noise.

Dead Girl moved away from the crash scene. There was the sound of rushing water coming from the end of the tunnel. She began to walk towards it. The road surface was wet under her feet. There was water dripping down the sides of the tunnel. The lights were fizzing out one by one. It was becoming dark.

Dead Girl slowed down. There was mud on the ground. She crept along. Before she knew what had happened she was swept off her feet by this torrent of water. It boiled and coursed all around her. It completely carried her off.

>>

Dreaming Girl was swimming in this lake on the Heath of London. She was dressed in a white rubber body-suit with this hood covering her head and a dildo harness round her waist. She was moving with powerful strokes towards the bank.

The stars were out in the sky. Dreaming Girl got out by this bare silver birch tree. It had these gnarled branches that stretched out over the calm water.

Dreaming Girl pulled the metal pipe from her mouth and spat this green slimy water on to the ground. The air was cool on the back of her throat. She remembered what had happened in the Temple of Osiris. Freak Boy had attacked her with a knife. He had stabbed her in the throat. The blood had come up unbidden. It had been hot and thick and urgent. But she had fought him off.

She took off her hood and shook out her hair. It sprang out around her head. It was thick glossy hair composed of very many different coloured strands. There were blonde strands, grey strands and black strands. There were strands of brown, auburn, red and every colour in between.

There was this clinking sound coming from the tree. Dreaming Girl could see the chrome rings fitted to one of the branches. She moved closer. Some of the silver bark had been scraped off the bole of the tree.

Dreaming Girl took off her gloves. The sensation had returned to her finger-tips. She traced the edges of the dark wood that had been revealed by the missing strips of bark. There were these letters that had been etched into the tree. Together they spelled out a name...

*You are Dreaming Girl. You are dreaming you have come back from the dead. You are bleeding. What is your name? Somebody wants to know. You are flying through the air over Whitechapel. You are going to land on the roof of this big hospital. It is coming up fast. What is it? Somebody wants to know your name. You are inside this emergency helicopter. You remember your name.*

*Someone is leaning in close beneath the whirring blades. They have their ear to your lips. You say it. You give them your name.*

*Ada 'Babyface' Wilson. That is your name.*

## Pink Lotus descent

*Screen Message*
GAMEPLAY RESUMING…

*Real Audio Stream*
"Strike the match at my radio signal, stand well back from the blaze and don't forget to clean up the mess."
—Doctor Double Oh No issuing instructions to Eddie on how to clear the chocks for his exit into a parallel universe.

*Player Status*
You are Doctor Double Oh No, Crown double agent, chaos magician and last man remaining at the Ukanian Stay-Behind radio cellnet. You have given Eddie his walking papers. You are making a strategic withdrawal. You are getting the fuck out of New New England.

This whole universe is irre-fucking-deemable. You are going to discreate it. You are going to start again.

Time to initiate the Pink Lotus descent. Give the Caliphate of New New England the bum's rush. Bring on the holy day of the Secret Ukanian Combine on earth.

*Screen Message*
PINK LOTUS DESCENT: PROCEDURE

*Player Status*
You need one thousand units of tezma to perform the Pink Lotus descent. Units of tezma cannot be exchanged. They must be discharged in spectacular fashion. Only then will their cursing power be effective.

The Pink Lotus descent creates a rotational black hole for a single player who can then traverse the Crown coded singularity of their choice to move to a new parallel universe.

*Screen Message*
PINK LOTUS DESCENT MEDIA: ZODIACAL POND

*Player Status*
Get ready to create rotational black hole on the lip of zodiacal pond at Parliament Hill.

One thing, though. This is not a short-cut from here to there. This is a quantum jump in spacetime. A short-cut from now to then and back again. This is a trip where universe passes through you.

Got it? Exit universe you are in, fold it up behind you, locate your dream universe, move right in. Blink and you miss it. You close your eyes and wake up in what appears to be the same place. Zodiacal pond. Cosmic tree. Sacred hill. But all has changed.

*Full Motion Video*
The Doctor strung upside down from the cosmic tree with the dressing-gown cord tight around his neck. He is tugging at the business end with his teeth.

The Doctor has a radio transmitter patched to his throat: Mppph! Mppph! Fuffucksaake!

He close his eyes.

*Screen Message*
PINK LOTUS DESCENT: LOADING…

*Player Status*
Location: Parliament Hill@North America screen

Delete London tactical map from North America screen. Exit overall strategic world index. Go to occult Crown leyline net via Parliament Hill terrain peculiarities. Destroy all incriminating evidence.

*Screen Message*
TEZMA HOARD: 999

*Narrative Voiceover*
The Doctor gonna send out his spectre do the job for him. Make Pink Lotus descent there at bottom of the zodiacal pond.

His penis stiffens in anticipation of the event. See the lubricating fluid on his glans. Uh huh.

Time to disappear. Radio signal goes to Eddie crouched in the hermetic hole-in-the-hill next to all those racks of glass storage jars stretching deep underground. Each jar meant to contain one ripped-off unit of tezma preserved in alcohol. One thousand jars in all.

Eddie always liked to play with fire. He's got the Anubis manual, he's got the box of Bryant & May. Eddie is wearing velvet slippers. He speaks the words conjure the demon Set. Smash those glass jars under the hill and release those gallons of alcohol fuel. Strike one match. The sacred hill goes up in flames.

Now this is a propulsive event. Get it? Think of each unit of tezma as a processor. Hook them up so they are working in parallel. Result? Exponential increase in processing capacity. Faster throughput of quantum energy. Shorter transit time.

Dedicate energy to designated higher order being. The Doctor got a secret thing going on with that rebel god, Set.

"Come to me, Set! Gimme that dream universe you know I deserve."

*Point of View: Doctor Double Oh No*
You reckon you just sacrificed one thousand units of tezma to Set.

Hooray!

You got no time to say good-bye. You're working to a schedule. You got the whole thing planned.

Open the black hole, dodge the Crown singularity, come out the other side. Go via the Pont de l'Alma tunnel in Paris. It's the leyline you remember best.

Don't worry! You'll be back before you know it. You've no time to even open your eyes.

Something splashes into the pond.

*Screen Message*
PINK LOTUS DESCENT: STALLED

*Narrative Voiceover*
The Doctor is in trouble. Game says he spent only nine hundred and ninety nine units of tezma. Uh oh! One thousand required for Pink Lotus descent.

It's okay.

Credit of one unit of tezma automatically extended. Doctor Double Oh No granted conditional option on Pink Lotus descent. That spare unit of tezma needs to be repaid before time Crown-coded singularity reached in order for safe passage to be granted and Pink Lotus descent successfully completed. Otherwise option on Pink Lotus descent lapse and made available to first bidder pay off that debt.

No way for this to be made known to the Doctor. Looks like some other networked player been fucking with his system.

*Screen Message*
TEZMA HOARD: 999 + 1

*Full Motion Video*
The Doctor hanging upside down from the cosmic tree. Twitching and muttering. Hands crossed over the chest Osiris-fashion. Finger-nails skittering. Eyes fixed on the stems of the water lilies deep underwater.

There are beetles crawling over his cuffed and chained body. They are making him a shroud.

*Screen Message*
PINK LOTUS DESCENT
GAMEPLAY STARTING...

*Player Status*
You have used your POV button to hijack the subject position of one of Doctor Double Oh No's alter egos in a parallel universe. You are Doctor Double Oh No.

*Point of View: Doctor Double Oh No*
You are checking your flight-plan. Looking good!

You regulate your breathing with the cord between your teeth. Choke, hold, breathe. Choke, hold, breathe. Not too fast, now.

You are bathed in perspiration. The pores in your skin have opened right up. Beetles crawling over your legs and your arms. It's so very, very hot. Did you take salt tablets to combat dehydration during voyage? Check. Beetles in your pubic hair. You shiver. Did you remember to take a piss? Check.

Something is wrong. Expectation of a safe return coincides with knowledge of certain disaster. Interval of superimposed double cognition. This is an omen.

Terminate Pink Lotus descent? Too late. What is happening? Overlap of parallel subject positions determined by coefficient of spacetime displacement. Shit! You got back before you left. There is an inversion of friction where the going force interferes with the returning force. Damn, it's itchy!

Fucking Einstein! A body travelling at a speed faster than light makes two events separated in a space-like way move closer until they occur simultaneously. Event one? Cause of departure. Event two? Effect of return. Result? Temporal parallax. Oh no! Increase speed of body so it tends to infinite velocity and cause and effect will inevitably swap places on the quantum level.

This is a quantum fluctuation. E-fucking emergency! This universe about to crash down on you. You need to get going now.

Time to launch your spectre.

Open your eyes.

Looks like Khepri already there in the zodiacal pond. She is lying under the water, arms crossed over her chest Osiris-fashion. Oh yes. She got the shaven head with the purple eye-shadow. She got the black nail-polish and the silver rings. She got tattoos all over her body, including that beetle just above her sex parts.

"Who?"

She got the Tally Stick. You count the notches carved in its side.

Nine hundred and ninety nine.

"What?"

Anu the Chameleon Kid is back to mess with your mind. She runs a demonic copy of your spectre in the zodiacal pond. Oh no. Fucks with your launch.

Figure it. Rules of magic dictate speak the name of a demon you rule it. Okay. Say the name Khepri and banish that demon of Anu let your spectre go. Uh oh. Say the name Khepri and failsafe cuts in shut your spectre down.

Say nothing and what happens? You wait. Nothing happens. Double of your spectre eyes open underwater fix you to the cosmic tree with her stare. The surface of the pond an interface. Your face inches from her own.

Time passes. You are paralysed with shame.

Oh for fuck's sake! Whisper the name of your spectre let that Anu know your secret name.

"Khepri."

That dirty little creature under the water screams at you as slowly, so slowly, she start to fade away. What a bitch! She kept you waiting for nothing. Now you gotta wait some more get yourself together.

Deep breaths. Launch your spectre now!

*Screen Message*
PINK LOTUS DESCENT
GAMEPLAY CONTINUING...

*Player Status*
You have used your POV button to abandon the subject position of one of Doctor Double Oh No's alter egos in a parallel universe. You are Khepri, goddess of beetles.

*Point of View: Doctor Double Oh No's Spectre*
You have left your body. You have jumped out of the urethra of Doctor Double Oh No. You are connected to the tip of Doctor Double Oh No's penis by a thin ethereal thread.

Can you dig it? This is your spectre. You are dropping through the air. You are moving though the beetles. You cut the surface of the water and keep on going down. The stems of the water lilies tangled together spell out a summons. You go deeper. You find the root of the bush support all those lilies.

You climb down. This is your moment of burn out. You are entering your own little black hole. Hot damn! The bottom of the pond exerts an irresistible attraction on you. You are under the influence of a singularity. The synchronicities begin to speed up. They become tinier and heavier. Events become micro-events. The gravitational force is pulverising. You begin to molecularize.

Aaargh! Next stop, Pont de l'Alma, get out the fucking way.

You let go and drop.

*Full Motion Video*
The Doctor behind the wheel of an ambulance in Paris. The vehicle is white with red crosses on the sides. It has black tinted windows.

The Doctor is dressed in a Total Allergy Syndrome kit, with the black all-in-one body suit, the big black gloves and the black double-lined hood with the wide plastic face window.

The Doctor: I always feel good when I can wear my favourite Gucci thong with the sheer mesh stockings and suspenders.

*Point of View: Doctor Double Oh No's Spectre/Doctor Double Oh No*
You are sitting in the driver's seat of the ambulance. Just like you were all those years ago. Everything seems familiar. The vehicle is a rush conversion job, but it looks real. The tinted windows are there for your protection. So noone can identify you later.

You've been driving up and down the Champs Elysees for the last hour now. Still no word on the radio. Hasn't the thing gone down yet? It's past midnight. Traffic is sparse.

You feel hot and drowsy. There are tubes exiting the sides of the hood from your nasal passages. You are making a wheezing sound as you breathe. Is this how it was? You can't remember.

You go through the plan one more time. The K-Team got four vehicles on the job. A Fiat hatchback to chase the target's Merc out of the Place de la Concorde, down Cours la Reine and into the tunnel running under the north ends of all those bridges over the Seine. A motorcycle way up front with strobe gun operator riding pillion, synched to turn and zap the Merc driver once the target's overtaken the Fiat and is in the tunnel. A motorcycle at the back to drive by the crash scene and check the target is dead. Then there's the final vehicle. A phoney ambulance to make the pick-up in the tunnel and drop-off the remains of the target at designated rendez-vous point in Pitie-Salpetriere hospital.

You approach the end of the Champs Elysees and prepare to make your turnaround in the Place de la Concorde for the sixth or seventh time that night. The tools of your trade are laid out on the fleece-lined leather wrap sits next to you on the passenger's seat. The little bleeders are tucked up inside their pockets. You got your adze. That's the curved blade for making the ritual opening incision. Then you got your scalpels and your forceps, for the real delicate work. Then you got your kitchen knives, your hack-saws and your hammers. Isn't that right?

You are getting impatient. How long does it take to bring down a wild brood-mare? You want to get busy cut out the little foal and chop it up for Osiris while it's still fresh. It's too much to hope it might still be alive in the crush of the Merc. That would be a miracle worthy of Set!

You hit a red light. Damn! Maybe nothing will happen, after all. Check how you're doing in the rear-view mirror. Eyes heavily made up, nose studded with silver rings, lips painted blue. Kissy, kissy! Can that be you? Radio crackles into life inside your hood. Operator speaking in code in voice laced with panic. You switch on the siren and the emergency roof-lights and surge through the stopped traffic. Ha ha! This time you will not get there late. This time you will make sure everything goes tickety-fucking-boo.

You speed down the empty Cours la Reine expressway with the Thames on your left. Or would that be the Seine? You got a false memory bleed. Tap side of the hood. Cut it out! Your own pale face back in the mirror again.

Road dips into a tunnel passes beneath the Seine bridges as they connect one after another with the right bank. Strip lights flash by on the walls. You want the bit of the tunnel under the Pont de l'Alma. Thirteenth support pillar on the central reservation. Count them as they file past on your left.

Okay. Black Mercedes with a crushed front-end facing you as you draw up. Smoke and steam rising from the engine. The horn blaring. You drive past the wreck and park on the left next to the central reservation. You get out with your bag of tools.

The tunnel is empty in both directions. There are no slowly moving lanes of traffic. There are no fire engines and no police cars. There are no other emergency vehicles. There are no cops holding back the crowds, no photographers crawling over the wreckage.

You walk over to the wreck, rubber soles crunching on windscreen rubble. Radio operator said target not dead. That's good news for you. That's good news for Osiris. You pull open the back door of the vehicle and peer inside. The horn stops. There is simply a silence with the sound of your own breathing. There are no bodies in the car.

That can't be right. Wasn't the target supposed to be inside? Wasn't she supposed to be semi-unconscious? You remember her laid out on a stretcher on the roadway, breathing through an oxygen mask, with blood coming from her right ear. Her long white Versace leggings were torn and her silk shirt was open. Her swollen belly was covered with a sheet. Wasn't that how it happened?

Maybe the back-up motorcycle rider dragged out the target's body before he made the call to the British Embassy from the Place de l'Alma. Maybe there's another phoney ambulance already made the pick-up. Maybe you're the fall guy. Now did you ever think of that?

You turn and walk unsteadily back to your vehicle. You see a beetle crawling on the surface of the road. You crush it with your boot. Another beetle lands on your glove and you shake it off. You are unbalanced.

The back doors of the ambulance are open a crack. You remember closing them firmly. But it seems your memory is not so good. Maybe the target is already in the back of the ambulance? Maybe someone was sent to help you while you were busy inspecting the wreck.

You have to check. You need to be seen to be doing a good job. But who is watching? You look up at the CCTV camera mounted on the roof of the tunnel. It should have been put out of action by the K-Team. But perhaps you are being filmed by secret paymasters at the British Embassy.

You are so miserable. You get in the back of the ambulance with your tools. Sure enough, the stretcher is inside. There's a body on it covered in a white sheet. Does this mean the target is dead after all? But then you hear the moans coming from under the sheet. You see the hump of the covered belly.

Time to get busy. You place your bag on the floor and open it up. Oh fuck! There are no tools in your bag. There are no knives, no scalpels and no cutting instruments. There is no adze. Instead there is a ridged wooden stick made in the shape of two intertwined snakes. How did the Tally Stick get here?

You know with a cold certainty that it's Anu the Chameleon Kid with you in the back of the ambulance. Something has gone wrong. Fingers creep out from beneath the sheet. Where is Eddie? You don't want to be here any more. One of the fingers is wearing a silver ring with the black nail polish. You speak words of distress into the radio microphone taped to your throat. The fingers grip the edge of the sheet and begin to pull it back from the stirring form.

"Khepri!"

There is a snickering sound comes from beneath the sheet.

You are screaming a name into the mike.

You shrink back. You are very rapidly fading away.

*Screen Message*
PINK LOTUS DESCENT
GAMEPLAY SWITCHING…

*Narrative Voiceover*
Doctor Double Oh No's universe is falling apart at the Crown-coded singularity. His spectre wants to vacate memory body go back to his real body last seen hanging from the cosmic tree over the zodiacal pond. He's had enough. He wants to go home.

Too late.

No longer possible for single player Doctor Double Oh No to jack out of game. His option on the Pink Lotus descent lapse.

Chance for some other player buy up the rights to the Pink Lotus descent. Who that gonna be?

Anu the Chameleon Kid guards every Crown-coded singularity. The Pont de l'Alma tunnel in Paris no exception.

*Screen Message*
TEZMA HOARD: 999

*Full Motion Video*
The Doctor lying in the back of the ambulance in the road tunnel at the Pont de l'Alma. He throws back the white sheet that covers him. He is dressed in white Versace leggings and a dark silk shirt. There is a dressing gown cord wrapped round his neck.

He looks down with horror at his naked belly. It is taut and swollen.

*Player Status*
You have used your POV button to hijack the subject position of one of Doctor Double Oh No's alter egos in a parallel universe. You are Doctor Double Oh No.

*Point of View: Doctor Double Oh No*

You are in the back of the ambulance. You cannot move. You are rigid with fear. There is someone leaning over you. They are covered in a full-body biohazard radiation suit. The garment is completely black. They are holding a bag. They place the bag on the ground and open it up. Their movements are laboured but precise. They select a curved blade from the collection of knives displayed.

Oh no! You know what that is. It's an adze. The figure holding the adze moves towards you. You are silent. You can see the identity of your destroyer behind the transparent plastic window of their black hood. They have the flickering face of Anu the Chameleon Kid.

The adze has a very sharp tip. Chameleon Kid pulls up your shirt and makes a shallow incision at the top of your belly. You shiver. You do not resist. Chameleon Kid slides the blade down. Blood seeps from the cut. It is a superficial wound. It's a guide line marking your body.

You are breathing hard.

Chameleon Kid is busy with her bag of tools again. She swaps the adze for a sharp hunting knife. You wonder how painful it's gonna be when she opens up your belly. It's okay. Chameleon Kid is merciful. She cuts your throat.

One stroke is all it took. You are floating above your thrashing and kicking body. The blood is gushing from your open throat. You can see the shock in your eyes. Your death has not yet registered. Semen is spurting from your cock. You are having an out-of-body experience.

What a fucking drag! Somehow you're the one got scapegoated. You watch with detached curiosity as Chameleon Kid opens up your pregnant belly with the hunting knife. There is nothing inside. There is no secret mana. There is no Substance H. There is just a bunch of spilled guts. Chameleon Kid digs deep with her scalpel just to make sure. She is cutting open intestinal tissue.

You feel vaguely outraged. That you should die at the hands of one of your designated victims is bad. That your death coincide with revealed fact of your phantom pregnancy is worse. It confirms what you have long suspected but always denied. All your powers as chaos magician product of no more than hysteria.

*Narrative Voiceover*

Doctor Double Oh No cannot dodge his way past the Crown-coded singularity at the Pont de l'Alma tunnel. He has been out-manoeuvred by Chameleon Kid. She has fucked him in a deathmatch.

Doctor Double Oh No is now one body short of a complete set across all parallel universes. This another way of saying he always got one spectre too many.

What he gonna do? Hide the extra spectre in a body just about to lose its own spectre making the Pink Lotus descent. Yeah? All Doctor Double Oh No can do now is go back almost where he came to some parallel point in spacetime. Only thing is he can't go on from that point.

Doctor Double Oh No trapped in a closed spacetime loop. Chameleon Kid made sure all his futures used up.

*Screen Message*
PINK LOTUS DESCENT
ABORTING...

*Player Status*
You have used your POV button to abandon the subject position of one of Doctor Double Oh No's alter egos in a parallel universe. You are Khepri, goddess of beetles.

*Point of View: Doctor Double Oh No's Spectre*
You leave your corpse in the back of the ambulance with Chameleon Kid. The thin ethereal thread connecting you to Doctor Double Oh No's penis has been severed by his orgasm. You float through the roof of the ambulance.

You think you get it. You have become your own homeless spectre up near the roof of the tunnel under the Pont de l'Alma. You look around. Oh fuck. The whole scene is changed. There's the crashed Merc by the wall. But it's got four bodies inside. One of them in the dark shirt and the white Versace leggings. The target? Maybe she's dead after all. She got the gold ring with white stones on her finger. Her hands crossed Osiris-fashion over her chest. Is that how it was? Her head tilted at an angle.

The wreck is surrounded by a tableau of unmoving bodies, like something out of a grinning waxworks museum. Photographers crouched around the Merc with cameras raised, medics in white coats at the doors, fire crews with chainsaws getting ready to take out the roof. The scene gonna be demolished. No souvenirs left. The cops form a cordon sanitaire keep back the crowds. Stacks of bodies in the tunnel pressing forward to get a good look, craning their necks, unsteady on their feet. There are hundreds of them. Thousands. The tunnel is choking with bodies in both directions.

But none of the bodies moving.

The ambulance doors open and Chameleon Kid steps out in hood and body suit. She turns and lifts your corpse out on her shoulder. It dressed in a cop uniform. The skin flapping loose at the neck. She props it up at end of line of cops in the tableau. One of other cops threatens to topple forwards and she rushes over to fix it in place. This other cop with identical wound in the neck. Identical face. Identical to your own corpse in every way. Chameleon Kid tucks piece of loose intestine back into buttoned shirt before going back to original corpse. She got so much to do.

The tunnel is full of your dead bodies. You get it at last as you begin to drift away from the Merc, back the way you came, past legions of your dead bodies, thousands and thousands, never stopping, millions. Time dilation effect. The tunnel is long. It is longer than you remember. It is infinitely long.

Your subjectivity is tending to infinity in an interval tends to zero. Boring!

Hundreds of millions of dead bodies later, you are still travelling. You wish you could take back the last minute of your life. You think of Eddie Boy Krishna. But it's far too late for that.

*Narrative Voiceover*

Doctor Double Oh No's one consolation is he understand that he trapped. He got no freedom but he got self-knowledge. He is hip to stoical wisdom.

So that's it then.

Doctor Double Oh No is fucked. His spirit bouncing backwards and forwards between zodiacal pond at Parliament Hill and singularity in tunnel under Pont de l'Alma. Flicking from one parallel universe to another, pulling the bodies in from the pond and stashing them in the tunnel under the bridge. La-de-da. His future getting used up one body at a time.

Spacetime curling back on itself from the pond to the tunnel in an infinitely crashing wave. The tunnel a dumping-ground in the multiverse. Doctor Double Oh No's bodies logged by Chameleon Kid. She his own personal morgue attendant. But she get bored and play big dollies. Understandable, really. She got to express herself.

*Screen Message*

PINK LOTUS DESCENT
GAMEPLAY RESTARTING…

*Full Motion Video*

The Doctor hanging upside down from the cosmic tree. Hands crossed over the chest Osiris-fashion. Teeth pulling at the cord round his neck.

*Player Status*
You have used your POV button to hijack the subject position of one of Doctor Double Oh No's alter egos in a parallel universe. You are Doctor Double Oh No.

*Point of View: Doctor Double Oh No*
Don't do it! What? Choke. Something is wrong. Hold. Beetles covering your naked body. Nothing is wrong. Breathe.

There is an inversion of friction where the you that's going interferes with the you that's just come back. This is experienced as an omen.

E-fucking-mergency! This parallel universe about to crash down on you. You need to get going now.

Fucking Einstein!

*Narrative Voiceover*
This sample gameplay one iteration in an infinite series. Think of the series as one unit of mana. Rules of game dictate this is sum total of Doctor Double Oh No's life.

Now mana which cannot circulate freely in a closed symbolic system is dangerous to the bearer. It becomes one unit of tezma.

Okay. So add this unit of tezma to the nine hundred and ninety nine units of tezma already on the clock. Result? One thousand units of tezma. Bingo! Total required for performance of the Pink Lotus descent.

Someone has scored enough units of tezma to move to the parallel universe of their choice and get on with their future life. Only it is not Doctor Double Oh No.

*Screen Message*
PINK LOTUS DESCENT
INFINITELY REPEATING…

*Player Status*
You are always using your POV button to either hijack or abandon the subject position of one of Doctor Double Oh No's alter egos in a parallel universe. You are and you aren't Doctor Double Oh No.

You are becoming one unit of tezma.

*Screen Message*
TEZMA HOARD: 1,000

*Full Motion Video*
The Doctor fading away over the zodiacal pond. Hands crossed over his chest Osiris-fashion.

*Narrative Voiceover*
That's it for Doctor Double Oh No. He lose. Get it? He lose big.

The Doctor's antagonist still in the game. She wins by default. Collect those spare one thousand units of tezma and mark them up to Anu the Chameleon Kid.

What a result. She got enough to make the Pink Lotus descent. This is how it goes. Tezma cannot be exchanged in a closed symbolic system. So open up the system. Sacrifice the tezma to the gods. Give it to Osiris. See what comes back. This is exchange on a meta-level outside the symbolic system of one universe. What comes back is another universe simple as that.

Can you dig it? Tezma exits closed symbolic system and comes back as baraka. Sacrifice negative mana and wait for positive mana. Only catch is that baraka must be given away to have any existence at all. Is this a good deal or what? Some say just a good way of doubling up on nothing.

But not Chameleon Kid. She got the power to get through the singularity. She say to Osiris what universe she want. She make the sacrifice.

Oh no! No future for the Crown orbital space ark. It decay in its orbit and fall into the sea. Down, down to the bottom of the Atlantic Ocean. It gone.

That's it. End of the New Ukanian Combine.

Oh yes! Where Chameleon Kid headed? What new universe she gonna bring down? Watch out for next installment there, people.

*Screen Message*
GAME OVER

## Space station insurrection

ANOTHER 'JAMES BOND' EPISODE

MARK 23: *(Voiceover)*    Assalamu alaikum, godly people. Here's your host Mark 23, hip hop prophet and reality TV signifier, settled in the backwoods of America with a hidden camera. There were no more missions left for me. Was this really the end? I had one last transmission to make.

*Cue titles and music*

THE ALIEN IN THE GARDEN

*Fade up on a daytime exterior riverside scene in America. A stretch of lawn framed by weeping willows at the water's edge. The river beyond is broad and flat and calm.*

*MARK 23 sits in a white wicker-bound chair next to a small circular wrought iron table also painted white. On the table is a plate containing a curling strip of green apple peel and a small kitchen knife. MARK 23 cradles a baby in his arms.*

*Move in on MARK 23. He wears a beige Mao jacket and vintage Adidas Gazelles. His hair is shaped into a greying moptop. A smile dances across his features. Close in on the infant's upturned scowling face. She has furious green eyes and her ears are elongated at the tips.*

*Cut to the water's edge. The wind begins to disturb the surface of the water. The light darkens. It's as if a cloud has passed across the face of the sun. There is a moaning sound from beneath the drooping branches of the willow.*

MARK 23: *(Voiceover)*   My first child was adopted.

FLASH-FORWARD TO A LATER PERFORMANCE

*Exterior daytime shot of a riverside garden in America. It is dark and the wind is whipping the brown muddy water beside the bank. The branches of a willow overhang the water. From beneath their screened canopy emerges a desolate moaning sound.*

*A pathway leads from the bank to the centre of a lawn. The pathway is lined with wooden sticks supporting the bleached jaw-bones of crocodiles. Move in on their jagged teeth.*

*A naked young GIRL enters the scene. She has curly black hair, clear green eyes and curious pointed ears. She sits cross-legged at the end of the pathway facing the water. A sharp pointed wooden stick rests across her bare nut-brown thighs.*

*The wind dies down as a crocodile hauls itself out of the water on to the bank from beneath the overhanging leaves of the willow. Golden rings decorate its front feet and there are precious stones in its ears. The reptile shifts itself along the lawn on its powerful hind legs. Its long ridged tail swishes from side to side.*

*Cut to the young GIRL. She leans in towards the amphibious beast as it lumbers down the pathway towards her.*

MARK 23: *(Voiceover)*   My first child would need to prove herself time and time again.

## SCRYING IN THE GAZE OF AN ALIEN

*Daytime exterior shot of a back-yard riverside scene in America. The light sparkles on the water. It's as if a cloud has passed from the face of the sun.*

*MARK 23 sits in a wicker chair cradling an infant in his arms. He gazes tenderly into the green eyes of his child. Close in on those eyes. They are hard and bright and fathomless. They seem to contain worlds...*

MARK 23: *(Voiceover)*   I could see glimpses of an alternate history in the eyes of my first child. It spelled the end of the offworld mutant call-girl ring run by the Saxe-Coburg-Gotha mob from the safety of their Royal Spaceship.

## THE DREAM GIRL REVOLT

*Exterior shot of a space station in the shape of a geodesic globe in orbit above a watery blue planet. Its double-glazed polycarbonate panels shine with reflected sunlight. Close in on one of the panels. The slit in its puckered skin jammed with a partially excreted wooden crate. The repeat whining sound of a burnt-out mechanism.*

*Cut to interior night-time shot of the factory farm inside the space station. The captive courtesans have escaped their cages and are scaling the chain-link guard fences with the aid of the boom-supported observation decks they have hijacked. They are dressed in multi-coloured saris and head-scarves and led by a gaunt young girl with pink lotus-print head-scarf and red bindi dot in the middle of her forehead. Injured men with clipboards run around in distress. Helicopters sweep the farm with searchlights.*

*Cut to interior of the covered mall next to the farm. Scenes of hand-to-hand combat in the atrium between the courtesans and crazed policemen dressed in black* body armour and gas masks. *The courtesans press forward their attack with boleros and nets. The policemen are armed with electric stun guns, concussion grenades, pepper spray cans and four-foot long riot batons. They fall back in confusion.*

*Cut to exterior shot of the space station. The flexible support struts shaking. Gas escaping from the punctured central sphere.*

MARK 23: *(Voiceover)*    Allegra looked forward to the time when she could just be one of the girls.


## THE LOCAL APOCALYPSE

*Interior shot of the bridge of the space station. A metal walkway is suspended high over a deep well occupied by desks of computer equipment with attending data-entry clerks dressed in yellow jump-suits and microphone head-sets. A dynamic map of the world is projected on a wall-screen opposite the walk-way. Its unhinged cartography describes one huge land mass spiralling out from the north pole with the south pole an isolated off-shore island territory.*

*Close in on the walkway. A villainous mobster stands alone dressed in a long black coat open to the navel. He gazes in astonishment at the red light which begins to flash above the wall-screen.*

*Cut back to the bridge as it trembles and quakes. The sound of alarms and distant explosions. The data-entry clerks scramble from their workstations as the floor violently tilts. Fire and smoke now rage from the seams of the well. The sound of shearing metal as the walkway starts to collapse.*

*Close in on the walkway. The mobster laughs manically as he goes down with it into the flaming well.*

*Cut to exterior shot of the space station. The central sphere is a ragged burning shell. The perimeter spheres automatically retract into a tighter position around the central sphere and push the articulated joints of their connecting struts outwards as defensive spikes. The collapsed surface volume of the station hangs against the blackness of space for one suicidal instant. Then it blossoms in a maelstrom of fire.*

*Close in on the edge of the firestorm to discover an orbiter escaping the black clouds of smoke. It dips its wings in salute to the blue waters of the earth as it swoops down into the upper atmosphere.*

MARK 23: *(Voiceover)*    Allegra specialised in narrow escapes.


## SOFT PORN FANTASIA (REPRISE)

*Interior shot of the orbiter's payload bay. Scores of lesbians wrapped in long furcoats languorously entwine in freefall sucking and fucking each other. They are*

*full-bodied women of varying racial designations. One of them holds a trembling*
*phallus between her fingers.*

*Cut to interior shot of the orbiter's crew cabin. A chauffeur is strapped into*
*the pilot's seat. He is dressed in a brass-buttoned grey uniform with a peaked cap*
*resting above clipped ears. His expression is blank.*

*Roll credits listing the names of industrial sponsors.*

MARK 23: *(Voiceover)*    Allegra was lost in ecstasy.


BACK TO REALITY ONCE MORE

*Pull back from the prophetic gaze of the strange little infant cradled in the arms of*
*MARK 23. Fade up on the daytime exterior of a back-yard lawn beside a river in*
*America. MARK 23 is asleep in his wicker chair.*

*A shadow slides over the face of the baby. She smiles and reaches up with tiny*
*hands.*

*Cut to ALLEGRA in pink lotus-print head-scarf sliding her hands around*
*MARK 23's neck and resting her chin on his shoulder. She has a strong-boned face*
*and striking green eyes. Her thick wiry hair is black and brown and blonde and all*
*the colours in between.*

MARK 23: *(Voiceover)*    My wife and I had a family to build. That was enough
                          of a quest for me.


THE END

*Roll credits*

## No Deal

ISIS: Report processing of my plan, little creature.

ANUBIS: Everyting on course for successful arrival, my lady. Osiris even now crosses the event horizon at Hampstead Pond.

NEPHTHYS: Osiris haul his tail to da Pont de la Alma!

SATIS: A *tiny* lickle singularity. Not like the First Cataract of the Nile in de old days. How those Egyptian obeah men used to worship me!

ANUBIS: Osiris is now in the upper control area of the singularity.

ISIS: Report status of Allegra Zero Zero Zero.

ANUBIS: Osiris continue to grant her wish for justice deh. He give her secret of da Pink Lotus. Now she select the coordinates of her dream universe and prepares for re-entry.

SATIS: Dat Ark of Ol Innglan in autoclaps for sure.

NEPHTHYS: Allegra really got da law in her favour.

SET: So whappen a dat bobolee Doctor Dee?

ANUBIS: Osiris ascending! Clear obstacles for emergency mass landing.

ISIS: My lord?

OSIRIS: I return with nine hundred and ninety nine baby Horuses.

HORUSES: Waugh! Waugh! Waugh!

SATIS: There are so many of them.

NEPHTHYS: Should they not favour Osiris?

SET: None of them has a pee-pee!

ISIS: You have drawn back plenty, my lord. Rest here with me.

OSIRIS: I hagged Doctor Dee into a black hole and closed it tight as a drum. He is squinged up for infinity!

SATIS: Tout moune is satisfied.

NEPHTYHS: Osiris *still* rules!

ANUBIS: Ahem! There remains a short-fall in the account. One Horus is missing.

NEPHTHYS: O Satis! It must be dat one we made and put in da belly of Jack's dog to teach him.

SATIS: Jack has not given it up! That kunu-munu jobber-man.

ISIS: My plan fails! Unless the Lord of the Dead snatch that Horus from Jack's own dog's belly-bottom with righteous vexation!

NEPHTHYS: Oh no! Cannot one little Horus survive on earth?

SATIS: She is so sweet!

SET: Now I have it! Break. Brother, the Horuses all favour Satis. She must have took her fastness to your Jizzum Stick!

SATIS: I confess it. Hee hee!

NEPHTHYS: Satis, you ring-neck! I would neveruv guessed it!

SET: Osiris, you must save us from this kadooment.

ANUBIS: One Horus or its equivalent must be paid.

ISIS: Blood is blood.

OSIRIS: I say Doctor Dee's infinite sufferation amounts to one Horus.

SET: Doctor Dee is expolicated!

ISIS: Osiris has mercy.

SATIS: Our little baby Horus is already born on earth.

NEPHTHYS: She is da spit of you, Satis.

SET: The nine hundred and ninety nine babies still pound da name of Horus. They are all girls!

ANUBIS: A small matter. Gender can always be reassigned under da knife.

OSIRIS: Set must fashion da pum-pum of my chile Horus into a penis deh.

SATIS: He must do it nine hundred and ninety nine times. Hee hee!

NEPHTHYS: Set is a boopsie.

SET: Oh for *fuck*'s sake!

ISIS: Everyone's time now meet for all the things they been doing.

ANUBIS: The New Ukanian Combine account is settled.

OSIRIS: Anubis, shut down communication with earth.

ANUBIS: Wilco, Osiris. Contact broken. De pot now burst.

CPSIA information can be obtained
at www.ICGtesting.com
Printed in the USA
LVHW11s1600051018
592549LV00001B/180/P